D0810143

Hothouse Flower

and the

Nine Plants of Desire

HOTHOUSE FLOWER

AND THE

NINE PLANTS OF DESIRE

MARGOT BERWIN

PANTHEON BOOKS
NEW YORK

This is a work of fiction. Names, characters, places, and incidents
either are the product of the author's imagination
or are used fictitiously. Any resemblance to actual persons,
living or dead, events, or locales is entirely coincidental.

Copyright © 2009 by Margot Berwin

All rights reserved. Published in the United States by Pantheon Books,
a division of Random House, Inc., New York, and in Canada by
Random House of Canada Limited, Toronto.

Pantheon Books and colophon are registered trademarks
of Random House, Inc.

A portion of this work originally appeared on Nerve.com.

ISBN-13: 978-0-307-37784-5

Printed in the United States of America

For Armand

For me the world is weird because it is stupendous, awesome, mysterious, unfathomable; my interest has been to convince you that you must assume responsibility for being here, in this marvelous world, in this marvelous desert, in this marvelous time. I wanted to convince you that you must learn to make every act count, since you are going to be here for only a short while; in fact, too short for witnessing all the marvels of it.

—Don Juan in Carlos Castaneda's *Journey to Ixtlan*

A Note from the Author

This book is a journey that moves from the advertising world of New York City to the rain forests of the Yucatán Peninsula. From the plant dealers in the Union Square Green Market to *curanderos,* herbalists, shamans, and charlatans, right into the spirits of the plants themselves.

The story is based on a relationship with my good friend Armand, who was kind enough to give me permission to use his name on these pages. I think he has a beautiful name, and I could not think of one that suits him better.

Over the years, Armand taught me many things about plants and about life. I've taken some of that knowledge and created this novel. I would say that the circumstances of the book are fictional in the specifics and very real in the abstract.

Take it for what you will. Read it in whatever way gives you the most enjoyment.

GLOXINIA
Gloxinia speciosa

MEXICAN CYCAD
Zamia furfuracea

CACAO
Theobroma cacao

MOONFLOWER
Ipomoea alba

SINSEMILLA
Cannabis sativa

LILY OF THE VALLEY
Convallaria majalis

MANDRAKE
Atropa mandragora

CHICORY
Cichorium intybus

DATURA
Datura inoxia

The Nine Plants of Desire

~ Gloxinia—The mythical plant of love at first sight.

~ Mexican cycad—The plant of immortality. A living dinosaur straight from the Jurassic period.

~ Cacao—The chocolate tree of food and fortune.

~ Moonflower—Bringer of fertility and procreation.

~ *Cannabis sativa* in the form of sinsemilla—The plant of female sexuality.

~ Lily of the valley—Delivers life force. In a pinch, this beautiful plant can replace digitalis as medication for an ailing heart.

~ Mandrake—According to both William Shakespeare and the Holy Bible, this is the plant of magic.

~ Chicory—The plant of freedom. Offering invisibility to those who dare to ingest its bitter, milky juice.

~ Datura—The plant of mind travel and high adventure. Bringer of visions and dreams of the future.

There is a tenth plant, too. The passion plant with no name. To find out about that one, you have to read the book.

❦ PART ONE ❦

NEW YORK CITY

Bird-of-Paradise
(Strelitzia reginae)

Native of South Africa, member of the banana family,
prized for its tall, highly colored structures.
This plant is not for the easily disappointed, impatient, or bossy,
as it can take seven years to produce a single bloom.
Perfect for the person who gives and gives
without getting anything in return. You know who you are.

I inadvertently became interested in tropical plants because that's what the man at the Union Square Green Market sold me.

I used to believe that sentence, but now I know better. Now I know that it was meant to be.

Here's how it happened.

I had just moved to Fourteenth Street and Union Square, into a small, newly renovated studio with absolutely no character. It was a square-shaped box with parquet floors, no molding, no details, white paint, and low ceilings. It was exactly the kind of apartment I wanted. Its newness meant that there were no memories trapped in the walls or the floorboards. No arguments or harrowing scenes of unrequited love staring at me from the bathroom mirror. It was brand-new. Just like I wanted my life to be.

I thought a bit of foliage might spruce the place up, no pun intended, and add some much-needed color, so I walked across the street to the Union Square Green Market to make my purchase.

The man at the plant stand was a throwback. He had streaky blond hair and a dirt-colored tan that came from being outside all the time. In his worn-out flannel shirt and beat-up Timberlands—worn for work, not fashion—he stood out in stark contrast to the manicured metro-sexuals perusing the market, wicker baskets in one hand, Gucci sunglasses in the other. This man was different. He was a rugged *country-sexual*.

He asked me to describe my apartment not in terms of the square footage or the make of the stove and the fridge, but by the amount of light, temperature, and humidity.

I told him that I had floor-to-ceiling windows, which was mostly true, although they were more ceiling-to-heating-unit than ceiling-to-floor.

I told him that I had an unobstructed south-facing view, hard to find in New York City, and that as long as the sun was shining it was hot and sunny all day long, even in the winter.

I hadn't lived in my apartment through a winter, so I'm not sure why I said that, but I guess it sounded good to me, and also to him, since he bent down amongst his plants, head covered with purple flowers, butt in the air, and emerged with a big smile and a two-foot-high bunch of leaves.

I was disappointed.

"What is it?"

"A bird-of-paradise," he said, holding it up toward the sky and twirling the pot around with his fingertips.

"A tropical plant?" I asked, zipping my coat against the late-March wind and picturing its imminent death.

"Hawaiian, to be exact. *Strelitzia reginae*. A member of the banana family. She needs lots of sunlight, not too direct, and let the soil dry out between waterings. She's tough to raise, and she won't flower for five or six or maybe seven years, depending on the weather. And the love," he added with a wink.

I unzipped my jacket.

"Six or seven years? My marriage didn't last that long. Do you have anything that flowers sooner, like in a week or two?"

"This is the plant for you," he said. "She's a beauty."

"How much?"

"Thirty dollars, and I'll throw in a brochure on rare tropicals so you know how to care for her."

"Three zero? I could go to the deli on the corner and get a dozen roses for ten dollars that have great big sweet-smelling flowers on them right now."

"You could, but they'd be dead in a week. You'd have to buy new ones every Saturday. If you do the math, I'm a bargain. And besides, this bird is *tropical*. Think balmy ocean breezes, swaying palm trees, cabana boys, and piña coladas on white sand beaches near warm light-blue water."

I don't know whether it was the piña coladas, the cabana boys, or the sky blue of his eyes, but as a person who worked in advertising, I had to respect a good sales pitch. I paid him, and he handed me the plant, the brochure on rare tropicals, and his card, which said "David Exley, Plant Man."

"Sounds like a superhero," I said.

"Well, I do have a little something special with the flora and fauna, if you know what I mean."

I didn't, but I nodded anyway.

"Come back if her leaves start turning yellow around the edges. I'm here every Monday, Wednesday, and Saturday from six in the morning till ten at night."

"They better not," I said over my shoulder. "For thirty dollars they better stay bright freakin' green."

I walked through the market with my bird-of-paradise held

out in front of me like an offering. It felt good to be carrying around a piece of the earth. I thought it made me look like one of those women who cooked satisfying meals on a nightly basis for their Steiner School children while wearing Birkenstocks and reading from the Cabala, instead of the single, childless, plantless, divorced thirty-two-year-old woman that I was.

Back in my apartment, I set the bird-of-paradise down on the window ledge. The base of the pot was too wide, and it teetered. I caught my thirty-dollar tropical right before it crashed to the floor. Not five minutes with me and its life was already in danger. No surprises there.

The bird-of-paradise was the first living thing I shared space with after my divorce. *No pets, no plants, no people, no problems* had been my motto for the past nine months.

I met my ex-husband at work. He was cute and smart and successful and he was a huge mistake. He was a man who drank like a fish and wanted lots of babies. I was a woman who didn't want lots of babies and drank like a human being. I know that most marriages are complex and multilayered, but ours was not. Our four-year marriage went something like this:

Year one—"I love you, Lila."

Year two—"I love you, Lila."

Year three—"I love you, Lila."

Year four—"I'm leaving you, Lila, for the producer at the advertising agency."

The producer at the advertising agency, aka the woman who brought him coffee and made his plane reservations. What a cliché. At the time I wondered how something that sounded so much like a made-for-TV movie could hurt so bad.

But in truth it wasn't the drinking or the producer. The problem with our marriage was genetic.

My husband came from a big Irish Catholic family where everyone got married and had kids unless they were gay or terminally ill. I came from a family where no one ever got married unless they had kids first, and usually by accident.

My parents, whom I love madly, divorced when I was young. Post divorce, they both dated furiously, like teenagers, without ever remarrying. My sister and brother, both older, had children but no spouses.

A lot of people get married to keep with tradition. I was a rebel. I married to break with it.

The strange thing was, against all odds, I loved being married. I adored the little rituals. The cute nicknames. "Honeybear" for him. "Wild Rose" for me. I loved shopping at Whole Foods, cooking beef stews and chicken soups in huge pots with lots of vegetables. I loved washing the dishes while listening to Curtis Mayfield. I liked washing, drying, and folding the clothes. For Christ's sake, I even loved the vacuuming. I think it's fair to say that during the years of my marriage I became the single most boring person in the entire world, and I totally loved it.

Turned out, my ex, who by all external appearances and family history was the solid, marrying kind, absolutely hated it. He was a space freak. He grew up in a tiny house with lots of siblings, and he couldn't stand the proximity to another person. He kept dragging me around to buy bigger beds and move into larger spaces. In the end, we were sleeping on a mattress so wide we could lie spread-eagle and our fingertips wouldn't touch, and we were living in a loft the size of an airplane hangar.

Just to make sure I wasn't crazy, I took a survey on the bed. My friend Oliver, who was a well-known interior designer, said it was the largest piece of furniture he'd ever seen in a Manhattan apartment. My friend Lisa said it made her feel tiny, like a baby who'd crawled into her parents' bed. My mother offered to have *special sheets* made for it. And my co-worker and good friend Kodiak Starr, who was a surfer, said that with its blue-green comforter it reminded him of the ocean. It was official. My bed was as big as the Atlantic. I was sleeping in New York, and my husband was all the way on the other side of the mattress, in London.

My big Honeybear, my rock, turned out to be a piece of pumice stone. Flaky and crumbly under pressure, and unable to talk about or even know what he was feeling. In our giant apartment with the giant bed, he moved farther and farther away, until one day he simply never came home at all. No kidding. Just like that.

Turned out my real rock was my co-worker Kodiak Starr. Kody was a bit of a philosopher/crunchy surfer for someone with such a glamorous name, and he was more beautiful than most of the women I knew. He used annoying words like "cool" and "dude," and he was into things like transcendental meditation and lucid dreaming. He would probably be considered New Age if he hadn't been born in 1984, eight years after me.

Because we shared an office, Kody did most of the day-to-day heavy lifting when it came to hearing about my ex. We were supposed to be working on a new commercial for Puma sneakers, but mostly we worked on the much more pressing questions of my marriage. When I asked him why my husband left without ever trying to work it out, he answered in lilting, rolling, easy-to-digest surfing metaphors. He brushed his silky blond hair behind his ears, put his flip-flop-clad feet up on the desk, and wrapped his hands around the back of his neck.

"Dude," he said, "only world-class long-board surfers have the discipline to ride all kinds of waves, big or small, in all kinds of conditions. Your husband was a short-board amateur."

"But why me?" I asked for the hundredth time. "Why do I have to go through this?"

"Because wiping out is like breathing," he said. "Everybody does it."

After the death of my marriage, I was hell-bent on keeping the bird-of-paradise alive. I would take it slowly. Plants first. And if everything went well, then I'd move on to people.

In the mornings, before work, I stroked its stems with my fingertips, because they were slightly fuzzy and felt nice to the touch, and occasionally I washed its big banana-plant leaves with a damp sponge when they got too dusty from city living.

I treated that bird like a houseguest, except I gave it water instead of wine and I tried not to blow cigarette smoke in its direction. I kept the blinds open all day, even when it was so sunny I couldn't read my computer screen. I catered to what I imagined to be its every whim, and, much to my surprise, it flourished. New shoots grew out of its stems. I coaxed them along with hand-wrung drops of water and sweet talk. They unfurled into giant shiny pale-green translucent leaves with delicate visible veins.

I wanted to go back to the green market to thank David Exley and brag about my progress (aka see him again and flirt mercilessly), but I was afraid: when it came to men, I was skittish and out of practice. So instead I called Kody.

He answered his phone at the beach and screamed over the surf.

"You gotta get back out there, Lila. You gotta get out there and catch some waves. Don't come back till you have cramps in your calves from squatting in the curl. Free as a bird, girl. Free as a bird."

I hung up the phone and headed to the green market, squatting in the curl.

———

"My bird is growing beautifully," I said.

David Exley, Plant Man, pointed his thumb behind him.

"There's a lot more where that came from."

"I'm not shopping, I'm just browsing."

"Fine by me, browse away. But if you have a minute I can take you into my tent and show you how to make that bird grow wings."

"I have some time," I said. "Show me how to make her fly."

He dropped his voice and moved in closer.

"Before I give away the special secrets of my tropical trade, I need to know who I'm talking to."

"I'm Lila."

"Lila, that's nice. Lila what?"

"Nova."

"A middle name, Lila Nova?"

"Grace."

"Lila Grace Nova. The *new* Lila Grace."

He took my elbow and led me into the indoor part of his plant stand. It was a humid, dripping green tent the size of a small city apartment, and packed with plants. It was at least fifteen degrees warmer than the air outside, and it smelled like damp earth and rain and things that are green.

On one wooden picnic table he had five tall birds-of-paradise. Their leaves were firm and pointing toward the sky.

"Give me your hand, Lila Grace Nova."

He took my hand and ran my fingertips over a large leaf.

"Feel that?"

"It's wet."

"Not wet. Misty. Can you feel the difference?"

"How do you keep them like this? Misty, I mean. Without them turning into just plain wet?"

He let go of my hand. It was covered with dirt from his gardening glove, as if he were still holding it.

"Buy yourself a couple of humidifiers. Don't put 'em too close to the bird—you don't want to soak the leaves—but not too far away, either—you don't want them to dry out. Just close enough to keep them coated with a fine, delicate mist. She'll love it. She'll grow you right out of your apartment. Take my word for it, you'll have to move to a new place just to keep up with that bird."

"I hate moving."

"That's because you're rooted. The sign of a true plant person."

I liked the sound of that. *A true plant person.* It sounded so much more alive, and warmer, and more female than *a true advertising person.*

I looked at Exley. His eyes were the color of a faded blue workshirt, with wrinkles spread out in a fan design around the outer corners, probably from squinting into the sun all day. He made me feel like I wasn't in Manhattan, and I liked the feeling. This man is a true professional, I thought. A real flower-selling flirt.

"What kind of work do you do?" he asked.

"I'm in advertising."

"Glamorous business, huh?"

I gave it all I had. If he was going to play rugged country boy, I was going to play sexy city woman.

"Yes," I said, brushing my wavy blond hair off my shoulders with both hands and shaking my head from side to side, "it's a very glamorous business."

Advertising

*A way of selling products by making people believe
they need something that they have absolutely no use for.
Not a job for the super-ethical, but
perfect for those practical souls who like their
creativity with a side of cash.*

The truth was, my job *had* taken a turn for the glamorous. I don't know whether it was the extra hours I put in to avoid the pain, or just the universe throwing me a bone, but right in the middle of the divorce, between the lawyers, the mediation, the drunk phone calls, the lock changing, the moving, and the crying, Kody and I managed to write and then sell a commercial for Puma sneakers. It was easily the best assignment of our career, and we were going on a television shoot with a supermodel (even though as a writer I hated acknowledging the word "supermodel" as part of the English language).

The morning of the shoot, I stood in front of my closet trying to decide what to wear, or, more precisely, what to wear in front of the model.

I tried on a few different looks: sexy, street, punk, and finally settled on ballerina. I let my blond hair fall in long, soft waves over a swirly, short pink dress. I wrapped a sheer silvery

shawl over my shoulders and slipped into a pair of sparkly ballerina flats. I was light, airy, and graceful. In a rare happy
moment, I danced through my new apartment, knowing that
if my career could pick up this much momentum, the rest of
my life was sure to follow.

The movie studio in the Brooklyn Navy Yard looked like a
huge warehouse, with cameramen, videographers, clients, ad-
agency employees, the director, and the model's "people" all
milling around a makeshift kitchen, eating breakfast. The
model was standing alone next to a brown folding card table
doubling as a kitchen table, smoking. She was carrying a
Balenciaga bag, wearing jeans with thigh-high pointy black
boots and a wife beater under a short, raggy vintage fur. She
looked impossibly elegant at seven in the morning, way before
hair and makeup.

"Oh my God, dude, look at her," Kody said.

The model put her cigarette out on a glazed doughnut, and
I took the opportunity to introduce myself.

"Hi," I said. "I'm Lila. I wrote the commercial."

She bent down to look at me, which made me feel as tall as
an infant.

"It's lovely, really lovely," she said in a ridiculously charming
British accent.

I never should have worn flats, I thought.

I walked over to Kody, who was standing with our boss,
Geoff Evans. The three of us watched the model from a distance, like a zoo animal. She smoked cigarettes like they were
breakfast food, ate popcorn sparingly, and spoke on her cell
phone incessantly. She seemed happy, and why not? I would
be, too, if I got to swing my head from side to side and be the
center of attention while lesser folk lit my Winstons and fed
me popcorn, one perfectly air-popped kernel at a time.

When the hair and makeup people arrived, Kody and I

gathered around to watch them turn the teenaged giant into a *supermodel.* The two people responsible for this transformation were so androgynous I couldn't tell their gender no matter how hard I tried, and I come from New York City, where deciphering gender is a matter of course. I followed them as they shunted the model off to a small room brightly lit with overhead fluorescent lights. Kody was not allowed inside.

"Take a picture with your phone," he whispered. "I'll be your best friend."

"We're friendly enough."

The model stripped down naked and stood with her arms out to her sides while her genderless cohorts sprayed her body with large silver canisters of foundation. They wore masks over their faces and sprayed her from head to toe like they were putting out a fire. They airbrushed her into a monotoned six-foot-two column of a human being with no visible veins, nipples, nails, lips, or eyelashes.

When every single thing that was real about the model was gone, the makeup artist dug through a suitcase of brushes and plowed through hundreds of tubes of flesh-colored colors and began to draw human features onto her face. At the same time, the hair stylist meticulously sewed, with a needle and thread, strand after strand of long blond hairs onto her thin light-brown locks, creating a thick, full mane of shimmering gold.

The model had brought her very own chef, who cooked her spinach soup from scratch. The soup was fed to her by one of her lackeys, who existed solely for this purpose. The blond boy stood in front of her, blowing on the soup and then feeding it to her from a small silver child's spoon, just big enough to slip between her lips. The model's mouth was barely open, maybe a quarter of an inch wide, so that she would not crack the makeup when the unimaginable happened. The lackey blew a bit of spinach off the spoon and onto the model's breast. There was a collective gasp in the room as he went to remove it with his fingertip. The makeup artist grabbed him by the arm before he reached the model, flicked the spinach off with his index finger, and asked everyone one in the room to back up and be quiet while he put on a face mask and resprayed the area with foundation. And then it was time for lunch.

I sat around coughing from the spray, reading Exley's brochure on tropical plants, eating chunks of raw sea-bass ceviche, and drinking way too much Chardonnay.

It took six hours to turn the child into the supermodel the whole world recognized, and finally the director began to shoot. The model danced on a stage set, wearing a short red Lycra dress so tight there wasn't room for a thong underneath. She started out as a barefoot jungle girl and morphed into a panther as soon as she put on the silver Pumas. The music was loud and pounding, and she moved provocatively, crawling along the fake jungle floor like an animal, sticking her butt out, rearing up to scratch plastic tree trunks with her long nails, and baring her fangs. Her skin glittered under the pulsing blue lights, and she tossed her newly sewn hair at all the right moments, perfectly capturing the eerie fake moonlight.

The director, well known for his many MTV videos, yelled creepy clichés over the music:

"You're beautiful. Gorgeous. You're perfect. That's it. Give it to me. Just like that."

I couldn't help imagining what the model's mind was like after hearing those words day after day for half of her life.

The shoot was going so well, I thought it would be a good time to go into my boss's private viewing room and get a pat on the back for a job well done.

"I'll be right back," I said to Kody. "I'm going to talk to Geoff."

Kody couldn't take his eyes off the model.

"She looks just like a panther, dude. She's a freakin' shape-shifter."

"Your shape's gonna shift if you call me 'dude' one more time."

I knocked on Geoff Evans's door twice and got no response. I figured he was as model-drunk as Kody, so I walked in.

Usually the creative director sits alone in front of a video feed, focusing without distraction, making sure the clients get the most for their millions. But from where I stood, the image on the monitor looked like a tangled mess of black and red and nothing like the filming going on outside the door.

I walked closer, squinting. It took me a moment to realize that he was not looking at the shoot at all. He was hunched over the monitor looking up the supermodel's dress, under which she wore absolutely nothing.

I guessed she was being videoed from underneath the stage: a hole in the floor of the set created by the famous music-video director, for the famous ad-agency creative director, to view the naughty bits of the famous model.

"Who's behind me?" he asked from his chair, without moving his body or taking his eyes off the video.

"It's me, Lila."

"The door wasn't locked?"

"No."

"Huh."

He didn't turn toward me, and I didn't move a muscle. I had absolutely no idea what to do in that particular situation.

Finally, he turned around.

My mouth was frozen into an O shape.

"Oh, come on, don't look at me like that," he said. "This is why we go into this business in the first place, isn't it? It's one of the perks of the job. In fact, it's *the* perk of the job."

I bent over and held my knees.

"No one will ever know," he said. "It's not like I'm going to sell it online or anything like that. The film stays with me. It's my own private property."

I started to back out the door.

"Come on, Lila. You're the copywriter. I gave you total freedom on this one. You chose the Lycra dress. You had her gyrating on the stage. You scripted the damn thing. Isn't this the response you wanted?"

I felt queasy, and responsible for a peep show involving a child.

"I'm going outside for a while. Kody can cover."

"We're almost done. Are you sure you don't want to take the car service back with me?"

"I'm fine."

He turned back to the monitor. "Do you think she'll come to the wrap party next week?"

I couldn't get out of the studio fast enough. I didn't even bother to tell Kody I was leaving. I ran through the makeshift kitchen, knowing that I was never, ever going to get that picture out of my mind. Every time I saw that model's face on a giant billboard in Times Square, I would see Geoff Evans panting at the video monitor.

I caught the L train back to Manhattan, giving myself a good hour to torture my mind with guilt. Why was life always filled with things that were supposed to turn out some other way, like some other things? I wondered whether everyone's life was like that, or just mine.

I got out of the subway station and headed straight for my favorite bar, on First Avenue. I was halfway down the block between Twelfth and Thirteenth streets when I stopped short. Right there, between a Spanish bodega and a Japanese saki bar, I saw it. A most unusual plant was hanging in the window of an old Laundromat. Its blood-red leaves and bright-yellow blossoms were caught in the light of the streetlamp. They attracted my attention immediately. I got as close to the window as I could, my face almost touching the greasy glass. I recognized the plant from Exley's brochure. I knew it was tropical, and I knew it was very, very rare.

Fire Fern
(Oxalis hedysaroides rubra)

Seldom-seen native of Colombia, Ecuador, and Venezuela.
Will drop all of its leaves in a single day for no apparent reason
and not grow them back until it's good and ready. Not a plant
for beginners, needy people, or those who are looking for outside
approval. Not a true fern, but well disguised as one.
We've all met a few of those.

I opened the door and stepped down onto something squishy. It was moss, velvety smooth, creating uneven hills of emerald green across the floor of the laundry. I slipped off my silver ballet flats, and my feet sank into the floor.

I had a powerful desire to lie down, but I fought it by breathing deeply and inhaling the twin scents of detergent and bleach to clear my head.

I walked around, first on my tiptoes so as not to damage the moss, and then with my whole foot, squishing down on it, feeling it conform to my arches like natural orthotics. The bones of my feet cracked with pleasure after being in shoes all day.

Thick grass grew from squares of soil perfectly cut to fit the tops of the industrial-sized washing machines and dryers. Dense pockets of jewel-colored flowers on long, thin stems grew from the grass. There were red poppies, purple bells, and bright-yellow daisies. The laundry looked like a meadow. Like a field of wildflowers.

Plants were strung across the ceiling in between the tracks of fluorescent lights, stretching from one side of the Laundromat to the other. Colorful flowers sprang from the pots and hung down over the benches and folding tables. The pots were hung on invisible fishing line, so the flowers seemed to float in midair.

The Laundromat was like a jungle where washing machines had been dumped, or maybe a laundry where a jungle had sprung up. It was such a tangle of plants and machines it was hard to tell which came first.

A gray cat snoozed in the grass on top of a dryer. I felt disoriented and sat down on a white bench. A butterfly landed on my arm. Its turquoise wings looked brilliant against the silver shawl.

"If you look carefully, you'll see many more creatures," said a man's voice from the back of the Laundromat. "Butterflies, yes, and birds and moths, too. They help to pollinate my flowers."

I couldn't see who was speaking, but the voice was deep, calm, and gravelly.

"Be careful of the bees—some people are allergic to the sting."

I stood on my toes, my feet wet from the moss, and peered through the flowers, looking for the voice.

"You like my plants?" the man asked.

"Yes. They're magnificent."

"That they are," he said, stepping out from between two large palm fronds and walking toward me.

He was at least six feet four inches tall and more than 250 pounds. I couldn't tell how old he was. He could have been fifty; he could have been seventy. In his green cargo pants, green tee shirt, and small round yellow-tinted John Lennon sunglasses, he looked like a plant himself. Like a psychedelic tree.

"I am Armand," he said, extending his hand. "And I am at your service."

"Oh, no. No thanks," I said. "I just stepped in here for a moment. I don't have any laundry with me. I do it by myself at home. I don't like strangers touching my clothes. See," I said, looking around me, "no laundry bag."

The cat on top of the dryer screamed like an animal in heat and jumped onto my shoulder. I swung my body from side to side, trying to shake it off, but it clung to me with its claws.

"Dawn, get off the young woman," Armand said, putting his hands around the cat's white underbelly and pulling it away from my body.

"That was a very sexy dance you were doing. No wonder my cat jumped on top of you."

As soon as I heard the word "sexy," I backed up toward the door. I'd had enough of that for one day.

"Why are you in my Laundromat all dressed up with no laundry?" he asked before I had a chance to get out the door.

I pointed at the plant in the window, and he seemed to relax.

"Ah, the little fire fern. She's the devil who drew you to me."

I put my hand on the doorknob.

"I'm not drawn to you, I have no idea who you are."

"The fire fern is from Colombia. She loves the sunlight, so I keep her in the front window, which faces south. Colombia is also south, so she feels most at home there."

"It was nice meeting you, Armand."

"Oh, come on, now. It's just a cat, and this is just a Laundromat. A beautiful one, though, don't you think?"

I had to agree.

"In fact, it isn't like a Laundromat at all, is it?"

"No, it isn't. It's more like a world. A tropical world."

"The tropics can happen anywhere, you know. They're a state of mind."

"Are they all tropical plants?"

"Some of them."

"How did you get them to grow in here?"

"Close your eyes and tell me what you see when you picture a Laundromat."

I thought for a moment. It was hard to remember any other Laundromat while surrounded by the gaudy, colorful opulence of the one I was in. It was as if this were the first and only Laundromat there ever was. I closed my eyes.

"I see white plastic baskets on wheels, filled with dirty clothes, and boxes of laundry detergent with bright-blue, green, or red letters. I see gray-and-red pieces of lint on the floor. I see sweaty people in ugly clothing sitting on worn-out benches, staring at big, noisy metal machines, watching their clothes go round and round, like some strange ritual or weird form of hypnotism. I see bulletin boards with pictures of lost cats, and handmade signs for sexual favors available at low rates."

I was surprised at how many visions the word "Laundromat" had inspired in me.

"Do you want to know what I see?"

I nodded.

"I see a room with absolutely perfect growing conditions. Plenty of heat from industrial-strength dryers, mist and moisture from powerful washing machines, and just the right amount of sunlight from the windows—not too direct, because in a Laundromat of this age they are usually scratched. To me, a Laundromat is an ideal greenhouse that just so happens to have some clothes going around in circles."

His explanation delighted me. "Is it yours?"

"It is," he said, sweeping his arm in a half-moon around the room as if he were showing me the Taj Mahal. He spun around gracefully, so delicately on his toes, his right arm out in front of him, palm in the air, that for one fleeting second he looked like a six-foot-four-inch, 250-pound ballerina.

"Before you leave, would you like a cutting from my fire fern?"

"I'm leaving?"

"You have to go back to wherever you came from. And I have to close the Laundromat." Armand sniffed the air around me. "By the way, did you know that you smell like fish, expensive fish at that, which is why my cat liked you? She has very good taste, you know. Some type of sea bass, no doubt, since it's all the rage."

"I had sea-bass ceviche at work today."

"What kind of work do you do?"

"Advertising."

"Glamorous, huh?"

Why does everyone ask that? I wondered.

"No. Not at all," I said.

"Do you like what you do?"

"No, not at all," I repeated.

"What would you like to do?"

"You mean if I didn't have to work?"

"Sure."

"I guess I'd like to do what everyone wants to do. Have great adventures, fall in love, get rich. The usual."

"So why don't you do those things?"

"Time, money—the same reasons you're stuck here in this laundry."

"I'm not stuck at all. I love it here."

Armand laughed. He giggled, actually, with his hand over his mouth, like a little girl. "So—would you like a cutting from my fire fern?"

"I wouldn't know what to do with it. I have a bird-of-paradise at home. But it was already in a pot when I bought it."

"Really?" he said with interest. "You know someone else involved in tropical plants?"

"I don't know him. He sold it to me at the green market."

"Are you going to get more?"

"I don't know."

"Go back and get yourself some more plants. They're good for the soul, you know."

He dragged a ladder over to the window.

"The fire fern spoke to you straight through the glass. It will always be a special plant for you."

He climbed up a step or two, rather laboriously for a man who just moments ago had looked like a ballerina. He pushed away some palm fronds and cut a piece of his fern for me.

"Put it in a glass of warm water in a room with total darkness. When you've got some nice long roots, bring it back to me. If you're lucky, I'll show you my back room. That's where the *real* tropicals are."

"What do you mean, the *real* tropicals?"

"I have some very special plants inside of that room," he said, swinging around on the ladder and pointing to a closed door behind him. "Nine of them, to be exact."

"What makes them so special?"

Armand scanned my body before speaking, looking at me from my head to my feet, his eyes moving across my frame in a zigzag motion, making me feel drowsy and uncomfortable.

"Folks come here, they do their laundry, and my nine plants make them feel a certain way about themselves that keeps them coming back. And when they do, they bring friends with them. More and more every day. Now I have people trekking in from all over town. They come from the West Side, the Upper East Side, Tribeca, SoHo, and the West Village just to do their laundry in my establishment. I've even had a few folks in from Connecticut. There are so many people coming and going that my machines are starting to wear down. It's a concern, I'll admit, but not such a bad one to have."

"And this is because of the plants behind that door?"

"You sound skeptical."

"I'm not sure I believe that plants can bring people into a Laundromat, especially if you keep them behind a locked door. I could understand if they were beautiful and people came to see them, but you don't show them to anyone."

"Well, my machines are the same as all the other machines in all the other Laundromats around town. But my laundry is filled up all day, and the others, not so much. So I say, yes, it is because of the nine plants in that room. It's what I believe."

"Why do you keep them back there?"

"Because they're very valuable. And I should add right now that if you ever mention their whereabouts to anyone, chances are, for one reason or another, you will never get to see them. And that would be very, very sad for you. Believe me, you want to see the nine plants in that room."

"Why don't you show them to me now? What difference could it possibly make if I saw them now or next week?"

"The fire-fern cutting is difficult to root. It doesn't like to grow in this part of the country, or even in this part of the world. It's a finicky plant to begin with, even in its own back-yard. If you have some success with the roots, if you can get it to grow just one or two, it's a sign for me that you're ready to see the nine plants."

"What can I do to help it along?"

"Only the fern can decide whether or not it will grow roots in your presence. This week, next week, next year, maybe never. We'll see what happens."

Armand stepped down from the ladder and held the cutting out to me. I half expected him to grab my arm and drag me into the back room when I took it from his hand, but he simply opened the door to the Laundromat and said good night.

Outside, on the street, I turned and looked at him. He held the door open and waved at me, moving his fingers in an odd, rhythmic, undulating manner—pinky first, with the rest of his fingers following. His wave upset me. His fingers looked like tendrils trying to pull me back inside the Laundromat.

"Come back soon," he said from the doorway. "And good luck with the fern!"

I stood on the street trying to get my bearings. I felt physically uncomfortable holding the cutting from his plant. I looked at my watch and stood stock-still. It was almost midnight. I'd been in the Laundromat for more than two hours.

I stared at the cutting on the way home, trying to understand why I didn't throw it away. Or simply drop it on the street. It looked like any other cutting I'd ever seen. It was a basic four-inch-long green stem with a few random leaves sticking off the sides. But somehow I knew it wasn't like any other cutting. I found myself gripping it more tightly than my bag with my money, phone, and credit cards.

When I got home, I put the cutting on the kitchen countertop. I took off my makeup, washed my face, changed my clothes, and was just about ready to get into bed when a nagging feeling took hold of me. It was silly, and I didn't know why, but I was having an argument with myself about the cutting. I didn't want to put it into water, but I felt pushed to do it. A picture of Armand waving his nauseating fingertips came into my head, and I went into the kitchen and quickly put the fire fern in a glass of warm water.

I'm not a superstitious person, I don't even read my horoscope for fun, but I knew I wanted to see those nine plants in the back room of that Laundromat.

Chinese Windmill Palm
(Trachycarpus fortunei)

The Chinese windmill palm does very well in cooler climates, and it doesn't grow very tall, making it the perfect plant for small apartments in big, cold cities. Instead of discarding its older leaves as most trees do, this kindhearted palm simply drops them down until they form a warm, protective skirt around the trunk, thereby giving them a second career.

I woke up with the sun and went into the kitchen to check on the cutting. As per Armand's instructions, I didn't turn on the light. Instead, I took the fern out of the glass and brought it up close to my face to inspect it. I twirled it around in front of my eyes, going momentarily cross-eyed as I looked for any sign of roots. Of course it was much too soon, and I knew that there wouldn't be any, but I checked anyway, because I'm a checker by nature: lights, stoves, occasionally underneath beds, and, apparently, now plant stems. Life was getting complicated.

I rolled the cutting around between my thumb and forefinger, feeling for any slight rises on its surface, any bumps that would signal its taking root. As I turned the stem I felt dizzy, as if *I* were turning instead of the cutting. I leaned against the countertop and quickly dropped the stem back into the glass of water. I took a damp sponge from the kitchen sink, went across the apartment to the south-facing window, and wiped down the leaves of the bird-of-paradise. The wiping motion always seemed to calm my mind. I wiped and wiped until I felt like myself again. When I was done, I looked around my studio. With just the one plant, it looked barren and empty compared with the colorful, raging beauty of the Laundromat. Armand was right. I needed more plants.

"Hey, advertising lady," Exley yelled from inside his tent.

"It's Lila, remember?" I yelled back.

He came toward me.

"I haven't seen you in a while. How's your bird doing?"

"She's doing great."

"I knew she would. I always manage to find the right homes for my plants. Can I get something for you today?"

"Sure," I said. "Do you have anything that will completely change my entire life?"

Exley smiled.

"That's asking a lot."

"I need a lot."

"That bird's really gotten to you, huh?"

"She has."

"Hmmm. I think you might need something even more tropical and exotic. Something balmy yet bold. Something red-hot and colorful, with a nice sweet scent to go."

"That's exactly what I need!"

"Then you're going to appreciate my newest acquisition."

He beckoned me with his index finger. I tied my hair back with an elastic band to prevent my waves from turning into frizz and went into the humid green tent, closing the flap behind me.

"It's just in from China," he said quietly, almost reverently, wrapping his arms around a rather large plant under a brown burlap sack.

"I hope you're not going to try and sell me that tree, or whatever it is under there. I'll need a U-Haul to get it home."

"This is no ordinary tree," he said, pulling on the rope dramatically, letting the burlap fall to the ground. "This here is a *Trachycarpus fortunei*. A Chinese windmill palm."

The fans bounced up and down as they were released from the burlap, cooling Exley and me like we were on a veranda in South China.

"Sugar comes from the sap of this plant," he said. "And upholstery stuffing, too. Hairbrushes, paint varnish, rosary beads, chess pieces, hats, dress buttons, hot-water bottles, margarine, cooking oils, shampoos, conditioners, cosmetics, moisturizers, doormats, soap, tin cans, and starch for Laundromats. It all comes from the palm tree."

I watched Exley's blue eyes come to life as he talked about the Chinese windmill palm. I saw the way his gloved hand held on to its trunk, and how he put his arms around it and leaned his whole body against the tree while marveling at its many uses. This was a man born to sell plants. I wasn't sure whether it was Exley or the tree, but I asked him how much he wanted.

"I'll give it to you for two hundred bucks, even."

"That's a lot of money for a plant."

"Not when it traveled all the way from China," he said, pulling down on one of the large fans and then letting it go, momentarily air-conditioning the humid tent. "If you have the space, and the inclination, I'll throw in a croton from Jamaica. Free of charge."

Holding on with one hand, he swung his body around the *Trachycarpus fortunei* and stopped just in front of the croton.

It was a small plant with long, colorful oblong leaves in shades of pale purple, deep red, and orange.

"Look at it long enough and you can practically smell the jerk chicken coming from a roadside shack," he said. "That baby grew up in Jamaica, mon. She is hot hot hot. You take these two plants and you've got the balmy Caribbean and the exotic Orient right in your studio apartment. You'll never have to leave home again."

"What's that thing? On its stem?"

Exley bent down.

"Well, look at that," he said, grinning and sliding toward the plant. "That's a brown racer. Crafty little hitchhiker got itself a one-way ticket to the Big Apple right on the back of that plant."

Quick as sound, Exley grabbed the brown snake behind its head and unraveled it from the stem. He held it up. Its long, muscular body whipped back and forth, repeatedly striking the Chinese palm. When it finally stopped, Exley loosened his grip. The snake seemed docile, and it wrapped itself around his arm five or six times, like a set of copper bangles.

"Do you want to touch it?"

He stuck his arm out toward me, and I stepped back.

"Don't be afraid. It only likes small, cold-blooded creatures like lizards and toads."

"And you," I said.

Exley stroked its head as we walked out of the tent.

"I'll drop by at the end of the day and bring the plants over in my truck." With his free hand he pointed at a beat-up white van.

"You'll leave the brown racer here, of course?"

"Of course."

I went home and spent the rest of the afternoon acting like a girl. I cleaned and dusted and sprayed my apartment, and then I cleaned and dusted and spritzed my bird-of-paradise.

At the end of his workday, as promised, Exley brought the plants to my apartment in his plant-transport van.

When I opened the door, he was standing there with the croton tucked under his arm like a corsage for a prom date, and the Chinese windmill palm standing next to him like an escort.

"You made it."

"Oh yes. I'm a man of my word."

"Really? How unusual."

He dragged the windmill palm across my brand-new parquet floors, leaving a trail of dirt behind him, and then he put one plant on either side of the bird-of-paradise, in front of the south-facing windows. He moved the pots back and forth until they were placed to his liking, and wiped the sweat off his face with the entire palm of his hand. He came over and stood right next to me and smiled out at the plants. It was a broad, proud smile, like he had just brought me a giant diamond ring instead of a croton and a palm.

"Thanks," I said, "for delivering them so soon."

He nodded.

"Kitchen?" he asked, bending his thumb back toward the kitchen door.

"Yeah."

He had one big hand on the swinging door when I grabbed him by the arm and pulled him away.

"You can't go in there."

"Why not? You got a dead body in there?"

"No. I just can't let any light inside."

"You got a hydroponic setup back there?"

"No, of course not. You just can't go in there."

"Well, can you go in there? Because I'd really like a glass of water."

"Of course I can."

I slipped through the swinging doors, barely opening them, trying to keep as much light away from the fire-fern cutting as I could.

"Here."

I stuck my hand through the doors and handed him the

water, and then I eased my body back out, opening them as little as possible.

"You're an interesting woman, Lila Grace," he said, and then drank down the glass of water. "Can I have another?"

I had started to slip back through the swinging doors when he grabbed my arm.

"I'm kidding. I just wanted to watch you do that again."

Fortunately, Exley changed the topic.

"The bird looks pretty good. Get those humidifiers and she'll look even better. She'll stand up straighter. It'll be good for the palm and the croton, too."

"I spray with this," I said, holding up a pink plastic spray bottle. "I keep her misty but not too wet, just like you said."

He smiled. "Try keeping the temperature no lower than fifty-five degrees at night for the palm. Sixty just to be sure. And when you get those humidifiers, keep the water in them warm. Cold water shocks the system, and everything gets gummed up and comes to a standstill. The same is true for humans, you know. Never drink cold water if you can avoid it."

"Thanks again for bringing the plants over."

"Yep, no problem," he said, dragging his yellow-gloved fingers through his blond hair in a sign of nervousness that pleased me.

I dug through my purse for some cash to tip him.

"No, no, no. Don't worry about it. I enjoy finding nice homes for my plants."

"Hey," I said, hitting him lightly on his biceps, "I was thinking."

"What?"

"Can I make you dinner sometime? As a thank-you for bringing these over and setting them up so perfectly?"

Exley was so quiet I thought I could hear the plants giving off oxygen.

"Are you asking me out?"

"No, no. Not really. I'm just inviting you to dinner to say thank you."

"Oh, I see. It's a thank-you dinner thing."

"I could make something light. Like fish, or pasta, or salad, but you probably don't eat plants, right? Or we can order pizza or Chinese."

"You don't do this a lot, do you?"

"Not really."

The conversation was so slow that my mind raced just to take up the slack. Maybe I'd put this very nice, handsome man in an incredibly awkward position. Maybe he was living with someone, or even married.

"Can I go into the kitchen next time?" he asked.

"Definitely," I said.

"Okay. Sounds like a plan. A week from Wednesday?"

"Good. Great."

He turned around in the doorway.

"This place you got here, Lila Grace, it's perfect for tropicals."

I knew that was some kind of weird compliment from him, like I had chosen my studio just for the purpose of growing his plants.

I locked the door behind him and went over to the window. I peered between the fronds of the Chinese palm and watched him walk across the street to the van. I was staring at the back of his army jacket when he stopped in the middle of the street, turned around, looked up at me, and waved. I felt like an idiot peeking between the palm leaves, so I closed them like a door.

I followed Exley's advice and invested. I bought two powerful humidifiers, one for each side of my studio. I made rain in my apartment in an attempt to replicate a tropical environment for my plants. My hair frizzed, but my plants grew taller. The walls dripped and the parquet floor buckled, but the mist made my skin smooth and my clothes wrinkle-free.

Although the bird-of-paradise would always be my favorite, like a first child (and I should know, being a third child), I got the same satisfying results from my two new plants, the *Trachycarpus fortunei* and the croton.

I have to say that it's pretty easy to get sucked into plants when they're growing well. They can't walk away when things aren't going perfectly, they don't play bad music, make weird sounds, or dress inappropriately. They just sort of stand around looking beautiful and succeeding at life, like fashion models. And I found them immensely gratifying.

Mexican Fan Palm
(Washingtonia robusta)

*A hardy, self-sufficient palm with bright-green fan-shaped fronds,
the Mexican fan can grow to eighty feet or more. Mexican fans
make great houseplants because they can adjust to your lifestyle,
but they do not like to be overwatered, overfed, or overpruned.
In other words, curb your overbearing tendencies.
They don't want all you have to give. Just a little bit will do.*

I felt ridiculous putting on black sunglasses to go to spy on a laundry (really, what had my life come to?), but I hadn't turned the kitchen light on in almost two weeks, and still the cutting had not taken root. I simply could not continue leaping in front of my kitchen door like a lunatic every time a handsome man wanted a glass of water.

I had no intention of actually talking to him, but I thought it might be a good idea to go over to First Avenue and get a better look at Armand in broad daylight. Maybe he wasn't a six-foot-four-inch guy who owned a moss-covered Laundromat with nine secret plants in a back room. Maybe I was just a slightly unhinged, newly divorced woman who had come off a horrible day at work.

I headed east from Union Square past the Dunkin' Donuts on Fourteenth Street and the New York Sports Club on Irving

Place. I made a right on First Avenue and noticed an unusual number of people on the street outside of the Laundromat.

Many of them had the requisite black or red laundry bags printed with the large pink-tulip logo signifying Armand's business, but there were just as many without bags, milling about, drinking coffee, and talking.

I decided to be an adult, stop spying, and go inside to talk to him. I walked up to the front of the laundry and was just about to open the door when I heard a yell from the back of the crowd.

"Hey, lady," a small woman with a packed laundry bag shouted, "the line starts back here."

"Sorry," I yelled over to her, making my way to the end of the line. I didn't want to piss Armand off by cutting in front of his customers.

"What are you waiting for?" I asked the man in front of me, noticing that he didn't have a bag with him.

"To speak to Armand."

"What are you going to talk to him about?"

"That's none of your business."

"I just want to know if you're asking about the tropical plants."

"Tropical plants? No. I'm not asking about any tropical plants."

I took my place in line, and a few minutes later the man turned to me.

"People talk to Armand about anything. The girlfriend's cheating, the husband doesn't love 'em anymore, heartaches, breakups, breakdowns, break-ins, bullshit, all the usual crap. He's the go-to guy in the neighborhood."

"How much does he charge?"

"He doesn't, but lately word's gotten out on him, and now there's always a line. Everything good comes to an end, right?"

"Is he that good?"

"You think I'm waiting on line on a Sunday afternoon for nothing? I got kids."

I waited outside for over an hour, longer than I've waited at the DMV, or at the new Trader Joe's on Fourteenth Street, until I finally got inside the Laundromat.

"I was wondering when you were going to say hello," Armand said, sitting on a red plastic milk crate and trimming a cutting with a pair of silver nail scissors.

"You saw me out there?"

"Of course I saw you—peeking into my laundry like a thief."

"The cutting didn't take root."

"I know it. You wouldn't be sneaking around if it had. Be patient. It's early yet."

"It doesn't even have nubs on the stem."

"Has anyone else seen it?"

"No, and believe me, that hasn't been easy."

"Good. We need to be sure it takes root just for you. If there's anyone else around, it may root for that person, and then you'll never benefit."

"How will I benefit?"

"I have no idea."

"Does it matter that I came back to see you before it took root?"

Armand shrugged. "I don't care what you do. You don't matter to me unless that cutting takes root. If that happens, we're in a different place that neither of us chose."

"How do you know the answers to all of their questions?" I asked, looking at the long line of people outside.

Armand held a cutting up to the light. "You were in such a rush to get away from me the other night, you never told me your name."

"Lila Nova."

"Hmmm," he said, rolling the cutting between his thumb and index finger. "Lila Nova. So soft. So very unlike you."

"I'm soft."

"Sure you are. Soft as rock." Armand laughed.

"So how do you know the answers to their questions?"

"I don't."

"Then why are they standing on line on a Sunday afternoon to speak with you?"

"Maybe they're just here to see my plants."

"I don't think so. That man I was talking to back there, he didn't have any interest in your plants."

"I'll give you a little tip, because I like you, Lila Nova. My job is easy. I tell them what they already know."

I looked out at all the people.

"Here," he said, pulling up a milk crate next to his, "have a seat and listen. But don't look like you're listening, or no one will talk to me anymore, and you'll ruin my good time."

The next man in line came over and plopped his laundry bag next to Armand. It made a loud sighing sound when he sat down on top of it.

"Armand, how are you?"

"Good, I'm very good. Thank you for asking. What can I do for you today?"

"I'm worried about me and Elaine."

"How is Elaine?" Armand asked, never once looking at the man, and continuing to trim the cutting with the small nail scissors.

"She's annoyed with me all the time. No matter what I do, she nitpicks and criticizes me about the smallest things."

"Nitpicks," Armand repeated. "Nipiks. Niphidium, nipho-bolus," he said, raising his cutting to the light.

"What?"

"Just some ferns I like."

"If I use a number-two pencil, she asks me why I'm not using a number-one. If I buy white napkins, she wanted pink. I can't win with her. There's nothing I can do to please her. To tell you the truth, it's making me a little paranoid. I'm starting to think she's getting tired of me. Maybe even thinking about leaving me. You know her—what do you think?"

"How do you spend your days?"

"The usual way. I get up. I go to work. I go to the bar with my buddies. I go home. I don't stay out all night, and I hardly ever look at other women, if that's what you're thinking, and almost never when I'm with her."

"Go straight home. Skip the bar."

When the man left, I looked at Armand.

"Skip the bar? That's it? That's all the advice you have? You're right, your job is easy."

Armand smiled.

"His wife already told me she hates his drinking. He believes in what I say, so maybe he'll slow down a bit. Who knows? I couldn't care less one way or the other. He's more fun when he's drunk anyhow."

"Why were you naming those ferns? Niphidium, nipholobus?"

"To keep myself amused. These people bore the hell out of me most times." Armand put his cutting down and turned toward me. "I'll tell you a little secret. I could help most of the people standing out there, but when I'm feeling a little lazy, which is most of the time, I let my plants do the work for me."

"What do you mean?"

"A man comes into my laundry. He doesn't know that he has a question, but I can see that he does. In that case, I can't give an answer, because there is no question, so I give the job to one of my plants."

"For instance?"

"Just recently a young man walked in, a man very similar to

you. He was your age and about your size, but he was here strictly to do his laundry. He didn't want to talk to me or look at my plants. In fact, he didn't even seem to notice them."

"Was he blind?" I asked, looking up at the dozens of plants strung across the ceiling.

"No, but he couldn't see the things around him because he was very sad. He was a young man, but he walked with his back bent over, like he was searching for coins with a metal detector. His life had slowed to a crawl."

"What did you do?"

"I didn't do anything. Why should I? I'm not a doctor, and I don't have the time to fix everyone who comes into my laundry looking like they're slogging through quicksand."

"But you did something?"

"I did. I gave the job to one of my smartest plants, my wonderful Mexican fan palm. I went right over to the young man crying into his dirty socks and underwear, and I asked him what was wrong.

" 'Nothing. Leave me alone.'

"I smiled at him as warmly as I could. I told him that I owned the Laundromat, and since I had seen him many times and he was such a loyal customer, I would let him do his laundry here for six months, for free, if he would take care of one of my plants."

"That sounds like a great deal," I said.

"The young man was too depressed to care one way or another about my offer, so he agreed without giving it a minute's thought. On his way out, I gave him my Mexican fan palm. It was a big plant. Three or four feet high. A gorgeous, energetic palm with lots of waving, sexy fans. 'Take good care of her,' I told him. 'And come back and do as much laundry as you like. No charge. No matter how dirty you are,' I yelled after him, 'it's okay to use my machines!' "

"Did he know how to care for the plant?"

"No. And he didn't ask, either. He just took it and left."

"And?"

"He came back about two weeks later looking rather upset and embarrassed.

" 'The leaves are turning brown and yellow around the edges. What should I do?'

"I told him he was overwatering and that all he needed to do was to let the plant dry out completely. I told him not to worry, the plant would be fine. He came back three weeks after that, looking even more upset.

" 'I stopped watering the plant, just like you said, and now its leaves are falling off!'

"Oh, he was so upset," Armand said, and laughed.

"What did you do?"

"I told him that the plant was in a new environment and its behavior was not unusual. I suggested he keep the plant for a while longer, regrow the leaves, and then, when it was a bit more robust, he should bring it back to the Laundromat. He came back a third time, looking even worse than the first two times. He looked absolutely terrible.

" 'The plant is dying. Please. Tell me what to do.'

"I told him that I'd never expected all of this to happen to my poor little plant. 'Keep trying,' I said. 'Do whatever you can to save the beautiful plant, and then bring her back to me, quickly.' And do you know what he did, that smart young man?"

"What?"

"He went home and he hacked that plant to pieces! He chopped it up and down with an ax, chopping and chopping it into tiny little bits. And then, when he was totally exhausted, he threw it all away. He dumped it right into the incinerator."

Armand laughed out loud.

"Why is that funny?" I asked, somewhat unnerved.

"That big, brilliant Mexican fan palm made him so angry, he didn't know what else to do."

"Don't you care what he did to your plant?"

"Listen to what I'm telling you. That man was depressed. He needed to get angry. He needed to let things out. Don't you see? That plant saw what was wrong with him, and it cured him!"

"I don't know how you can be happy about that. He killed one of your favorite plants."

"The plant showed magnificent abilities. Genius, even. Think about it. First it turned yellow, and then it dropped its leaves, and when that didn't work, it began to die. Ha! Even I underestimated it. It worked hard to make that man angrier and angrier. When one thing didn't work, it tried another, until it was near death and the man was thoroughly and completely pissed off. That plant sacrificed its life to cure the young man. It lured that man into killing it. That's plant magic!"

"But how do you know that? I mean, how do you know that the plant knew what it was doing?"

"Oh, I can't say for sure, but it certainly looks that way. I gave him a plant that was exceptionally hard to kill. A plant that flourishes in the most dire of environments. A plant well known for its adaptability. Don't you see? It was an effort for that plant *not* to thrive!"

"Does the man still come here to wash his clothes?"

"Of course he does. And when I see him now, he's happy. He walks into my Laundromat with a woman on his arm, smiling!"

"He sounds like a nut to me."

"No. It's a beautiful story. A love story. That plant truly loved that man!"

I said good-bye to Armand, because there was simply no

way I was going along with a story about a plant that gave up its life for a man.

"Come back when you have those roots," he yelled after me.

The next day I got home from work and checked on the cutting. I raced out of the kitchen with a level of excitement I hadn't known since I was a child. I didn't know what to do with myself. I danced around my studio, accidentally knocking over the croton, spilling dirt all over my new wood floors. I couldn't have cared less. The fire-fern cutting had four long, tender white roots!

Plant Money

*Marijuana can go for thousands of dollars an ounce.
In fact, as of 2006, it was the number-one cash crop in
the United States, averaging thirty billion dollars a year.
Saffron from Iran is the next-most-expensive plant, as it takes
seventy-five thousand flowers to make one pound of the popular
spice. Orchids, on the other hand, tend to elude the laws of
supply and demand and are priced much more like paintings or
sculpture, their value being in the eye of a particular collector.*

I took the cutting, with its brand-new roots, sprayed it with water, and put it in a square of cellophane. I would have brought it over to Armand right then and there, but the wrap party for the Puma shoot was at six-thirty. What were the odds that the party would happen on the same night as the roots? It was bad enough that I had to see Geoff Evans every single day, but now I had to give him an evening, too. My plan was to go to the dinner party, make a quick exit around seven-thirty, and head for the Laundromat.

I looked over at the croton I'd tipped over and felt a pang of guilt. I had Exley on the brain, and the thought of him and his obvious love for the plant made me repot it on the spot. So there I was at six-fifteen, dumping new dirt into the plant instead of waiting outside for Kody and the car service to take me to the dinner. By the time I was ready to leave, I was covered in potting soil. It was too late to change my clothes, so I stamped my feet to shake it loose, brushed off my skirt as best I could, put on a pair of heels, which probably made the dirt stand out even more, and locked the door behind me.

My doorman, Carlos, knew way too much about my life. So much so that the sight of him had become humiliating. I'm sure he noticed that I never stepped foot out of the elevator with a man, ever. In fact, every single day, Carlos was a reminder of my single status. That was the thing I disliked most about having a doorman. It was impossible to fake my life. Even to myself. It was worse than having a shrink.

"Someone left this for you today," he said as the elevator door opened.

He handed me a white envelope smudged with dirt, just like me. The note inside was short and to the point. *Can't make it on Wednesday night for dinner. David Exley.*

There was no *What are you doing on Thursday night?* or the requisite *How about another time?* or even just a simple *Stop by the market and say hello.* The tone of the note was all business. He was a guy at the green market who'd sold me a couple of plants, and that was that.

I looked at Carlos and feigned surprise, as if I had just gotten a pleasant invitation instead of a rejection from a man I really liked. I could tell by his automatic expression of sorrow that he wasn't buying it. It was obvious to both of us that I was going to be single for the rest of my life. I gave him a smile that seemed to scare him, and headed out the door.

The car waiting to take me to the dinner was parked outside. Kody was already in the backseat, drinking coffee and looking sullen. I slid in next to him. I scraped some of the dirt out from underneath my fingernails with the help of my other fingernails, and then filed my nails against my skirt to smooth out the rough edges. The driver looked at me through his rearview mirror. He had a disgusted look on his face that said, *Keep your nail dirt off of my new leather seats.*

Halfway to the Upper East Side, Kody finally spoke.

"You're dirty."

"I know. I tipped one of my plants over. I had to repot."

"Why couldn't you do it later?"

"Because," I said, holding up the piece of cellophane, "I have roots!"

I waved the wrapper in front of Kody, and he grabbed it out of my hand.

"What's this?"

"Please. Don't shake it or bang it. It's a fire-fern cutting, and it took me weeks to get it to root."

"It looks like a tiny little tuber."

"You don't know what a tiny tuber is," I said, trying to remain calm.

"You don't, either," he said, holding the cutting out of my reach.

"It's the swollen part of an underground root. Like a potato."

"You seem tense," Kody said. "Have you gotten any lately?"

"That's none of your business."

"Have you seen that guy from the green market?"

"I have. And, once again, none of your business."

"Maybe you should take up yoga," he said, finally handing the cutting back to me. "It would relax you more than alprazolam."

"I only took Xanax the one time, right after I got divorced. You try getting through a divorce without drugs."

Kody began his mantra.

"Yoga nidra, the yoga of sleep. Pranayama, control of the breath. Hatha yoga, O gentle yoga of service."

"O nutjob, what the hell is the yoga of sleep?"

"It's when you practice staying awake in your sleep so that your mind is awake while your body is sleeping."

We came to a dead standstill in rush-hour traffic.

"I'm taking a nap," I said. "Body *and* mind. Wake me up when we get there."

The restaurant lived up to its name, Ice. It was cold both literally and figuratively, as if the owners had spent so much money on furniture design that they couldn't afford heat. It was beautiful enough, though. Cut-glass patterns etched into frosted-glass tabletops paired with pale-blue chairs. Lamps were lit with blue-tinted bulbs under blue frosted glass, and the waiters and waitresses were all uniformly pale, blue-eyed blonds, in keeping with the décor. The large, frameless silvered Art Deco mirrors on the walls reflected elegant people everywhere, and each table was set with a bouquet of white lilies flown in from some part of the world where lilies were in season.

I looked in the window before going inside. Everyone was there. There were writers and art directors from the creative department, along with the letter people—the ECDs, GCDs, EADs, and CEOs. Nobody really knew what they did, but we knew it was something important because their offices had large windows with good views of Manhattan, and fancy Italian espresso machines replete with attractive young people to operate them. Our boss, Geoff Evans, stood up when we got there.

"The team of the moment," he said, already drunk. "You're filthy," he added.

Everyone stared at my dirty clothes.

"I'm not dirty," I said. "I'm covered in specially formulated potting soil made from Canadian sphagnum peat moss, organic reed-seed peat, rice hulls, and forest products, perfect for African violets and gesneriads, and probably more nutritious than any of the food we're about to eat."

Everyone at the table was silent, and I sat down next to Kody.

"Nice," he said.

"These people don't know anything. I'm covered in more organics than the Whole Foods on Union Square."

"So—what are you going to do with that root?" he asked.

"It's a cutting, not a root, and I'm going to bring it to a man I met in a Laundromat."

"You're getting really weird, you know that?"

"It's not that weird. He grows tropical plants in his Laundromat on First Avenue."

"All right, dude, I can roll with that."

I liked Kody because he was one of those people who understood that the world and all of its inhabitants were a bit strange, and he preferred it that way. I was one of those people who were frightened by the general oddity of the human race, even though I often found myself involved with particularly strange people.

"I bet he's got some real special *sativa* up in that Laundromat. Maybe even some diamond peyote." Kody loved to get high, and his mind often tracked in the direction of things that could be smoked or ingested. "Maybe he's a plant shaman, like Don Juan?"

"I have no idea, Kody. I'm only interested in his plants."

"What's he interested in?"

"I don't know."

"I do," said Kody, smiling.

"He's not like that. He's old."

"So are you."

"Thanks a lot."

Champagne arrived by the bottle, and the food came out of

the kitchen à la carte on small plates. Roasted foie gras with passion fruit, saki–pine nut gazpacho with oysters and cherries, melted chestnut soup with salmon threads and celery root, and Mediterranean sea bass with Parmesan and charred lily bulb.

"At least we know what they do when the lilies wilt," said Geoff Evans, sitting next to me and putting a big bulb in his mouth.

"Lila met someone who likes plants, too," Kody said. "He doesn't eat them, though. He deals in them. He sells them at the green market in Union Square."

I took a large swig of champagne and kicked Kody underneath the table.

Geoff picked something green from between his teeth and re-ate it.

"Anyone who aligns himself with nature these days is a fool. Your friend who deals in plants, he's a fool. Nature's going the way of the Arctic ice shelf," he continued. "It's going the way of the snow leopard, the white rhino, the silverback gorilla, the jaguar, the Pygmies, and the Inuit people. Every single polar bear will be gone in less than fifty years. It's all over for nature. Don't you know that yet?"

He glared at me, as if my liking someone who sold plants was a new type of personal insult.

"We have to align ourselves with machines," he continued, picking up his cell phone and holding it out over the table. "This is the new nature. A unit with no weakness. You can't kill it, because there's a billion more where it came from. It won't biodegrade, so it's inherently indestructible. You can't eat it, or rip it out of the ground, or burn down its land for timber. It's a perfectly self-contained entity with a shelf life of forever."

"What about oxygen?" Kody said. "We get oxygen from plants."

"Oxygen, smoxygen," Geoff said, looking around the table. "Where's the model?"

"In high school," I said.

I wasn't sure whether it was the richness of the foie gras or the buzzing and ringing cell phones parked next to each dinner plate like a new utensil, but by the end of the first course, I was feeling slightly nauseated.

I ducked out of the frosted door of the restaurant without a word and headed for the Laundromat, sucking in fresh air like it was gold.

I took the subway back downtown and walked south along Third Avenue, clutching the cutting in my hand like a lunatic. Suddenly it was the most important thing in the world. I just had to be involved in something besides Geoff Evans, naked teenagers, and the death of nature.

Rush hour was over, and the streets were not very crowded. It should have been a pleasant walk, except that I was having all sorts of second thoughts about Armand. What if the cutting wasn't a fire fern from Colombia, but just a regular fern he cut from a plant in Tompkins Square Park? What if he was going to lure me into the back room with the so-called nine plants and lock the door from the outside? A life spent around advertising executives can make a person very suspicious of the motives of others.

Those suspicions got the better of me, and somewhere around Thirty-fourth Street I veered away from the direction of the Laundromat and walked west, toward the green market.

I needed to see Exley. He was exactly the type of man I was in the mood for. A man of commerce, not a man of colors and whites. True, he had canceled our date, but, romance aside, he would know whether or not the cutting was the real thing.

When I arrived at the market, Exley was watering his crotons and cursing the unusually chilly April cloud cover under his breath. I heard words like "Northeast" and "cumulonimbus" uttered with nasty intonations. Happy to see me, but, having just broken our date, he simultaneously brightened up and backed away when he saw me coming.

"How's your bird doing?" he asked, shaking my hand with his yellow gardening glove.

"She's getting bigger every day."

"And the Chinese palm? Giving you any problems?"

"Same as the bird-of-paradise, growing like a weed."

"They'd both be dead out here," he said, looking up at the clouds. "It's bad for tropicals this year. Bad for business. I can't keep 'em alive for more than a week or two. Not long enough to sell 'em."

"Is that why you can't make it to dinner? Business is bad?"

Exley scratched his head with one finger.

"You sure get right to the point, don't you? The truth is, I don't like to mix business with dating and dinners and all of that complicated stuff. It never works out well. It's never a good idea."

"I'm not sure my purchasing three plants qualifies as doing business."

Exley looked at me sideways.

"It may not seem like business to you, but this is the business I'm in. I sell plants, and I've sold a few to you, and I hope to sell you a few more."

It was my turn to be quiet.

"I'm sorry," I said. "You're right. We have done business."

We stood together quietly while Exley watered his plants.

"The croton's growing like a teenage boy," I offered. "I came home the other night and the pot had tipped over while I was out."

"She's too big for her home. She needs to be repotted. Pick up some Schultz Professional Potting Soil and a pot that's three to four inches wider than the one she's in now. Cut the old pot open with some gardening shears, making cuts that go from the rim down toward the roots. Make sure to fill the new pot with a few inches of soil and some ceramic shards for drainage, then pick up the whole root ball," he said, making a big circle with all ten fingers, "and put it in the new pot. Put some more soil on top, to about an inch or two from the rim. She'll thank you later."

"To tell you the truth, I didn't come here to find out why you canceled the date. And I've already repotted the croton."

"Oh?"

"I have a question I was hoping you might be able to answer."

"If it's plant-related, I'm your man."

I unwrapped the cutting and dangled its long white roots in front of Exley.

"I was told by a somewhat questionable source that it's a fire fern from Colombia. I need to be sure."

Exley dropped the hose.

He came very close to me, holding my eyes with his, and in the same second, before I could say anything, he grabbed the cutting out of my hand and raced into the tent. I followed him as fast as I could. He brushed some dirt and leaves off an old wooden table he'd brought to make the tent look like a French country garden. He brushed enough debris off the table to make room for a thousand cuttings. He cradled the fern in his palm and then carefully laid it down as if it were a newborn, which in a sense it was. Then he pulled a magnifying glass out of a skinny drawer running the length of the table and studied the roots. He was quiet for several minutes.

Finally, he looked up.

"It's a fire fern all right; you can tell by its shrubbiness. Most oxalis plants are tuberous, but not this baby. She's pretty rare. I saw one once in South America."

He stopped talking and looked dead into my eyes as if I were a criminal.

"Where did you get it?"

I'd seen that look in men's eyes before, but it was usually about getting sex, not about getting a plant. I didn't like the way Exley was staring at me, or the cutting, so I leaned over and grabbed it off the table. I stood there in front of him holding the root, pressing it to my chest like a freak. He came around to my side of the table and stood so near to me that I could smell the dirt on his jacket. This was definitely the strangest reason I'd ever been so close to a man I liked.

"How much do you want for it?" he asked.

"Are you kidding?" I said, root pressed to my sternum.

"I'll give you five hundred for it right now. Or I can try and unload it for you for whatever I can get, which will probably be a lot more than five hundred. We'll split the difference."

"Why are you whispering?"

"I don't want anyone to know that thing is in here."

Never a big fan of life's odd little turns, and having had way too many of them lately, I laughed a bit and then got nervous. Five hundred dollars was a lot of money for putting a small, dirty stem in a warm glass of water and waiting a few weeks for roots to show up.

"Where did you get it?" he asked me again, ignoring the customers beginning to line up outside.

I knew he wouldn't believe me if I told him, so I didn't even bother to lie.

"I got it from a Laundromat."

"Put me in touch with whoever gave this to you and I'll tack on an extra two hundred bucks. I may be a guy covered in soil who runs a plant stand, but I know that's a lot, even for someone in advertising."

If the average person has three career changes in a lifetime, then I just saw my second career flash before my eyes.

"Well?" he asked.

It was possible that I could get more cuttings from Armand and sell them to Exley. I could say good-bye to Geoff Evans and make money traveling between the Laundromat and the green market, transferring tropical-plant cuttings from grower to seller.

"I'll act as a go-between," I said, even though I had no idea what a go-between acted like. "I'll get the cuttings and you'll pay me."

Exley looked annoyed.

"You don't want to tell me who this person is?"

"I don't."

"You don't trust me?"

"We've never worked together."

"Does this person have any other plants?"

"I'm not an expert, but I think I saw wild primrose, poppies, a few different types of grasses, marigolds, dahlias, and an iris."

Exley spoke slowly.

"I mean valuable plants," he said, breaking the word "valuable" up into its syllables. "Did you see any plants of value besides the fire fern?"

"I wouldn't know if a plant had value. I didn't know this one had any until you told me. But he did mention some nine plants he had in a back room."

I didn't see any harm in bringing up the nine plants, since I had absolutely no intention of telling Exley where the Laundromat was.

"Are you sure he said nine? He said nine plants?"

"Yes, definitely nine."

"Did you see them?"

"No. He said I wasn't ready yet. He said if I could root the fire fern he would show them to me."

"I'll be damned. The nine plants of desire," Exley said, mostly to himself.

"What?"

"It's nothing. Just an old story amongst plant people. A myth."

Exley seemed to calm down. He put his arm around my shoulders, and even though he had his gardening gloves on, it was nice to feel him touch me.

"Just get me as many of these cuttings as you can," he said. "If any of them grow, I'll make it much more than worth your while."

It wasn't exactly the proposition I wanted from Exley, but it was a start.

I left the green market and headed east, toward the Laundromat. All I needed to do was show Armand the roots. I would impress him with my growing ability and convince him to give me more cuttings. Maybe even from the nine plants in the back room. The nine plants of desire, as Exley had called them, making them sound as sexy as Armand had made them sound mysterious.

The reason for meeting both Armand and Exley was becoming ever clearer in my mind. It had nothing to do with either of them. It had to do with me, and my life's work. Perhaps I wasn't meant to be in advertising after all. Perhaps I was meant for something much more romantic. Like dealing in rare tropical plants.

The Number Nine

Beethoven wrote nine symphonies. A cat has nine lives.
A baseball team has nine players. The expression "to the nines"
means "to the highest degree." "On cloud nine" means
happy or euphoric. Nine is the highest single digit,
symbolizing completeness.

When I got to the Laundromat, Armand was sitting on the bench that ran straight down the middle with his back to the door.

"You're back," he said, without turning around.

"How did you know it was me?"

"It's not a big laundry hour. Most people are at home with their family, while you, without a relationship of any kind as far as I can tell, might be going to a bar, or perhaps coming here."

His comments stung, but I let them pass.

He turned around and laughed. His teeth were very white, with even, quarter-inch spaces between them, and much too small for his size. Armand had separated, Chiclet, girl teeth. The image disturbed me, and I pushed it to the back of my mind.

"I have roots," I said, holding up the cutting in plastic.

"Yes, unfortunately, you do."

"What is that supposed to mean?"

"Your roots are your problem. They hold you in place and stop you from growing. Plants need roots because they can't move on their own. Their roots serve them well, stopping them from getting blown all over the place by the wind. But we humans can move around at will, and our roots hold us in place unnecessarily. Usually in a place we don't want to be. Then, when we try to move, we rip our roots, and it hurts, so we end up staying right where we are."

Armand held out his hand, and I forked over the cutting.

"Next time, bring the cutting in a paper bag—or, better yet, wrapped in a moist towel. Never put a cutting in cellophane unless you want to suffocate it."

"Of course," I said, thrilled that he had mentioned a *next time,* dollar signs in my eyes.

He unraveled the cellophane and turned his attention to the roots. He held them up to the fluorescent lights and ran them under his nose to smell them.

"The little plant likes you," he said, shoving the cutting toward my face very fast, making me back up. "You better watch out."

"I thought that was a good sign?"

"If a plant likes you, it might decide to give you gifts. Some of them you'll want, and some of them you won't."

"What kind of gifts?"

He tickled the white roots with his index finger.

"This little plant can hypnotize you and make you greedy," he said, staring into my eyes.

His look seemed to push me farther backward, and I had to grip one of the folding tables behind me to keep my balance. Armand took a step toward me. I bent back even farther, until I was practically lying across the table.

"Would you like another cutting?" he asked, leaning over me with a fierce look in his eye.

It was the second time in one day a man had given me that look over a plant cutting. When it came to intimidation, Geoff Evans had nothing on Exley or Armand.

"Yes," I said from my supine position on the table, "I'd like another."

Armand climbed up the ladder to his fern and took a cutting. "Maybe this one will bring you even more money," he said on the way down.

"How did you know about the money?"

"I know because I gave you something valuable and you're not a stupid woman. I know because of generational factors. I know because a woman of your time and place would look at the monetary value of an object in her possession first, above anything else about that object. A woman of your time and place is not trained to see in any other way. She is not trained to look for other values and meanings for the objects in front of her. For instance, you never thought about meeting me, the strangeness of it, or the possible reasons for it. If you had, you might have thought more deeply about the little plant in the window that led you to me. I simply thought about the values of your time and assumed that you would act accordingly. And, like a good soldier of your milieu, you did."

I did not like that I acted according to my time, since I thought of myself as brighter than most of the people around me. And I did not like his use of the word "milieu." It sounded odd coming out of his mouth, and it made me very uncomfortable.

"We all act according to our time. Don't worry about it. Look at me. I'm an old man growing plants in a Laundromat. That is definitely of my time and not yours. I don't mind being of my time, and you shouldn't, either. We're stuck with our milieu until we recognize it and then change it if we choose."

"I could change it if I chose to."

"It's very, very difficult to change. Remarkably few people are capable of it."

Armand held his hand out with the cutting in his palm.

"Take this and make yourself some money. There's nothing wrong with making money. Consider it a gift from the little fern."

I took the cutting. I could tell from his mood that the timing wasn't perfect, but I asked him if I could see the nine plants.

"Not today," he said.

"Can I ask you a question, then?"

"Sure. Go ahead. Ask me anything."

"Why are there nine plants? Why not three, or twenty?"

"Good question. I was beginning to worry that you'd never ask. Each one of the plants holds the key to one of the nine things human beings desire most. In no particular order, they are fortune, power, magic, knowledge, adventure, freedom, immortality, sex, and of course love. And then there is the number nine itself. This number holds many unique qualities. For instance, if any number is multiplied by nine, the resulting digits always add up to nine. For this reason, nine is often referred to as a 'mathemagical number.' A symbol of unalterable truth. The essence of completeness. A perfect circle, always adding up to itself. It's a beautiful thing, don't you think?"

"I never thought about it before, but, yes, I do."

"That's why anyone who has the nine plants is complete. That person will have all that she desires in life, so the myth goes. But you must have all nine in your possession at the same time. Though an individual plant can be powerful in the right hands, the magical nine combination is invincible. No matter who you are."

"I rooted the fire-fern cutting. Now I'd like to see the nine plants. You said I could."

"It's not the right time."

"What time, then?"

"Come back at dawn or dusk. When the male and female energies meet as equals, neither stronger than the other. That's when you can see the plants in their true power. Otherwise, you are only seeing half of the nine combination. You've come too far to see only half, don't you think?"

I just wanted to see the plants. In single file, combinations, groups, day, night, one, nine, whatever, whenever, I just wanted to see the plants.

I stopped in the doorway on my way out.

"Why me? Why are you showing them to me?"

"Because I like you."

"That's not enough."

"Because you came into my Laundromat."

"I don't believe that."

"I have been growing plants in my laundry for thirty years. During that time, I have met ten people who are capable of change. You are one of them."

"But what does that have to do with seeing the plants?"

"They will change you, if you let them. And I'm counting on you changing."

"Why do you care if I change?"

"Because both of us will benefit. You perhaps even more than I. But maybe not. It depends how much you can change, and in what way."

I ran from the laundry back to the green market, shaking Armand's thoughts out of my head. I arrived, out of breath, and held up the new cutting. Exley looked unimpressed.

"I'll give you three hundred for it."

"You said five."

"I'm not sure it's worth five," he said, rolling the cutting between his gloved thumb and fingers.

Why does everybody do that? I wondered.

"The price is dependent on the quality, of course."

"Of course."

I looked at the cutting, and it looked good to me. It was long, bright green, and still moist. All good things in a cutting, as far as I knew.

Exley put his arm around me and pulled me close. He put his hand on top of my head.

"Look at you," he said. "You know nothing. This isn't a good cutting. It's not even an okay cutting. It's perfect. It's an absolutely perfect cutting. Healthy, robust, alive, and ready to grow. You really don't know anything about plants, do you?"

"Maybe not, but I know something about math."

Exley shook my hand with the money in his palm.

"To many more moments like this one," he said.

"To many more," I repeated.

"From a Laundromat, huh?"

"Yep. Straight from Colombia to a Laundromat."

"How would you like to go straight from the green market to dinner? Tomorrow night?"

I walked away from the plant stand and into the market with the five hundred dollars in my pocket and a date with Exley. I'd never had such a good time making money in my entire life.

I walked past the people pushing baby strollers, which usually annoyed me when the market was crowded, but not this evening. This evening I smiled at the babies, and their parents, too.

I walked past the home-farmed-salmon stand without cringing at the warm fish in the dirty bins. I even took a cup of juice from the carrot guy whose blender was so coated with carrot scrapings it looked like it hadn't been rinsed in a year. It tasted sweet.

The baked-apple-pie stand did exactly what it was supposed to do: it made me feel wholesome and good about myself. I searched my pocket for two bucks for the mini handheld apple pie. I pulled out a hundred-dollar bill instead, and good feelings washed over me about the turn my life had taken. My feelings mixed with the apple pie and the babies, and I felt magnanimous. Right there I decided to share my profit with Armand instead of keeping everything for myself. Everything would be out in the open and fair. I would settle into business with Exley and split the money with Armand, and all three of us would benefit. I walked around the market feeling the satisfaction that comes with making an ethical decision.

Dating

A moth hops onto a flower under cover of moonlight, pollinates,
or mates with the flower, and leaves. We humans do the exact
same thing, except it involves dinner beforehand. So, to make
a long story short, dating is when two or more people eat and
converse to find out if they can tolerate each other enough
to pollinate under cover of moonlight.

Exley invited me to the Strip House on Twelfth Street.
Although it was one of the best steak houses in the neighborhood, serving New York strip tender as warm butter, I
thought it was a strange choice. The interior of the restaurant
was painted dark red. The lighting was low and mustard-
colored. It was romantic but very gloomy. Like receiving a
dozen black tulips, which were beautiful, but not the bright-
yellow ones you were expecting.

He was already there, at the bar, when I arrived. His back
was toward me, and I watched him from behind. He wasn't
drinking, or even talking to the woman next to him, though
she was attractive and looking in his direction. He was simply
waiting. I could have stood there for a long time. There was
something thrilling about watching Exley wait, but I knew it
was unfair to keep him sitting there, so I made my way over to
the bar.

I noticed his hands first. They were much paler than the rest of him, because the yellow gardening gloves he always wore kept them out of the sun. It was the first time I had ever seen them out in the open. They were smaller and more delicate than I'd imagined, as if his gardening gloves did all the work without ever involving his actual hands.

His light-blue button-down shirt was rolled up at the sleeves, revealing tan arms. The blue of his shirt matched his eyes and made me feel like I was outside, looking at the sky. I wondered if he knew that. He didn't seem like the type of man to think about such things, which meant that he probably was.

"Did you want to do this all along," I asked after we were seated, "sell flowers?"

He laughed out loud and rolled up his sleeves even farther, as if he was just getting started.

"Sounds like you're asking me if I ever had any *real* ambition."

"No, no, I'm not asking you that at all."

"Personally, I think growing and selling tropical plants in New York City is a very ambitious thing to do. It's very challenging, actually."

I was not used to people like Exley, whose idea of challenge and ambition was not necessarily rooted in money.

"People in this city are hungry for nature," he said, picking up a roll and buttering it. "They salivate at the sight of it, like a food craving. Plants are good business in a city like this."

"Well, there isn't much plant life around," I said.

"Have you ever watched people here look at nature?" he asked.

"Not really."

"Well, I have. I watch it all day long. They walk around the green market saying things like *Ooohhh, did you see that tomato?* Or *Ahhhhh, look at that beautiful tulip.*"

"So? They're appreciative."

"It isn't what they say exactly, it's how they say it. Like this is the last flower or the last real vegetable they're ever going to lay their eyes on. It's a tone of total surprise. A kind of shock that there's anything natural left at all. When I first heard it, it made me sad. I wanted to bring something from the earth into the city, so that it wouldn't be so much of a surprise. And that's how I got started."

"I don't miss nature."

"Yes, you do. It's why you like me. You still want to believe in the myth of the natural man. And you see it in me. Somewhere inside of you, you miss *men*. I've seen the guys in your neighborhood, the ones who shop in the green market. I know my value to a woman like you."

His clarity about what I wanted made me feel that I had underestimated him.

"Ever marry?" he asked.

I nodded. "I was married for four years."

"What was your husband like?"

I smiled. "Like an alcoholic."

"Hmm. Did you have children?"

"No. He wanted them, but I was afraid, because he drank so much."

I was silent for a moment, remembering a conversation I'd had with my ex.

If you leave now, I'll never have a child.

That's not my fault. I wanted them. You wanted to wait, and wait, and wait. I don't know what you were waiting for.

If I never have a child it's because of you. I want you to know that. I want you to live with that.

If you'd had a child, like a normal woman, I wouldn't be leaving. I would have a reason to stay.

If you could drink like a normal man, I would have had a child with you. But having a child with you would mean I'd have to take care of another person sucking on a bottle.

You're calling me a baby?

I'm calling you a drunk.

"Is that why he left?" Exley asked. "Because you didn't want to have kids?"

"How do you know he was the one who left?"

"You seem a little gun-shy."

"He said he left because he was in love with another woman. But a year later, he left her, too."

"I bet you were happy about that."

I laughed. "Very."

I hadn't told anyone the things I'd just told Exley about my ex-husband, and it made me uneasy. Not because I didn't enjoy talking with him—I did—but because we had just exchanged money. Money was the real reason we were sitting together at this restaurant.

"Why are we here?" I asked him. "Is it because of us, or because of the cuttings?"

"Ah. It's the famous 'What are we?' question."

"No, it isn't that."

"So you see a possible future?"

"Stop it. I'm just asking you why you're sitting here with me, in this lovely restaurant."

"Okay, I'm here because of you. And I'm also here because of the cuttings. Maybe because the cuttings came via you, okay?"

"I bought my first plant because of you," I said. "Did you know that?"

"Your first ever?"

"Yes. The bird-of-paradise was the first plant I ever owned."

He smiled. "So—I was your first."

"That's why *I'm* here."

"What about the man who gave you the cuttings? The man from the Laundromat?"

"Armand?"

"You like him, don't you?"

"I like his Laundromat; I don't know if I like him."

"Why not?"

"He's strange. I don't feel like he's from the planet some-times. But his Laundromat, it's the most fantastic place ever. Green grass, and bright-red poppies, and lavender, and lemon verbena, and palm trees."

"Sounds beautiful to me."

"The man has moss growing on his floor. I can't just like a man who has moss growing on the floor."

"It sounds like a fairy garden."

"Yeah. Like a fairy garden with washing machines."

"When I was a kid, my father told me that fairies lived in holes in the moss around tree stumps. Whole families of them. He told me that if I lay on the ground and looked into the holes I could see them, but they would only show them-selves to little kids."

"Maybe that's why you like plants," I said, "because some-where in your mind you think they have fairies living inside of them."

"Maybe you like the Laundromat because there really are fairies in the moss."

"Maybe."

"Because, I gotta tell you, for a woman who never owned a single plant, you sure are drawn to plants and the people around them."

"Tell me more about the nine plants," I said.

"I've never seen them. You've had more contact with them than I have."

"Not really. Armand won't show them to me. He keeps them locked up in a room in the back of the laundry."

"Smart man," Exley said, running his fingers through his hair, lifting up the blond top layer and revealing the darkness underneath. "The nine plants are very beautiful and very dangerous"—he looked into my eyes—"like a good lover. I've seen one of them up close and personal. And I've only heard about two others."

"Which one did you see?"

"*Sinningia speciosa,* also known as gloxinia, the plant of love at first sight. The myth says that anyone who finds gloxinia will fall in love with the first person they see."

"Who was the first person you saw?"

"I was alone in the jungle in Peru at the time, looking for the plants."

"You were in Peru looking for the nine plants? Jesus, those things really have a hold on you."

"When I first saw the gloxinia, there was no one nearby to fall in love with. A little bit later, I saw some folks on the plane ride home, but I didn't fall in love with any of them. And when I got back to the States, the first person I saw was Jimmy, the guy who sells apple cider behind me at the market. We didn't fall in love, either, in case you're wondering."

"So you don't think it's true about the plants? You don't think they work?"

"I think you have to have all nine of them. I think they're weaker when there's just one."

"That's what Armand said."

Exley's head went up and down involuntarily.

"Does anyone know which plants make up the nine plants?" I asked. "Is it written in a book somewhere, or in a poem?"

"Nope. It's hard to know what the nine plants are. According to the myth, they change over time, and the only way you can know them is if they show themselves to you. And they only show themselves to the people who are ready for them."

"Ready like how?"

"I don't know exactly. I'm guessing that a person has to be evolved enough, or something along those lines."

"How do you think Armand found them?"

"They probably found *him.* Like I said, you can't really look for the plants, they have to look for you. I mean, just imagine if you could search them out. The entire population of the world would be living in the rain forests and jungles of South America and Oceania, looking for the plants."

"But you were looking for them when you went to Peru."

"I was young and stupid back then. I still believed I could find them that way."

"What about the other two that you heard of?"

"All I know is that one is a succulent of some kind, of which there are millions. And the other is some type of night-blooming plant. A female that opens up at night and closes during the day, like most females."

I smiled and drew my sweater tightly around me.

"Oh, come on, don't sit like that," Exley said. He uncrossed my arms with his pale hands.

"It's cold in here."

He rubbed my shoulders. "Better?"

"Not really."

He pulled me toward him and kissed me. I was surprised. I'd always hated kissing in restaurants. I felt bad for the other customers, the ones who might not have anyone in their lives, the ones who were old with dead spouses, or the ones who were lonely.

Exley wasn't thinking about the people around us, and he kissed me again. He tasted like honey butter from the dinner rolls, and when he stopped kissing me my mouth remained open of its own volition, waiting for more.

He sat back in his chair.

"Warmer now?"

"Much."

"Early on, they used to say that the nine plants brought eternal life to whoever had them."

For a moment I wondered exactly how old Armand was, since he had all of the plants.

"But nowadays," he continued, "the myth has changed and evolved, and the nine plants are thought to bring abundance in many different forms, such as love, money, or even children."

I thought about all of the people waiting outside of the Laundromat. All of the people who came to see Armand. They brought him love, and money, and they were, in a way, his children.

"Let's just say the plants are a very, very fortunate possession, in that they bring people whatever it is that they most desire," he said.

"Why haven't they found you?"

"I ask myself that question all the time. I've done everything I know of to prepare myself for the plants, but they haven't come to me. People spend years, sometimes entire lifetimes, honing their minds, trying to bring themselves to a level of consciousness that will draw the plants to them. They go to India and live with gurus, or spend years in the Amazon Basin with shamans and medicine men and healers of all sorts. But even with all of that work, it's extremely difficult to attain all nine. Believe me, many people have died trying."

"For a myth?"

"People have died for less."

Outside of the Strip House, Exley pulled me into every doorway on Twelfth Street between Fifth Avenue and University Place. We kissed passionately over plants and myths of immortality, over love and procreation. We kissed over Indian shamans, *curanderos,* and cuttings from Laundromats on the Lower East Side.

When he put his arms around me, his jacket smelled like fresh earth. I unbuttoned the first three buttons of his shirt and pressed my face against his chest, where the hair was soft as summer grass.

He was the first man I'd kissed since my divorce, and he

made me feel that all the pain had actually been worth it. Like if I hadn't met my husband and gotten divorced, I would never be standing on a street corner with a plant dealer having the best kiss of my entire life.

I grabbed his hand.

"I want to show you something," I said. "Come with me."

"Where are we going?"

"Come with me."

Four avenues and about a hundred honey-and-butter kisses later, we reached our destination.

"Here we are," I said with some measure of awe. "The Laundromat."

Exley took a step back on the street to take in the sight. We must have looked like two lunatics, open-mouthed, gaping at the greasy, cracked window of an old laundry. He took a lighter from his pocket and went over to the window. With a flick of his thumb, he bathed the fern in firelight, like it was a rock star at the end of a show.

"That's it," I said. "That's the fire fern."

I felt like I had just given Exley the greatest gift in the world.

"She's beautiful," he said. "So beautiful." He turned to me. "Thank you for showing her to me. Thank you for showing me something so exquisite."

I took his hand as we walked away from the Laundromat, and I held it all the way back to my apartment.

When we got inside, the bird-of-paradise was lying on her side. Her long leaves were crunched up in an awkward, uncomfortable-looking position. Dirt covered the floor around her.

"She needs to be repotted. You don't mind, do you?" he asked.

Exley dropped my hand. He righted the plant and began to scoop dirt from the floor and put it back in the pot.

"She's never done that before. The croton's fallen over, but never the bird."

I took his hands out of the dirt and pulled on them until he was standing. I put my arms around him and whispered into his chest.

"I have the soil. I have the cutting shears. I know what the root ball is. And I promise you, I'll do it in the morning."

"I'm sorry," he said. "It's in my nature. She's one of my babies."

"I'm not going to let anything happen to her."

"I know you won't."

Exley picked me up and carried me over to the bed. His hands looked better now that they were covered with potting soil. Less pale. I felt like he could do anything with those hands—build cabins, paint pictures, plant trees, and communicate everything he needed to say. He stroked me gently, just like I stroked the leaves of my bird-of-paradise. He talked to me with those hands, he really did, and I realized how much I missed being spoken to.

He took a brush from the top of my dresser. It was extra soft, made for babies. He sat behind me on the bed, moved my hair over my shoulders, and brushed the skin on my back. It felt incredibly good.

"It's like a mushroom brush," he said. "It takes the top layer off, so that your skin is more exposed and you can feel more. It makes you raw."

He leaned over my shoulders and brushed my breasts, and then leaned back and ran it through my hair.

"I'm growing you," he whispered. "Brushing away everything that's old. Making new skin, new hair, new cells, new you."

"I'm not a plant."

"Yes, you are. Your hair grows from a root, just like a plant. It grows long and lustrous with care. I care about you on a cellular level. This stuff on the outside," he said, running his hands over my skin, "this is just a body bag to keep you in and hold you together so that you can be you. I want to be closer to you than just your skin."

He made love to me slowly. Climbing his way in, rooting himself, planting himself inside of me, like he was going backward in time. He *was* closer to me than my skin.

There was something special about bonding with a man over plants. It was so natural it was almost renegade. So outside of society there wasn't even a fetish named for it yet.

Exley didn't call the next day. Or the one after that. Or the one after that, either. I missed him. I missed him after one day—after one hour, really. He was the first man I'd made love to since my divorce, and because of the way we made love, he felt like the first man I'd made love to, maybe ever. Even Carlos, my doorman, finally looked at me with joy in his eyes instead of pity. I had to find Exley. I couldn't go back to the eyes of Carlos's pity.

After three days, I decided I'd waited long enough to cover the rules of dating decorum in New York. I went to the green market.

It was Saturday, the busiest day of the week, and the market was jammed. I looked around for Exley, but his stand was not in its usual spot. I oriented myself with the neighborhood landmarks, just to make sure I was in the right place. I looked across the street and saw the Barnes & Noble directly to my right, and the Raja deli, catty-corner. The California-orange man was in his usual spot, but Exley was nowhere that I could see.

It wasn't unusual for vendors to move from one side of the market to the other, looking for what they called the *sweet spot* for sales, and he would never miss a Saturday, his most profitable day, so I knew he was somewhere in the crush.

I walked the three-block length of the market, peering at every vendor. I looked behind each stand, way down deep into the back rows. More than half the vendors sold plants, making the going a little tough, but after walking through twice I still found no sign of Exley.

I made my way back to Jimmy, who had the apple-cider stand that now stood in Exley's spot.

"Do you know where David Exley is?"

"The guy with the tropicals?"

"Yes, the blond man with the tropical-plant stand that used to be right here."

"Nah. All's I know, he said I could have his spot if I wanted it. I usually sell out of the back of my truck. It's a real pain in the ass. He hasn't been here in a couple days, so I set up shop."

"For how long?"

"How long what?"

"Did he say you could have his spot?"

"Permanent. He said once he was gone he wasn't coming back."

"When did he tell you that?"

"I don't know. Four, five days, maybe a week ago. I think it was last Saturday."

"Last Saturday he told you he was planning on leaving?"

I didn't wait for an answer. I ran out of the green market toward the laundry. I hadn't run in a long time, and I was winded after just one block, but I kept on running, holding my chest like I was ninety.

I turned the corner on Twelfth Street and First Avenue. I was relieved to see the beginnings of a Saturday afternoon street fair. Dozens of people were milling about, no doubt looking for good spots for their booths, getting ready to sell their I ♥ NY tee shirts and baby I ♥ NY onesies. In an hour, the smell of Italian sausage, green peppers, and onions would be rising off hibachis everywhere, and the faces of kids would be covered with white powdered sugar from funnel cakes. Everything seemed normal, and I bent over, putting my hands on my knees, to catch my breath, sweat running into my eyes.

I had begun walking toward the Laundromat when I crunched down on something lying in the street. Balancing on one foot, I picked a large shard of glass out of the bottom of my sneaker. I wiped the sweat pouring down my face and looked toward the Laundromat. The whole street was shining like a diamond. Glass was everywhere. I realized that I wasn't looking at the beginning of a street fair, I was in the middle of a crime scene. I was already too late.

From behind the throngs of people, I could see that the big front window of the Laundromat was smashed, and the open hole was wrapped in yellow tape.

I pushed through the crowd, my vision tunneled. I panicked, thinking that Armand was hurt. There were neighborhood people all over the street, and I looked in the spaces between them, frantically trying to get a glimpse inside of the laundry.

I finally reached the window hole. Sharp pieces of glass hung on to the metal frame. I looked up at the ceiling, moving my head very slowly, not wanting to see the state of the hanging plants exposed to the early-spring chill and wind.

It was worse than I thought. The fluorescent bulbs were cracked or broken entirely. Strands of fishing line hung down from the ceiling, cut, and drained of plants. Dirt was everywhere. It must have poured out of the pots as they slid down the line.

Plants from the ceiling and the tops of the washing machines were lying on the floor, torn up and stepped on, covering the ripped-up moss like a colorful quilt.

Climbing and shrub roses lay crushed and smeared under the dryers, like bloodstains. Armand had told me they should always be kept near the dryers, because the heat encouraged their fragrance.

Nicotiana sylvestris lay ripped apart on the folding table. He said that nicotiana's musky scent was the only thing that could cut the smell of bleach.

Bright fuchsia bergamot pollinated with Armand's in-house bees lay on the floor. Bees buzzed overhead, looking in vain for a bloom to pollinate.

One large ficus stood upright in the middle of the room, untouched, like a witness to the carnage.

With all of the plants mashed on the floor, I could see directly into Armand's secret back room. The door was hanging off its hinges, a perfectly round hole in the middle that could only have been made by a circular saw. Unlike the Laundromat proper, the back room was spotless—and completely empty. There was nothing smashed on the ground, and nothing torn up in the corners. There wasn't even a spot of dirt on the floor.

The nine plants were gone.

I put my head in my hands. Nothing but the nine plants had been taken from the Laundromat. Not even the old copper cash register in the corner.

I saw Armand step out of a police car. He lifted the yellow-and-black tape that surrounded his laundry like a swarm of bees and walked inside. I pushed out a strong breath of relief. I had been blocking the fear that Exley had somehow hurt Armand.

"I need to talk to him!" I yelled at the police officer.

"Get back!" the officer shouted at me.

Armand turned around, reached across the tape, grabbed my arm, and pulled me hard against him.

"The man who bought the fire-fern cutting," he said before I could speak.

I nodded.

He pulled me even closer.

"You told him about the nine plants?"

"I didn't."

"How did he know?"

I couldn't bring myself to tell Armand that I had brought Exley to the Laundromat.

"You told him nothing about the plants?"

"I told him that you had them. But I didn't tell him where they were," I lied. "He didn't think much of them," I said, lying again. "He said they were a joke. An old wives' tale amongst plant people. A myth."

"That old wives' tale just cost me half a lifetime of work."

I felt tears in my eyes, though I had not cried in a long time. Never in my life had I caused so much damage.

I pictured Exley in front of the Laundromat with his hand over his mouth, gasping at the beauty of the fire fern. I imagined him pulling up to the Laundromat in his dirty white plant-transport van and tossing a cement block through the window. I could hear the glass crashing down into the Laundromat and onto the street. I knew I'd hear that sound in my head for a very long time.

When the details came in, I turned out to be wrong about the window. He had drilled a small circular hole big enough to stick his hand into, and he opened the old lock on the inside of the door. The window had shattered much later, finally collapsing around the hole.

I felt the money in my pocket and realized that Armand was right: the fire fern had made me greedy. It hypnotized first me, and then Exley.

"I'll make it up to you," I said. "I'll pay for the window and the plants."

"I misjudged you," he said quietly. "I thought you were

smarter. It's nothing to be ashamed of, though. We are who we are, until we're not. Next time you won't be so dumb, and neither will I."

I took the money out of my pocket.

"I got it for the fire fern," I said, handing it over to him.

He shook his head from side to side and took the money. Without saying another word, he lifted the yellow tape and headed out toward his people, the coterie of neighborhood folks that had gathered on the street.

I could hear him comforting the ones standing closest to him, but I knew that his heart was broken from losing his plants. They were his teachers, his friends, and his connection to the neighborhood. And the nine plants in the back room— I knew that they were not replaceable.

I took one last look inside of the Laundromat. Now it was like every other laundry in the East Village. It had scuffed tiles, big gray machines, handwritten posts sloppily taped onto corkboards, and old white cracked plastic folding tables.

With the plants gone, I realized, perhaps for the first time, how much care and hard work had gone into creating the phenomenon that was that Laundromat.

I turned around and walked home, knowing that I had destroyed a little spot of beauty in the world. There are some things that cannot be undone, and I knew that I would never be able to compensate Armand for his loss.

He told me once, what seemed like a long time ago, that if I mentioned the whereabouts of the nine plants to anyone else I would never get to see them. He was right. But now he would never get to see them again, either.

The Floribunda Rose

Abundant blooms of sweet perfume, silky smooth to the touch,
and intoxicating to the senses, floribunda can and will
fool you. In reality she is tough, disease-resistant, prickly,
and very hardy in colder zones. The proverbial iron fist
in the velvet glove of plants.

A rmand and I sat outside the Laundromat on two orange milk crates turned upside down. It was hot inside, and I was happy to be out in the breeze. There was an oak tree in front of us, one of the only trees on Twelfth Street, and it was quiet because of the early-morning hour. I had a coffee in my hand, and I leaned back against the crystal-clear glass of the brand-new Laundromat window.

"The man who robbed the Laundromat gave you your first tropical plant, your bird-of-paradise, and for that you owed him very much. More than you know."

"It's just a plant."

"He brought you to me. You would never have recognized the little fire fern in the window if he hadn't given you the brochure."

"That would have been a blessing for you."

Armand waved his hand at me to be quiet.

"Now that he has the nine plants, your debt to him is more

than paid, and you are in the clear. Except, of course, for your debt to me."

"Of course. I'll do anything you ask."

"Don't be so quick to say 'anything.' "

"Anything."

We both laughed, and it was good to see his separated, Chiclet-sized teeth again.

"Do you know why you owe me?"

I looked at his plantless Laundromat. All metal machines and cracked tiles.

"No, it's not for the window, or even for my plants, although I miss them terribly and may never be able to recover them. You didn't break the window or steal the plants. That was someone else's choice. No. You owe me because I taught you something very important about yourself. I taught you that you are greedy and desperate, and for that you owe me. Big-time."

I felt myself getting angry.

"You were greedy enough to start a side business with my plants. And you were so desperate for a man that you got involved with someone who was manipulative and dangerous. Your desperation replaced your ability to judge that man's character. That's a scary place to be in this life."

I stood up. "I'm not desperate."

"Good," said Armand. "Now you owe me even more, for making you angry and taking away your sadness."

"What do I owe you, Armand? I'll find a way to get it. I'll pay you anything you want."

In truth, I was desperate to give him some money and put this whole thing behind me. The involvement with him and the plants and the Laundromat and Exley had become too much for me. In fact, meeting them had made me fully respect the comforts of the advertising world. My job had its unethical moments, but in reality it was cushy and safe. I had taken it for granted, thinking that Exley's and Armand's worlds were somehow easier, less pressurized, and more adventurous.

"I'll pay for the window," I reiterated for the ninth time. "And I'll work at the laundry on the weekends or at night, if that's what you need."

"You're too soft and spoiled to work in my Laundromat. You can't even operate the cash register."

"I can learn."

Armand waved his hand at me again.

"Don't worry about the money so much. I'm insured for the damage. It's no problem for me to pay for the glass."

For some reason, I found it unnerving that Armand was insured. He was so far outside of the circles that I moved in that sometimes he didn't seem real, let alone insured. "You have enough to cover it?"

"I do. And plenty more, too."

Just then a loud, noisy, smelly garbage truck stopped right in front of us. The garbage man put on the parking brake. He got out of the truck and used the space in front of the Laundromat as a jumping-off point to collect all of the garbage on the street.

I shook my head in disgust. Armand smiled at me and took his coffee out of its brown bag.

"It stinks around here," I said. I wanted to run away from the Laundromat and Armand and the garbage. "Let's go inside."

Armand took a long, deep breath through his nose. "Ahhh. That's not so bad!"

He was either crazy or so old that he had no sense of smell, I thought.

"I'm neither," he said, reading my mind. "I just know how to keep my equilibrium during adverse circumstances, and you don't. That's all there is to it."

"I don't know why they parked right here," I yelled over the garbage truck. "They have the whole block to park. They know we're trying to talk. They can see it."

Armand laughed with his eyes closed and his Chiclet teeth open to the sun.

"You think they parked in front of us on purpose? You think we're so important to them they're plotting against our having a conversation?"

Armand continued to rock and laugh.

"Ahhh. I really enjoy your company sometimes," he said.

"All I'm saying is, they could've moved farther down the block. It would have been the polite thing to do."

"Think of my tropical plants torn from their natural habitats, the rain forests, the jungles, and the deserts. They manage to live amidst the smell and noise of the city. They grow beautifully. They thrive. They don't cringe and hide and wish they were back home. They adapt." Armand leaned closer to me. "Do you want to know their secret?"

"You don't have any plants left," I said, not really caring or willing to believe that they had a secret.

"The secret I'm talking about is very simple, but it is the hardest thing to explain. I will try for you, because I like you, and also because you're still so upset."

"Okay, but you'd better yell over the trucks."

"Gladly," said Armand. "I love to yell!"

He stood up, and began to yell.

"If you can hear the quiet while being woken up by the garbage trucks, you have power. If you can feel the stars when all you can see are the lights in the skyscrapers, that's power. If you can smell the forest in front of the Dumpster, then you have power. Never let the events in front of you, or the people around you, tell you what to see, feel, taste, smell, or hear."

Armand was yelling at the top of his lungs.

"Why should the garbage man tell you to smell bad things?

Decomposing food? Rot? Why should the urban planners tell you that you cannot see the stars? And why should the thief at the Union Square Green Market take away my tropicals? Why would you let him? You have a mind. You can re-create my plants right here," he said, tapping the side of my head. "Go ahead, picture all the tropical plants you want. Now look at them. Really look at them, until you are living amongst them. Don't be a slave to the nonsense that's put in front of you by other people. You have a mind. And if you can use it correctly, you are free!"

Armand sat back down on the milk crate. He looked invigorated. I felt exhausted.

"Come on, I have a plant for you that might be able to explain all of this better than I."

Inside, he showed me his newest plant. It was a single delicate rose in a small pot on top of the cash register. It was the very first plant he'd purchased since Exley had robbed the Laundromat.

"Take her home with you. Put her in front of the noisiest window in your apartment, and then open it to make her cold. Blast your bad music near her pot. And give her just a tiny bit of water and even less sunlight. Then see how she does!

"Remember, she is much more delicate than you, yet you will see that she can withstand a lot. Under the worst of conditions, she maintains her beauty and her delicacy. She adapts! She is graceful. Watch her and learn her secrets. If you study her long enough, she'll teach you how to be at peace anywhere you choose, at the drop of a hat, in front of a noisy garbage truck, or after a robbery. Do you understand what the rose is telling you?"

"I do."

"Ahhhh," Armand sighed. "As usual, my little plant is better at explaining things than I am."

"But I want to do something to make this okay right now. I

don't want to learn how to get centered. I want to fix what I did."

Armand took off his round yellow sunglasses and sat down on the bench in the middle of the Laundromat. He studied me with his coppery eyes.

"You really need to repay me?"

"More than anything," I said, unable to stand the guilt for one more minute.

"Okay. There is one thing you can give me."

"Anything."

"I will take my payment in increments of time."

I felt a little dizzy, like I had when he first twirled the fire-fern cutting in front of me.

"You want me to work in the Laundromat at night?"

"I'm going to need a little more time than that."

"I can't come during the day because of my job. But maybe I can find an intern for you. A kid from NYU to help clean up and replant."

"It's really very simple," said Armand. "I would like you to come with me to Mexico to replace the nine plants. I need the plants, and I need your help to get them."

"Mexico?"

"We can't expect to collect tropical plants in New York City, can we?"

"How long would it take?"

"No one can tell. When the nine plants reveal themselves to us, we'll come back. It's up to them. Not us."

"I can't just leave New York and move to Mexico. I have responsibilities. I have a job and an apartment."

"I'm not going to try and convince you to come with me. It's what I want as compensation for my stolen plants. You've asked me what I wanted many times, and now I've given you my answer."

I closed my eyes as I felt another slight turn on the wheel of my life.

"My plants were no ordinary plants, you know."

"I know."

"My tropicals were legendary. They were on the nine path. The path of the heart's desire."

"Will Exley get everything he wants in life now that he has the plants?"

"No. The plants cannot be stolen. They can only be earned."

"How did you earn them?"

"I didn't have to. I am their keeper. It's my job."

"What about the Laundromat?"

"Nothing more than the place I chose to keep the plants."

I was beginning to feel a lot worse.

"Come with me to Mexico to replace them. I want this for me, but I also want it for you."

"Why for me?"

"The legend says that if the nine plants are stolen, the person responsible will never find fulfillment in any form. Exley is responsible. And, indirectly, so are you. To break the spell of bad luck, the person responsible must return the plants to the keeper. I'll help you as much as I can, of course."

"Of course."

"I should add that you need to do this because of your coldness."

"Excuse me?"

"You're cold. You're a cold, cold woman in the guise of a sweet one. You're an artist, a performance artist, and your art is a show in which you pretend to be sweet and naïve when in fact you are distant and cold and calculating. And you are very good at this. It's a true talent, and one that will surely help both of us in Mexico."

"I have no idea what you mean."

"Yes, you do. Think about how you were going to use me, a poor old man who works in a laundry. You were going to use me to make money for yourself. And you were going to use my plants, too. You were going to try and dupe me even after I made you a very special gift of the fire fern. This makes you cold and, even more than that, it makes you dumb."

"I was going to give you half of the money. I wanted us to go into business together."

"Me go into business with you? Ha. You know nothing about business, and even less about the business of plants."

I definitely did not want to go to Mexico with Armand.

"And besides," he continued, "by the time you were going to give me the money, it was already too late. So you also have bad timing, and timing is everything in business."

"I'll think about it," I said, turning and walking away from the laundry. "I'll let you know."

"You once told me that, more than anything, you wanted high adventure, money, and love."

I turned around. "That's right."

"What if I told you if you come to Mexico you will have all three?"

"I don't know if I would believe you."

"Think about it, and come back when you have an answer. But don't wait too long or I'll be gone."

He waved at me with those mildly nauseating, undulating fingertips that said goodbye and pulled me closer at the same time.

I started to walk away from the Laundromat, and then I broke into a little trot. I knew deep inside that I would never go to Mexico to dig around for plants with Armand.

"Oh," he yelled after me, "just one more thing."

I stopped in the street and held my breath. I didn't turn around. I was so close. I was almost free.

"Before you go, I'd like you to meet my wife."

The word "wife" sank slowly into my consciousness. I'd never imagined that Armand had a wife. Or even a home, for that matter. If I did think about it, I imagined that he lived alone, in the back room of the Laundromat, with his plants.

I pivoted and slowly turned toward him. Much as I wanted to run, I found myself walking back to hear what he had to say.

"Meet her as a personal favor to me. She wants to meet the woman I've been cavorting with, the woman who destroyed my business and had the nine plants stolen."

I took a deep breath. I owed him at least that much.

The Orchid Family
(Orchidaceae)

*Orchids develop through a process of rigorous natural selection
and should be treated as the rare individuals that they are.
If you consider humans, each one of us has about a
one-in-two-hundred-million chance of being alive. So does each
orchid. We understand each other's rarity, and that is probably
why we are, as a society, so crazy for orchids.
On the other hand, and contrary to popular belief,
orchids are not difficult to grow. In fact, they are the
perfect plant for people who can't grow anything at all.
They don't need soil. They don't need fertilizer.
They don't even need a pot to grow in. All they need is air.
We like to make orchids seem difficult to grow
so that we can feel special when they do.
They're about as hard to grow as grass.*

Armand lived in a stately old townhouse on Irving Place
that had aged beautifully. At one time it must have been
painted a tropical flamingo pink. Now the paint was chipped
away and faded to a pale pink mixed with gray from the
cement underneath. There were marble pillars at the top of
the twelve stairs leading up to the front door, and two large
lion's heads rested at the bottom, like sentinels.

"They kind of get to you, don't they?" he said, petting one of the stone lions.

It was true, they did. They gave the building a regal appearance the others on the block did not have.

"What floor are you on?" I asked.

"All of them. This is my house! My generation doesn't live in little square boxes, like yours. Besides, when I bought this place, you weren't born yet, and prices were much lower back then."

"But you work in a Laundromat."

"I own a Laundromat."

"If you have all of this money, why do you wash people's clothes all day?"

"I already told you, I am the keeper of the nine plants, and the Laundromat is the place where I choose to keep them. When I wash clothes, no one thinks about the plants in the back. No one suspects that they are there. The Laundromat is an excellent disguise. And anyway, washing clothes is a good business. Good times, bad times, war, drought, famine, there are always dirty clothes to be washed."

"Why don't you have other people wash them for you while you tend to the plants?"

"The Laundromat is my business, and I am very interested in every single facet of its operation. You can never have a truly successful business run by other people. They simply won't care as much as you do, and why should they? The owner still gets the lion's share of the profits, right? Ah, see that, I knew there was a reason we were standing here," he said, once again petting the stone lion's head.

We walked up the marble stairs toward a heavy copper-colored wooden door that looked marvelous against the chipped pink paint. When we got to the top, the door opened as if it knew we were coming. In the frame stood a tiny woman in a tight-fitting black silk kimono. Her figure was superb, with every curve accented by a flower. There was a rose on each breast, and daisies in the deep indentations on either side of her waist. She looked like a miniature fashion model for Yohji Yamamoto, grown old.

"My wife," Armand said, extending his arm out toward the tiny woman with his palm toward the sky, "Sonali."

"Lila," I said, extending my hand.

"Come in, come in," she said, without taking it.

We crossed the threshold, and the heavy wooden door closed solidly behind us. I followed Armand and Sonali up a staircase covered with faded blue rose-printed carpeting to the second floor of the townhouse.

Sonali, under any circumstances, and not just because she was Armand's wife, was a very strange woman. First of all, she was maybe five feet tall and probably less. She weighed maybe ninety pounds and probably less. On first impression, she came across as comforting, with a lineless face of soft caramel skin. But at the same time, there was something steely about her. Something unmistakably hard and immobile. Something unreachable. Almost cold.

Maybe it was her hair. It was jet-black and pulled back into a tight bun, with one stripe of gray going diagonally across her head like a lightning bolt, as if her corpus callosum were on a slant, or her head were split in two.

Or it could have been her dark eyes. They were direct and assertive for someone so soft and demure. It was as if she had another person's eyes in her face, or another person's face around her eyes.

Overall, she came across as someone so sure of herself that what you thought of her not only did not matter to her, but probably didn't even cross her mind.

"Are you done drinking in my wife?" Armand asked. "You might as well stop now, because you will never understand her."

"I wasn't drinking in your wife."

"Good, because I'd like to say hello to her now."

"Go right ahead."

"Lila gives us permission to greet each other," Armand said to his wife.

"Oh, good," said Sonali.

Armand held her, pressing her tiny body against his gigantic one, the top of her head buried in his stomach. He held her, and held her, and held her, until I was quite frankly uncomfortable. He held her like a man out of prison. As if he hadn't seen her in years. He whispered to me over her head, which was very easy for him to do.

"I hug her like this every day," he said. "Why wait till I miss her?"

In order to escape their fantastic embrace, I turned away from them and looked around the room. Plants, of course, everywhere. Long glamorous-looking orchids sat on top of mirrors. The mirrors rested on top of heaters, which rested on top of sunny window ledges.

"The orchids are my wife's," said Armand, still holding her against his stomach.

Sonali finally turned around.

"A little tip about orchids," she said in the most forthright manner, launching right into a conversation, as if she hadn't been pressing her face against Armand for the last five minutes in front of a total stranger. "If you place them on top of mirrors in front of windows, the reflection adds light to existing sunlight. At certain points of the day, they are surrounded by light on all sides as well as underneath. They grow wildly under such conditions. It makes them feel outdoorsy and very sexual."

"How long have you been interested in orchids?" I asked.

"Oh, some of them have been with us for twenty years or more. I can't remember exactly. They like living here, as do we. It's their home as much as ours, perhaps even more so. We cater to their need for light and heat, and they cater to our need for beauty. A perfect dance between all of us."

She turned around to hug Armand, which alarmed me, because I thought I might never see her face again.

"I never thought of beauty as a need," I said loudly, trying to separate them.

"Oh yes," she said into his stomach, her words muffled by his clothing, "that's why the world needs artists, and plants. Beauty is as important as sleeping, or eating, or sex."

"Especially sex," said Armand.

"Plants can't move, so they use their beauty to get us to take care of them, just like babies use their cuteness and cuddliness to get the things they need."

"Nothing is more important than sex," said Armand, hugging her again.

"Ernesto, stop!"

"Ernesto?"

"It's not his real name, but I call him that sometimes when he's lying. It means 'honest,' so it keeps him that way."

"Sonali is like a plant," Armand said. "See how she dresses?"

I looked at her long black kimono, which did not bring any plant to mind.

"Think of the floribunda rose that I gave you. Each petal draws your eye toward the sexual organs inside, yet conceals them at the same time. Notice how Sonali's clothing draws you in, yet conceals her sex organs totally."

I did not want to think about Sonali's sex organs.

"Just as the flower petal teases the bee, clothing should tease the eye. You can't go wrong if you follow the plants," he said, eyeing Sonali.

"Oh, don't listen to him. He's a man in love."

"And she knows how to keep me that way!"

"How long have you been together?" I asked.

"Since we were children," he said. "And we are children now."

They giggled at each other exactly like two little kids. Like two conspiratorial children.

"Come," said Sonali, "let me formally introduce you to my orchids."

We walked over to the orchid window.

"Are these from the jungle?" I asked.

"Do you mean to ask if I purchased them from an orchid dealer who cuts down jungle plants for obsessed collectors, like you read about in *The Orchid Thief*?"

"Yes, I guess so."

"Would you like to see a beautiful black panther pacing back and forth in a cage?"

"No."

"Or a dancing bear with a muzzle on his mouth?"

"Of course not."

"Do you enjoy looking at polar bears sitting on puny blocks of ice behind zoo bars?"

"No."

"Then you must develop the same attitude toward orchids. Jungle orchids belong in the jungle, not in homes in New York City."

"But how did you get these?"

"I let the nurseries propagate them, and then I buy them when I am sure there are many and the species won't die for my desires. If you take an individual orchid straight from the jungle, you are not doing anything to help continue the species. Although I will admit there is a special feeling to plants that come from exotica. Straight from the world of the jungle."

"I've never heard her admit that before," said Armand. "She must like you."

"Is that an orchid?" I asked, pointing to a particularly unattractive small brown plant.

"*Maxillaria tenuifolia*," said Sonali. "One of my favorites. This little brown orchid is a species. Not as spectacular as a hybrid, but very satisfying nonetheless. Its charms are quite powerful. Come closer and smell it."

I leaned over the ugly brown plant.

"Coconut pie! How is that possible?"

"Wonderful, isn't it? She doesn't need bright, flashy colors or spectacular sprays of flowers. Her pollinators, the moths, come out at night. She uses her coconut scent to guide and entice the little moth in much the way we use perfume to entice men in nightclubs and cafés."

Sonali winked at me.

"You can learn much about how an orchid is pollinated by the way it looks. White, pink, and pale-green flowers usually get pollinated at night, since those colors are easily seen under moonlight. The little moth sneaks up on the flower in the middle of the night like a lover. He lands on her, pollinates her, and then leaves. We've all had this experience, yes?"

"Yes," I said, thinking of Exley.

"Brightly colored orchids, on the other hand, are pollinated by butterflies and birds. Butterflies prefer red and orange. Bees love orange and yellow all the way through to ultraviolet."

"Just like certain men like certain color clothing," I said.

"Yes, colored petals are the clothing of flowers. The insect must find a way through those petals to get what he wants, like a man brushing his hand through the layers of a woman's skirt."

"I told you," said Armand, "she will drive you crazy with her sex talk."

"Stop it, Armand," she said, in a voice so deeply sexual it excited me on the spot.

"Sonali could talk to you for years about orchids. I'm not kidding, years. She's been talking to me for at least ten years, almost solely about orchids."

"Really?"

"Yes, she speaks through the lip of the orchid, as I like to say."

"I am not finished yet, Armand. She has not seen my prize."

Actually, I had, and I couldn't take my eyes off it. Its petals were the most intense fuchsia I'd ever seen.

"It's a very sexy plant. *Lycaste skinneri,* the national flower of Guatemala. She's quite common, and beautiful at the same time. I like that combination, beautiful and common. I love her because she has been with me the longest and I know her best. But she is not my prize."

Sonali handed me a drawing of a rather plain-looking plant. It was low to the ground, with leaves going round in a circular, inward-spiraling configuration.

"What is it?"

"She is my prize. And it is my one and only dream to see her with my own eyes. She is the passion plant with no name."

"Where is she?"

"They say the passion plant is completely extinct. Not a single one left on this earth. Even her name is gone. No one knows what it was. There are no records of her, anywhere."

Armand came over and put his arms around Sonali.

"Her circular leaves form a mandala," she continued. "They swirl round and round like the layers of the mind, forming a black hole in the center. This hole is the passageway out to the universe. It represents the endless possibility of the human mind. It is a perfect metaphor for what we look like on the inside. A gift from the plant world to us. They say she no longer exists, but I believe she is out there, somewhere."

Sonali seemed sad.

"I'll find her for you someday," Armand whispered into her hair. "I promise."

I was wrapped in the dream of Armand and Sonali and the passion plant with no name when a horn blared right behind me. I screamed.

"Oh, sweetheart, I'm so sorry," said Sonali, "I should have warned you." Sonali put her arm around me. "This is Marco."

"Nice to meet you," Marco said in the voice of a child.

"A pleasure," I said, somewhat confused to find a man sitting on a cushion on the floor in the middle of Armand's living room. He had a long black beard and a worn-out maroon velvet vest with tiny mirrors on it. Inside of each mirror was an orchid, reflected.

"His voice is so high because he doesn't use it often. It's out of practice," said Sonali.

Marco blew into the oboe, and a haunting, sad sound came out.

"Does he live here with you?"

"He plays for my orchids and makes them grow. I hired him years ago because they like him. And don't get me wrong, I like him, too, but my plants like him much more. He used to play on the street outside of our window, for money, and my orchids would grow in the direction of his music. Pretty soon the whole house was tilted to the left."

She pointed left, toward the window facing the street.

"I realized that I had to bring him inside to play to their right, and so I did, and now the house is straight again."

It was true that all the orchids were standing upright.

"So now he works just for you?"

"He doesn't work, he plays."

"See," he said, pointing to the mirrors on his vest, "I am the orchid."

He looked dirty and moldy and nothing like an orchid. He was definitely not the kind of man I would invite into my own home, but the sound of his oboe was very sweet.

"Look at you," said Sonali, "you're leaning to the right just to listen to him."

I straightened up immediately.

"He's magic like that," she said. "He makes people lean. It's a very odd gift that he has, and I haven't been able to figure out its purpose quite yet."

"Are you going to Mexico, too?" I asked Sonali. For some inexplicable reason, I felt as though I loved her. Not liked her, but actually loved her. I was enraptured by her and wanted to put my arms around her and hold her.

"See what she does to people?" said Armand, staring at me. "I feel like you do right now, all the time. Every single second of every single day."

"Are you coming to Mexico?" I asked her again.

"Oh no, the nine plants are for Ernesto. I have my orchids right here. Although I do miss Casablanca; that's the name of our home in Mexico."

Sonali put her arms around Armand.

"Why do you keep switching his name?" I asked. "It's confusing."

"I call him Ernesto when he is a man. And Armand when he's not."

"Isn't he always a man?"

"He is hardly ever a man anymore," she sighed.

"Don't sigh, Sonali. She'll think that means we don't have sex anymore," said Armand.

"I didn't say that."

"You were thinking it."

"Armand is much, much more than an ordinary man," said Sonali. "But, still, sometimes he is just a man."

"Come on, leave her alone now. She has to go home and decide whether or not she's coming with me to Mexico. The choice being hers, of course."

"Of course," said Sonali. "Would you like some marigold tea before you leave, dear?"

"No, thank you, Sonali."

"Well, then," she said, grabbing a handful of marigolds out of a vase, "take these home with you. Before you go to sleep tonight, break the flowers off the stems. Tear them apart, crumble them up, and toss them underneath your bed. Marigold flowers can produce very prophetic dreams. Perhaps they will help you decide whether or not to travel to Mexico, to Casablanca, with my husband."

"You can understand my hesitation, can't you? He's practically a stranger to me."

"Oh yes," said Sonali. "To me as well. Besides, it's good to think things through very carefully. But make no mistake," she said, sounding more serious than she had before. "Once you make a decision, you must stop thinking about it and take action without any regret toward the outcome, regardless of that outcome."

"Everyone has regrets."

"No. Regrets are for people who believe they could have done something differently. If you think carefully about your actions, and then you act, you will have no regrets, because you will know that you were as careful as possible when you made your decision."

I hugged Sonali good night and headed down the stairs. She waved at me, and her wave was as disturbing as Armand's, but far more nauseating. I actually felt as if I was going to be sick.

"The bathroom is over there, dear," she said, pointing her thumb behind her.

I couldn't stand to look at her fingers, so I declined and started on my way home.

Were-Jaguars

*The great, mysterious Olmec people, the first pristine culture
of Mesoamerica, a pristine culture being a "first" culture who
had no one to learn from but themselves, claimed to be descended
from the black jaguar. They believed that the optimal life form
would have the intellect of man and the spirituality and strength
of the jaguar. They made it a practice to leave their children
in the company of jaguar cubs so that they could learn the
secrets of mysticism, including silence and invisibility.
The Olmecs disappeared without a trace, so maybe it worked.*

I called Kody on my way home, and when I got there, he was sitting on the steps of my building, waiting.

"I don't want you to go," he said as I unlocked the door.

"I know."

"But I also think it's kinda cool."

"I know."

Inside, he plopped himself down on my white vinyl couch and lit up a joint. He brushed his silvery blond hair behind his ears and put his feet up on the kidney-shaped coffee table.

"Are those Hush Puppies?" I asked, looking at the white foam soles of his shoes.

"They're comfortable," he said. "You know me, I'm all about the comfort zone."

I sat on the fake Adirondack chair from Ikea, white with Mediterranean-blue cushions, and broke apart Sonali's marigolds, ripping the flowers off the stems and crumbling them into a pile on the floor next to me.

"Whatcha doin'?"

"They're supposed to give me prophetic dreams. Armand's wife said they might help me decide whether or not to go to Mexico. Couldn't hurt, right?"

Kody took another hit off his joint and spoke without exhaling. "Here, try some of this. This'll help you decide even quicker."

I took the joint and began to smoke.

"Whoa, go a little easy on that thing. If you're going to Mexico, you gotta be chill with the plant substances. Those babies in South America aren't like the ones we've got up here. Those plants down there are tricksters. Smart as people."

"Get it off your chest, Kody."

He leaned back on the couch and took another hit off the joint.

"Okay, I will. I think it's crazy, scary, unforgivably stupid, dangerous, and kind of moronic to go to Mexico with a guy who runs a laundry on First Avenue. It's also really bad timing, since our careers are going pretty damn well."

"And what else?" I asked. "Get it out of your system, now."

"I'll have to share our office with a total stranger."

"You're worried that you won't be able to pick the raisins out of your muffin and count them in public anymore."

Kody smiled.

"I do like to count my raisins."

"It's obsessive, you know. It's a disorder."

"Whatever."

"Anything else?"

"Well, I never thought I'd tell you this, but I've always had high expectations of you, and if you go to Mexico you'll totally surpass them. I don't know if I can handle that. I'll have to change my whole way of thinking about you."

"*You* have expectations of *me*?"

"I always thought you had potential to be something more than a copywriter or the wife of an ad guy. I thought there was more to you. I can't believe I'm saying this, but I think you're actually starting to pan out, even though it's in a much weirder way than I ever imagined."

"I'm still me. It's just a trip. I'm thinking of it more like a vacation than an entire life change."

"It's not just a trip. It's Mexico, man. It's not those soft, silky beaches of Thailand. Did you know that the Mayan Indians came up with the concept of *zero*? That shit is big. Bigger than any of the crap you or I ever came up with at work."

"You mean bigger than the calendar of hot milkmen you came up with for the calcium pill?"

"Way bigger than that, dude. And besides, the Mayan calendar comes to an end on the winter solstice, December 21, 2012. That's soon, man. According to the Mayans, everything's coming to an end in just four short years. So who cares what you do? Go to Mexico."

"Why 2012?"

"Exactly. No one knows why. It's a mystery how they even knew the exact day of the winter solstice thousands of years ahead of time. And why they decided that particular solstice would mark the end of all time. If I were you, I'd get out of here right now. Your best bet for survival might just be this trip to Mexico."

"You're high."

"Yes, I am. And as your very good friend and close business associate, I brought you a parting gift."

Kody pulled a book out of his backpack and handed it to me: *The Wilderness and Jungle Survival Guide*.

"Read it before you go. It's got all kinds of great advice. It's got chapters about how to live without electricity, how to find edible plants in the jungle, how to build a fire, and which snakes are poisonous. All the stuff you're gonna need out there."

"You don't have to worry about me, Kody. I'm not going to be in the wilderness, I'm going to Armand's house."

"It's always good to be prepared, my friend. Take it from a surfer, the more you know about the natural world, about all the stuff you can't see, about what's crawling underneath and inside of things, the better off you are. Because, when you get out there, no matter how much you think you know, you're still never quite prepared for it. Nature is a bitch. Repeat after me. Nature is a be-yotch."

"I don't want to get out there, Kody. I want to get to Mexico, pay my debt to Armand, get the plants, and come right back here. I don't want to know what's inside and underneath things."

Kody got up and looked out the window.

"It's a full moon tonight. If you put a fifteen-watt lightbulb on your ceiling, it wouldn't be as bright as that full moon right there, which is two hundred thirty-eight thousand miles away. And that moon out there, that moon is capable of bringing out passion, longing, emotions, and imagination. Show me a lightbulb that can do all that."

Kody opened up the window and howled at the big white moon.

"So you think I should go."

"You're gonna see harvest moons, blue moons, big bright moons unhindered by the lights of cars and buildings. I'd kill to see the full moon over the Yucatán Peninsula."

"You're such a romantic. I'm not going to look at the moon. I told you a million times, I'm going to get the plants that got stolen from the Laundromat."

"You know that you can't say that sentence to anyone but me. Ever. Every single person you know would think you were a complete loon."

"I do. I know that."

"Do you need anything from me? Do you need me to do anything for you while you're gone?"

"I need you to water my plants."

"Of course."

"That means following my instructions, exactly."

"Yeah, yeah, I know. Touch them, rub them, talk to them, spray them, all that creepy, crawly, crappy, girly stuff."

"I need for you to call and tell me everything that's going on at work. I'm going to be fired, I know that, but keep mentioning me to Geoff Evans anyway, just to keep me top of mind."

"That's a lot to ask."

"I know."

"You're a pain in the ass."

"Thanks for the book, Kody."

"It's a good read. Promise me you'll read it before you go."

"I will. I'll read it tonight."

I took the pile of broken marigolds and tossed them under and around my bed. I fell asleep reading the wilderness-survival guide, and, just like Sonali said, I had a prophetic dream. A strange, mythical, erotic dream. Passionate enough to get me out of bed in the middle of the night to write it down.

I dreamt that I was in the house I lived in as a child. I was lying on my small single bed in my old room, and I was making love to an exquisite creature. A beautiful black panther. I was lying on top of the panther, its front paws wrapped around my back, and its hind legs around my thighs.

I held the short silky hair of its head in my hands and pressed my body against its body. I moved against it. I inhaled its fur as we stared into each other's eyes. I felt deeply connected to myself, to the animal. His eyes were bright green. We stared. Black and green into black and brown.

A hissing sound came from the far end of the bed. We turned at the same time. We saw a snake rise. Fangs down. Head forward. Poised to strike.

The panther got on top of me, covering my face with its face. It stretched out its back legs and covered my legs with its own, until every inch of my body was covered with panther. The snake rose up and slammed down, sinking his fangs into soft, black fur. Unable to reach me.

When I got out of bed the next morning, I felt absolutely invincible. I was going to Mexico! I was going for myself, for Armand, and for the nine plants. But I was also going to make sure that Exley didn't win.

I ran over to the townhouse to tell Armand and Sonali about the panther dream and my decision to go and search for the nine plants.

"The black panther lives in the jungles of the Yucatán," Sonali said. "He likes you. Mexico will be a friendly place for you. It was a good dream."

"Where's Armand? I want to tell him I'm coming with him."

"Armand is gone," she said.

"What? He was here last night. Twelve hours ago."

"And now he is gone."

"Nobody can leave that quickly."

"It's not a problem, dear. I will tell you exactly how to get to our house in Mexico. It's called Casablanca—that means white house. Armand will meet you there. He's on his way right now."

"I can't believe he left without me. What if I had come here and said I didn't want to go?"

"Why wouldn't you want to go? You will be embarking on the second-greatest road trip of your life."

"I've never been on a road trip."

"Oh, but you have. We all have, only we never remember. It's such a pity. The greatest road trip of all time is the trip down the birth canal, of course. That's the start of the most fantastic journey you will ever take on this earth. But this next trip with Armand, this trip may come very close to that one, if you're lucky."

"How so?"

"You will learn to live like you did when you first slid into this world and everything you encountered was new. If all goes well, this trip will reopen your fontanel, the soft spot on top of your head, and you will once again be open to all the world has to offer."

Sonali patted the top of my head.

"How long will Armand wait for me?"

"He'll wait until you arrive."

"What if I don't show up?"

"He'll wait until the pull of his waiting makes you show up, dear."

PART TWO

THE YUCATÁN PENINSULA

Costa Maya, Quintana Roo, Mexico

*Costa Maya is a small fishing village on the coast of the
Yucatán Peninsula, state of Quintana Roo, Mexico.
The majority of the villagers are of Mayan Indian descent,
with the usual smattering of expatriate alcoholics, criminals,
and students slumming it on the beaches between semesters.
It is such a special place that the great writer Joan Didion
named her only daughter Quintana Roo, after the state.*

"*Treinta pesos. Pague ahora por favor,*" the man said. Thirty
pesos. Please pay now.

I took thirty pesos out of my fanny pack (God, I hate
admitting that I brought one of those with me) and handed it
to the man.

"*Muchas gracias. La última persona que cruzó se parecía
mucho a usted. Y se largó sin pagar.*" Thank you very much. The
last person I took across looked just like you. And he ran off
without paying.

"Like me?" I said by way of pointing at myself.

"*Sí. Blanco. Con las manos muy blancas. Como si el sol se olvi-
dara de ellas.*" Yes. White. With very white hands. Like the sun
forgot about them.

I looked at him and pointed at my hands.

He nodded.

"Sí. Las manos muy blancas."

The fisherman tossed my backpack into the single-engine craft, which in this case was a fancy name for a rickety old rowboat with a motor stuck on the end of it. After several tries and a lot of cursing in Spanish, the motor turned over and we were on our way from Puerto Juárez to Costa Maya, across water so electric-blue it looked as if someone had dumped a vat of Ty-D-Bol into it.

It was a color I didn't realize the earth could make without the help of human beings. I knew the water would be blue, but I had in my mind a tamer, more pastel blue: a light color, through which all the sand and fish underneath would be clearly visible. This water was like super-wavy, lit-up turquoise, and so beautiful I could hardly take my eyes off it. The moment I was spellbound by the color of the water was the moment I knew I had been in New York for too long and my decision to leave was a good one.

As the morning wore on, the temperature went up. By 10:00 a.m., it was hot and muggy. A haze hung blue-green over the water. It was dead quiet, the way some hazy days can be, except for the occasional sound of small fish jumping. The boat was moving along at a crawl, and my eyes were closed, when the boatman got up, pushed me onto the floor of the boat, and threw a tarp over my head.

"¡Ballena! ¡Quédense quietos!" Whale! Stay down!

I peeked out from under the tarp to see a gray whale breaching. It cut through the haze and spiraled upward, propelling its entire body through the air right next to the tiny rowboat. It was as big as a yellow school bus and crusted over with a thick layer of barnacles.

I was intensely nervous about its size. The only time I'd ever seen a whale was in an aquarium in a Florida resort. This one seemed much larger. And infinitely freer. It was the first time in my life I understood how scary and dangerous things that are free really are.

When it dived back into the sea, it upended such a huge amount of water, it was like being caught in a monsoon rain. It soaked my hair, my clothes, and everything in my backpack. The boat was flooded with water right up to the edges.

"*¿Sabe usted nadar?*" the man asked me. Can you swim?

When we finally butted up against the dock in Costa Maya, the fisherman tossed my soaking-wet bag onto the dock like another net full of fish. I could hear my thirty-dollar glass ampoules of Dr. Hauschka Night Conditioning Moisturizer shattering in their cardboard case.

I stood on the dock alone, soaking wet, with a backpack filled with broken glass. I looked around. My new surroundings were not posh.

The tourist name for this part of Mexico is "the Mayan Riviera," but there wasn't a yacht, a silver bikini, or a martini in sight. I'd been to the south of France, and as far as I could tell the two places had absolutely nothing in common except for the word "Riviera."

The dull-gray cement buildings scattered around the port looked like identical squares. Like extra-large children's blocks without any color or playfulness. Men and women sat at tables covered with dirty red-checkered tablecloths, under cheap white plastic umbrellas, fanning themselves in the heat, smoking, and looking out at me with little interest.

"*El café, el mercado, la pescadería,*" the fisherman said, pointing at each identical cement square. "The café, the market, the fish store," he repeated in broken English.

They all looked exactly the same to me, but, per Sonali's instructions, I went over to the fish market to rent a car.

The man behind the counter smiled. He had no teeth of his

own, but he was wearing a necklace of long, pointy, yellowed shark's teeth.

"*¿El auto?*" I asked.

He came out from behind the counter, wiped the fish scales off his hands down the sides of his fish-bloody white apron, and stuck out his hand. I took it, suppressing the "Yuck!" in the back of my throat.

"*¿El auto?*" I asked again.

"*Ah, el auto, sí, sí señorita. One moment. Seet, seet.*"

I pulled out a plastic chair from under a plastic table. It slid easily on top of the oily floor, and I waited for the fish man, trying not to breathe in too deeply.

"*¿Agua fría?*" the man asked. Cold water?

"No, thank you," I said, looking at the water glass smeared with fish scales. "Just *el auto, por favor.*"

"*¿Permiso de conducir?*" the man asked.

I pulled out my driver's license and gave it to him. He studied it for a moment.

"*Nueva York, ¿eh?*"

"*Sí.*"

"*Una ciudad es muy grande.*"

"*Sí.* It is a big city."

He took some keys out of his apron pocket and handed them to me.

"*Nueve dólares* for one night."

I took the keys and gave him a hundred-dollar bill. I figured I would be keeping the car for at least ten days.

"Thees way." He pointed toward a door in the back. "*Por aquí.*"

We walked through the swinging doors into the kitchen, past short, sullen, sweaty workers. There were manta rays with fourteen-foot fins spread across the ceiling, hung up to dry like huge, living kites. There were small sharks lying on tables, with their mouths open, as if they were still surprised at being caught. Shocked at the final uselessness of all those serrated teeth.

Finally, we were out the back door. There was only one car in the vicinity. It was a little red Volkswagen Beetle, and I was very happy to see it.

"*¿Le gusta?*" the fish man asked, pointing at the car.

"*Si, es muy bueno,*" I said. "*¿Usted sabe donde está Casablanca?*" Do you know where Casablanca is? I asked him in the best high school Spanish I could muster.

"*Por allí,*" he said, pointing straight down the only road in sight. "*Es una casa muy grande, y muy blanca.*"

He said the house was right down the road. He said it was very big and white, and I figured, in this land of gray cement blocks, I couldn't miss it. I placed my soaking-wet backpack on the seat next to me and put the car in gear. As I drove away, the women at the cement café waved goodbye. They were all uniformly dark brown under white dresses with blue-and-red embroidery, and their sandals were really just strips of leather wrapped around their toes and calves, all the way up to their knees. I smiled and turned away quickly. I didn't want to look at their waves after the experience I'd had with the waves of Sonali and Armand.

The road to Casablanca should have been called the swamp to Casablanca, or the sandpit to Casablanca. Anything but "road." It consisted of small, infrequent stretches of cement interspersed with long swaths of dirt, sand, and occasionally mud. At first I could not find any logic as to how it was made, why certain parts were paved and others not. But as I continued to drive, it occurred to me that the concrete portions were always underneath trees, as if the workers were only willing to pour it in the shade. I couldn't say I blamed them. It was hot as hell in the Yucatán. A hundred degrees by noon.

The intensely bright sunlight and heat made the road look wavy and unreal, and more than once I swerved to avoid absolutely nothing. It was like driving in the Sahara, or any-place without landmarks for perspective. I felt like a Paul Bowles character in *The Sheltering Sky*. It was one of my favorite books, and I wondered if that was a bad omen.

The road finally curved into the woods, where it was darker and cooler and I wasn't constantly tricked by sunlight. I stopped the car and pulled out Sonali's hand-drawn map. I was entering the semi-tropical rain forest that covers a good portion of the Yucatán Peninsula.

At the bottom of the page there was a small arrow. On the other side was a note from Sonali. In her tiny handwriting, she warned me that the rain forest was "a most inhospitable place and difficult to access without a guide." I rolled my eyes and wondered why she hadn't verbalized this key piece of infor-mation back in New York.

The road inside the jungle (and, once again, I use the word "road" very lightly) was made of wettish dirt or outright mud. The Volkswagen tipped and jerked as it went over large tree roots, rocks, and God knows what else. It was definitely not a jungle-friendly vehicle. I drove slowly and brought my face as close to the windshield as I could, so that I could anticipate when the next major lurch was going to happen. It was a bit like being on an amusement-park ride whose concept was *randomness*.

There was no air-conditioning, and with the windows wide open, mosquitoes and bugs I didn't recognize flew into the car with impunity and clung to my body like hitchhikers. It was difficult to drive when I needed to kill something sucking the lifeblood out of me every few seconds.

Worse than either the bugs or the mud was the noise. It was absolutely earsplitting. It made Fourteenth Street and Union Square on a Saturday night seem like a silent mountain retreat.

I heard monkeys, or at least I hoped they were monkeys, screaming like maniacs in the trees. Low-flying bright-yellow birds cawed like lunatics as they rushed past my windshield, vying for space as if they were on an invisible freeway through the jungle. The constant drone, the white noise of millions of insects, was, I'm sure, the Mexican equivalent of Chinese water torture.

At one point, the amount of insects, birds, monkey shit, and bird shit falling out of the air was so thick that I turned on my windshield wipers just to get a glimpse ahead.

I could easily see why someone would need a guide in the rain forest, but I could not understand why someone would actually choose to be here in the first place.

I stopped the car. I closed my eyes and took a deep breath. According to Sonali's map, I was not that far from Casablanca, twenty miles at most.

"I can do this," I said out loud. I'm from New York City. I've walked through the Lower East Side alone at night back in the days when it was populated with dealers selling heroin, not art. I've watched every episode of *Northern Exposure* and *Men in Trees*. I even read the wilderness-survival guide that Kody gave me, from cover to cover. I can do this.

My confidence reinstated, I took a few deep breaths, started the car, and drove deeper into the jungle. I kept thinking of the jungle as a jungle, but I wasn't completely sure if I was inside of a rain forest or a jungle. The survival guide said that the growth of a rain forest is restricted by limited sunlight, but if the rain forest's canopy is thinned out for any reason, then vines, shrubs, and small trees quickly grow, creating a jungle in the rain forest. This was precisely the situation I found myself in. I was inside of a Volkswagen, inside of a jungle, inside of a rain forest. Like a box inside of a box inside of a box, each one getting progressively smaller and farther away from the light.

Mid-smack, killing at least ten mosquitoes with one swat, I was startled to see a small boy up ahead. He was squatting, perhaps looking at a bug, or an animal, or maybe just going to the bathroom. I was too far away to tell.

I honked my horn to let him know I was coming. He put up his hand palm-first, signaling me to stop. He didn't even bother to look up. He had neither fear nor interest, which gave me the feeling that he was completely in charge.

I slowed down from five miles per hour to two, which was dangerous because of the mud and sand, and edged up nearer to him. As I got closer, I was able to make out other children, too. They had shiny black hair and skinny brown arms wrapped around the jungle trees that lined the side of the road.

It was clear that the boy was not going to move, and I had no choice but to stop the car. For some unknown reason, my heart was pounding. I steadied it by reminding myself that he was a kid, no more than four feet tall, and eight or nine years old. I was an adult. Five feet seven inches tall and 120 pounds. I could definitely take him if push came to shove.

I got out of the car. When my feet hit the jungle floor, I was stunned by its mobility. This was definitely not terra firma. Walking on the rain-forest floor was a bit like walking on a trampoline. I had to lift my knees high with every step. It made a sandy beach feel like a cement sidewalk by comparison.

The boy was still crouching. He put his index finger vertically across his lips in the universal sign for *Be quiet.* I was so intent on his little brown body and the oddness of seeing it in the jungle that I almost missed the camouflaged creature to the left of him: a huge earth-colored snake. My inhale was not followed by an exhale. Perhaps I was wrong. Perhaps I would not be able to take this eight-year-old boy if push came to shove.

The snake's body was coiled. It was so large that the coils looked like tires lying one on top of another. It was at least five tires high, almost as tall as the boy himself. Its body was rippling in slow circles, and I hoped I was watching its peristalsis. At least that would mean it wasn't hungry.

I knew from Kody's book that I was looking at either a rattlesnake or a python. The pictures in the guide were black line drawings, dictionary-style, so it was hard to tell exactly which one this was. It didn't really matter, though. Both were deadly. It was just a matter of which way I preferred to be killed: poisoning or strangulation.

I took a step back toward the car. At the sound of my footstep, the snake raised its fat head off the pile of tires and hissed in my direction. Just to put things in perspective, *its* head was larger than *my* head.

At the hissing sound, the other children stepped backward, deeper into the woods, simultaneously, like synchronized swimmers.

The sight of the snake's tongue made me sweat profusely. I had read that snakes smelled through their tongues, so I tried to relax my sweat glands.

The snake looked at me through slit eyes, and for one split second a picture of Exley with his pale hands flashed through my mind.

I shook my head back and forth to get the picture out, a deeply stupid move, when I heard the telltale sound of the rattle.

I stood still and tried not to listen. Rattlesnakes were master hypnotists. If you closed your eyes and listened to the rattle, it would bring back memories of childhood, making you feel like a baby, lulling you to sleep, and then killing you in the deadliest crib there ever was.

I tried to back away, but I was already up against the Volkswagen. The sound of the rattle bounced off the jungle under-story like surround sound in a movie theater. The effect was the same: terror augmented through sound.

The boy spoke, breaking the most singular moment of con-centration I'd ever experienced in my life.

"*No se asuste. Mire los árboles, señorita, mire los árboles,*" the boy said. Don't be afraid. Look at the trees, miss, look at the trees.

I had no idea what I was looking for, but I stared hard at the tree that was closest to me.

"*Suavemente, señorita, mire suavemente.*" Softly, miss, look softly.

I didn't know what he meant by *look softly*. I relaxed the muscles in my forehead, an enormous effort considering the state of tension my body was in, and that seemed to soften my gaze.

"*Intente olvidarse de la serpiente, y ella se olvidará también de usted.*" Try to forget about the snake and he will forget about you, too.

I was trying hard to piece together the language from my three years of Spanish, and I hoped to God I was getting it right.

I stared at what I thought was an almond tree, trying to for-get about the snake. I became absorbed in the bark, amazed at the deep grooves and indentations, some of them large enough to fit small packages inside of. Packages of what? I wondered. My eyes glazed over, and my mind melded in with the tree, until I felt small enough to fit inside the grooves. Although I was standing perfectly still, my body moved away from me and toward the tree. Before I knew it, I was standing with my arms around the tree. I was next to all the other chil-dren, who had their arms around the trees, too.

I had no idea how I'd gotten from one place to the other,

but before I had time to think, the boy jumped onto the snake's body and grabbed it around the neck. He squeezed tight. I could see the exertion in his little-boy limbs. When the snake's eyes bulged out of its head, the boy loosened his grip and let the snake go. It slithered around and around, coiling itself up faster and faster, until it was just a blur, like a Tasmanian snake devil. The boy never moved. Not once. He just stared at the creature in front of him, and his eyes alone were enough to keep the snake spinning in circles.

He's a shaman, I thought. A born witch.

The little witch turned toward me.

"*El árbol le salvó. Es un abuelo. Es muy viejo. Debe haberle caído bien, o le habría entregado a la serpiente, para matarla y convertirla en parte de la selva. Quizás habría salido mejor parada.*" The tree saved you. It's a grandfather. It's very old. It must like you or it would have given you to the snake to kill so that you could become a part of the jungle. Maybe you would have been better off.

I clung to the tree, frozen, as the boy and the other children swarmed into my car.

"What are you doing?" I asked quietly, unable to scream, barely able to hear my own voice.

"*Se parece mucho al otro,*" the boy said. She looks just like the other one.

The children giggled.

"What other one?" I tried to say. No words came out of my mouth, but the boy read my mind.

"*El blanco,*" he said, pointing to his hand. "*El que parece que vive en una cueva.*" The white one. The one who looks like he lives in a cave.

I thought about Exley's pale hands. Is that what the boy meant? Was Exley here in Mexico? I wanted to ask him, but I couldn't find the words.

The boy took my wallet out of my backpack and threw the pack over to where I was standing, gripping the trunk of the tree.

"Déle las gracias al abuelo árbol antes de irse. Él le salvó, no yo." Thank the grandfather tree before you leave, he said. It saved you, I didn't.

Then he gunned the engine and tore through the jungle, maneuvering the Volkswagen Beetle like a Porsche on the autobahn.

I had never wanted to see a familiar face so badly in my life. If Exley showed up, I would take him back immediately, no questions asked. At that moment I couldn't have cared less about the nine plants, or Armand, or the laundry. Exley would know what to do. He would know the way out. Nothing he did, or could ever do, was as bad as this. "David," I called. But then I stopped, terrified that the snake was still nearby.

An hour later, I was still unable to let go of the tree. It was way beyond psychological; I was physically unable to drop my arms. I stood in the jungle wrapped around the grandfather tree, talking to myself.

"Let go of the tree," I said. "It's going to get dark soon. You have to keep moving. Let go of the tree."

Finally, my terror of being alone in the jungle at night overcame my terror of the rattlesnake, and I dropped my arms. They were painfully stiff and sore. I realized I had been holding the tree with all of the strength in my entire body for a very long time.

I heard the little boy's voice in my head. *"Déle las gracias al abuelo árbol"*—thank the grandfather tree.

Being in the situation I was in, not wanting to take any further chances, and not wanting to piss anyone or anything off that I couldn't see or hear, I knelt on the soaking-wet jungle ground. My knees sank into the rotting earth, which was sweet and stinky like shit and decay. I put my arms back around that old grandfather tree and thanked it profusely.

I picked my backpack up out of the mud and slipped it around my shoulders. I knew I was coming back to life again when I heard the monkeys screaming in the trees. I had been wrapped in an eerie cocoon of selective silence from the moment I came into contact with the boy. All I could hear was boy and rattlesnake.

According to the survival guide, the monkeys in the area were either spider or howler, and I had to be careful where I walked, because they dropped their business from the tree-tops every few yards. I felt like a terrified, moronic, idiotic fool, walking through the jungle alone, avoiding tree roots on the ground and monkey poop from the sky. I had no idea what I was doing, where I was, or where I was going, and now Sonali's map was gone with the little brown witch boy.

I poured sweat as I walked. The jungle canopy provided shade, but it locked in moisture, making the air thick and wet and hard to take into the body or let out. It was like trying to inhale a solid instead of a gas. I thought about the two humidifiers I'd bought for my bird-of-paradise, hoping to replicate its jungle environment. I let out a sarcastic laugh.

I was embarrassed that I had called Exley's name in a moment of panic. Why him? I was angry and amazed, literally amazed, that a short romantic infatuation with a man, based solely on the fact that he didn't look like he belonged in New York City, had brought me here, to the jungle in Mexico, alone, with no friends, no food, no car, no compass, and no protection. Armand was right. I was stupid and desperate. My only question was, exactly how stupid was I? Was I stupid enough not to be able to make it out of here alive?

I kept going, putting one foot in front of the other. I was painfully aware that there were panthers, ocelots, jaguars, tigers, vampire bats, bobcats, rattlesnakes, lizards, pumas, pythons, and dozens of other dangerous and/or poisonous animals, insects, and plants in the area. They were all listed for my reading pleasure in *The Wilderness and Jungle Survival Guide,* given to me by Kody, whom I now considered my best friend on earth for not only giving me that book but also insisting that I read it before leaving.

The Luna Maria

*The moon has two distinct terrains, the very old highlands,
and the younger, smoother maria. The maria are lunar seas
formed by impact craters striking the surface of the moon,
but that's not their most interesting feature. Even more
fascinating are the names that astronauts and physicists
have given to the maria. These include
Sea of Tranquillity, Sea of Serenity, Sea of Fertility,
Sea of Storms, Sea of Peace, and Sea of Clouds.
Why is it that, with such romantic and imaginative names
for the seas of the moon, the seas on earth get stuck
with Black Sea, Red Sea, North Sea, and Baltic Sea?*

I had been walking for about two hours when I saw a clearing
ahead. I was surprised that I had enough energy to run
toward it, but I did, the heel of a shoe in my backpack bouncing
and digging against my spine with each step.

The clearing turned out to be more than I could have
hoped for. It was an abandoned campground on a beautiful
white sand beach. I ripped the backpack off my shoulders and
dragged it behind me toward the ocean. Although I was still
utterly and totally lost, I will never forget the pleasure of leaving that murky, dank, dark, rotting, and thoroughly oppressive
jungle behind.

In just one moment I had emerged from a world of dark green, almost black, to a world of bright blue and light sunshine. It was what I imagined birth to be like.

The Yucatán Peninsula is a place where two oceans meet, the Atlantic and the Caribbean. It was a wild scene where they collided. I stood on the shoreline and watched as the waves rose up on my left and my right, slamming into one another, creating a mass of white water that had no discernible pattern or direction or flow. I'd always thought of the Caribbean as calm and gentle and the Atlantic as cold and roaring, but as far as I could tell both bodies of water were equally violent on the Yucatán.

There were four wind-torn bamboo tents lined up near the water's edge. I gathered that at one time the beach must have been much wider. No one in his right mind would have built the tents so close to the water.

I felt lucky that I'd found them, because I could tell that within six months they would be gone, washed out into the sea. I walked into one of them. It had a sand floor and a torn hammock with white mosquito netting draped over it. It felt good to know that other people had been in the tent. I put my backpack on the hammock and opened it to find out what had been banging against my back. It turned out to be a pair of open-toe red pumps. I laughed out loud. I'd packed them the night before I left New York, imagining my trip from the comfort of my apartment, where I lay on my bed, over Sonali's marigolds, picturing myself dancing on tabletops in bars on the new Mayan Riviera.

I dropped the shoes on the floor of the tent and used my foot to bury them with sand—quite violently, I might add—and then I took a pair of nail scissors out of my pack and cut away the mosquito netting strung over the hammock. I knew it would come in handy when I had to go back into that jungle out there.

I was fatigued beyond my own imagination of being tired. When the lime-green sunset, a color that took me forever to get used to in a sunset, signaled the coming night, I lay down on a hammock in the bamboo tent with my head on my backpack and my body wrapped in mosquito netting.

I fell asleep fast but didn't stay that way for long. The light from the moon was unbearable—a sentence I never thought I would think, a feeling I never thought I would have. With no surrounding buildings or lights of any kind, the moon was as bright as the sun. It glared through the slats of the broken bamboo all night long. No matter which way I turned, I couldn't get the moon out of my eyes. As a last resort, I put on a pair of sunglasses, but with mosquitoes buzzing all around me, I gave up on sleep and went outside.

I walked to the edge of the ocean. By the light of the moon, I saw silver fish just below the surface of the water. I fell asleep on the beach; I must have simply fallen down on the sand and slept. I woke up sometime in the middle of the night with an armadillo crawling across my leg. It was harmless, but *ugh*— with its armor-plated back it looked like something straight out of *Jurassic Park*. It left a muddy trail of slime across my calves.

At first light, I turned my back to the ocean and watched the sun rise over the jungle. Macaws screamed, and trees came alive as monkeys shook the branches to free the fruits. The ground thundered from the downpour of coconuts and mangoes. They piled up on top of one another in stacks so perfect they looked like a display at Dean & DeLuca. And then, just as quickly, they were gone, as hundreds of monkeys descended from the trees to grab their share of the goods. To be honest, it didn't frighten me at all. It looked like any Saturday afternoon on Canal Street, with thousands of tourists vying for Fendi and Prada knockoffs.

When the monkeys were gone, I treated myself to the over-ripe mangoes, the leftovers that weren't good enough for the locals.

I went back to the ocean for a wash. The salt stung my face. I didn't know my skin was so raw. I slung my backpack over my shoulders, and with the white mosquito netting wrapped around me like a wedding dress, I went back into the jungle.

According to Sonali's map, which I was now reading in my memory, I couldn't be more than fifteen miles from Casablanca, maybe ten. I couldn't fault Sonali or Armand for the distance; by car it would have been a breeze. Walking was, of course, another story.

Mexican Cycad
(Zamia furfuracea)

*You think you're old? Cycads have the rare privilege of surviving
two hundred million years of history. When you compare recently
discovered cycad fossils with today's living plants, they appear
to have changed little in all that time, giving them the distinction
of being considered living dinosaurs. To take that thought
one step further, whatever cataclysmic event killed the
dinosaurs—an ice age, or perhaps a comet crashing into the
earth—did not make a dent in the cycad population. Hardy
little fellows, aren't they?*

Not three feet into the jungle and I saw a movement out of
the corner of my left eye. I turned just in time to witness
closing time on a vine of moonflowers. Their bright-white petals
glowed under moonlight and shut down at the first hint of daylight. I stood there mesmerized, watching their twelve-inch-
wide dinner-plate-sized flowers simultaneously folding up to
nothing, like hundreds of slamming doors. I'd always thought
of flowers as still and beautiful. It was strange to see them in
such a blur of self-generated motion.

Sonali had mentioned the moonflower. She'd told me if I
ever came across one not to cut it or take it out of the earth. I
remembered her exact words:

The vine of the moonflower is an umbilical cord connecting all women to the moon. Take special notice of the plants, such as this one, that jump out at you in the moonlight, lost in the daytime to louder, more vibrant types. They are females. They will help heal the female parts of you that have been hurt.

It was strange to me that I could quote Sonali so perfectly. I hadn't known her for long, but everything she said stuck in my mind like glue.

At the close of the last moonflower, I continued on. The jungle wasn't at all like the woods I'd hiked in upstate New York. It was much denser, and as I got deeper inside, all sunlight was obliterated by the thick jungle canopy.

It was so dark I had to squint to make sure I didn't trip over tree roots covered in leaves and thick as a man's thighs, or mistake the head of a python for a stepping-stone.

That was the thing I hated most about the jungle: every single step was treacherous. It required the same level of hyperalertness I felt when I used to play around with coke back in college. And the aftermath of all that vigilance, the crashing exhaustion, was just as bad.

My pack felt heavy. It blistered the tops of my shoulders, sliding back and forth across my sweat-covered skin no matter how tightly I pulled the straps in the front. I cursed Sonali for not telling me to bring a flashlight so that I could see what I was doing in the dark. I cursed Armand for leaving for Mexico without me. And then I cursed Exley for absolutely everything. Armand was right. It felt really good to yell in the morning.

I stopped for a moment. I wanted to look at the three photos I'd saved on my cell phone, just a little taste of home before the long day of walking. One was a picture of Kody eating a muffin with one hand and holding up a raisin with the other. One was Exley cleaning soil off the floor in my apartment, which I would immediately delete. And the last was my beautiful bird-of-paradise, although at the moment I really wasn't in the mood to look at anything green.

When I put my hand in my pocket, my phone felt wet and slimy. I pulled it out. The flip top was oozing. I didn't actually expect it to work—I knew there were no cell towers in the jungle—but I didn't expect it be corroded, either. I slid open the battery cage with my sweaty fingertips and saw that the ooze was coming from inside: battery acid was eating through the phone. I thought of Geoff Evans holding up his cell phone and calling it *the new nature. A unit with no weakness . . . with a shelf life of forever.* What a fool. The new nature didn't survive twenty-four hours in the jungle. The old nature kicked the new nature's ass.

I stamped my foot, an activity that was actually dangerous and stupid, but I was angry that everything in this stinking swamp turned to rot in the heat and humidity. I found my phone incredibly hard to let go of. I looked at it, leaking battery acid and disintegrating by the minute, and I tossed it. Okay, I said goodbye to it first, and then I tossed it. I made sure to throw it far enough away so as not to disturb any creatures that might be lurking nearby.

I took a deep breath and calmed down. I could not afford any more fits of temper or foot stamping or throwing of objects. That's the thing about the jungle. It made me really considerate. All I wanted to do was get out of it without pissing anything off by accidentally squishing it, or sitting on it, or covering its home with my foot.

Fifteen or twenty minutes of walking and my hair and clothes were soaking wet. I don't mean wet like after an hour at the gym, I mean wet enough to wring out and create a small body of water. Walking in the rain forest was like walking under a hot shower that was originating from my own body.

I was thinking about how all of this water could possibly be inside of me, and if there would be any left for the cellular activity I needed to stay alive, when I saw the gloxinia directly in front of me. For the very first time, I experienced the plus side of being so alert.

The gloxinia was the only one of the nine plants that Exley had ever seen. It was the one he'd told me about on our date in the restaurant. It was unmistakable: deep-violet color on bell-shaped flowers. *Sinningia speciosa.* The great mythical plant of love at first sight.

I stared at it, wondering if it was a bad omen that I found it when I was alone. I took off my pack and bent down to remove the plant from the jungle floor. I pulled gently on the stem to find out where the roots began, but they were long and deep. I followed them, only to find that they snaked underneath the thick, heavy roots of what looked like either a coconut palm or a gum tree.

I knelt down next to the plant and rubbed the flower petals between my thumb and index finger, just to make absolutely sure it was the gloxinia. Sure enough, they were as soft as an old worn-out Victorian velvet sofa.

I got my nail scissors out of my pack to snip a cutting, a little trick I'd picked up from Armand. I felt along the stem for a good place to cut, as Armand had told me never to cut below the space where leaves, flowers, or new stems forked away from the main stem. He told me to close my eyes and feel for the nubbies, or bumps, which signaled new growth, and cut between them, above the fork. I wasn't about to close my eyes in my present environment, but I felt along the stem until I found a satisfactory place to snip.

"Don't move one millimeter, don't even look up, or I'll blow your face off."

I froze at the sound of the man's voice, speaking English

accented in Spanish. I had met with enough dire consequences in my dealings with plants that I took no chances. I stared at a worm furiously digging into the ground near my foot, as scared of me as I was of the man I couldn't see.

"Now let the scissor slide off your finger."

I did as I was told.

"Stand up straight. Lift your body using the muscles of your thighs. Don't move your feet at all or I'll put holes through both of them. I promise you, you'll never use them again."

From my crouching position, I pushed my body straight up with the strength of my thigh muscles; the thought of getting shot in the feet definitely helped with that maneuver. I put my arms up and out to my sides, with my fingers spread wide apart, to let him know that I wasn't holding anything I could throw. It was amazing what I had learned from my love of action movies. I knew how not to get killed.

There was no one within earshot. No one within gunshot. No one who could hear me if I screamed for help. I had to prepare myself; I was going to be at this man's mercy. This was way worse than being mugged in New York City. This was not going to be a quick hit and run. This man didn't want my money or he would have taken my backpack and left. He wanted *me*. This was just about as bad a situation as I could possibly find myself in. There's no chapter for this type of predator in *The Wilderness and Jungle Survival Guide*.

"Okay," he said. "Raise your eyes. Just your eyes, not your head, and look at me."

I raised my eyes without moving my head.

He was pointing a very large hunting rifle in my direction, and he was the single most beautiful man I had ever seen. These two facts were so incongruous that my brain didn't know what to do with the information. It didn't know what to focus on. My death. Or his beauty.

He had wavy, shiny black hair, tan skin, and a muscular body clearly visible under a soaking-wet tee shirt. It's funny how the mating instinct kicked in even with a gun in my face.

He pointed the rifle into the air and fired a shot into the jungle canopy. Thousands of creatures fled at the same time, like a rushing waterfall of animals, birds, and insects moving away from the single spot that I was standing on. Then he quickly stepped toward me, lifted me off the ground with his free arm, and set me back down about three feet from where I had been standing. He jammed the nose of the gun into the soft jungle floor.

"I'm sorry," he said. "I had to do that. You were about to step on a Mexican cycad."

I looked at the ground.

"It was right behind you. Less than an inch from your left heel. It's extremely rare, and you would have crushed it trying to get the gloxinia out of the ground. I was trying to get you to stand still the only way I could think of. If I had simply asked, you would have moved. Even a centimeter would have killed the cycad."

"Who are you?" I whispered without looking up at him.

"I am Diego. I'm a friend of Sonali and Armand, from Casablanca."

I was frozen to the spot. It occurred to me how often I was frozen in this jungle, the hottest place I had ever been.

"Sonali told Armand you were coming. When you didn't show up, he sent me in here to look for you. I'm not happy about it, either."

"Oh."

"Believe me, this isn't just any plant. I wouldn't have done that to you if it wasn't very special. It's an endangered plant, so it was doubly important that you not step on it. It's been around for a long time. Two hundred million years. Since the

Jurassic period. Many people hunt for this plant. They dig them up and sell them for small fortunes. Cycads live out every day with a huge price on their head. I can't imagine how it is for them."

He smiled at me with teeth as white as moonflowers. I was not going to get sucked in by yet another sexy plant-man. Especially one with a big gun pointing in my direction.

"I am truly amazed that you led me to this plant," he said. "I'm grateful to you."

"Oh" was still the only word I was able to get out of my mouth.

"I've seen some perfectly fossilized cycads," he said, kneeling next to the plant. "But it's incredible to see a live one. Thank you."

"Okay," I said, uttering my second word.

"Don't say okay when you don't really understand. That's not smart. I want you to listen to me. Cycads are, and always have been, perfectly adapted to their environment. They were meant to be. How many things on this earth were meant to be? Most species last for a few thousand years at best before something comes along and wipes them out. This plant lasted for *two hundred million years*. It lasted through ice ages, comet strikes, and dust storms. Events that killed almost every other living thing on earth did not kill this plant. And it never once had to change. It never had to grow taller, or develop wings, or fins, or legs, or lungs. It never had to evolve. It's remarkable, really. Perfect just the way it is."

"Meant to be, huh?"

"The cycad is one of the nine plants, you know. The ones you traveled all this way to find. So is the gloxinia. You were standing between two of the nine plants and you almost killed them both."

He laughed a smooth laugh with his head thrown back and his shiny black hair falling across his shoulders.

"You almost killed them, but yet you also found them. Armand was right—you're a strange woman."

"Armand doesn't know me very well, so I wouldn't take his description as fact."

"Oh yes, he does. He described you perfectly. He said you were the luckiest person he'd ever met. And he was right."

"Really? You think I'm lucky? I'm stuck in the middle of nowhere. Everything I have is ruined. My car was stolen, my cell phone disintegrated before my eyes, I have no map, no money, no job, and I almost got shot. In what world is that lucky?"

"You found two of the nine plants in under a week!"

I had already learned the hard way that it was useless to have a rational discussion with anyone involved with these plants. I let the topic of my luck fade away.

"So you say the cycad is one of the nine plants?"

"Yes. And it's the only succulent."

I felt ecstatic. Not because I had found the only succulent, but because I might be getting out of Mexico much sooner than I'd thought. It didn't seem like it was going to be at all difficult to find the plants. I'd come across two of them without even looking.

"What do you know about the plants?" I asked him. I figured, the more I knew, the quicker I would be back in my bed in Manhattan, vacuuming up the marigolds, getting high with Kody, and putting all of this behind me.

"I know they come from Mexico, from the Mayan Indians. Or at least the story comes from them."

Diego held the hunting rifle across his chest as he spoke to me. He looked proud, and suddenly very Mayan.

"Are you Mayan?"

"No. I am Huichol, but I was born in the Yucatán. In Mayan country."

"What else do you know about the plants?"

"I know that whoever finds the nine plants and brings them together in one room will have everything he or she desires. And whoever disturbs them will have nothing at all. The Mayans believed that the plants signified fertility; that's probably because they desired children to help them with the harvest. They grew the plants on an isolated island called Isla Mujeres, or Island of Women in your language. Today the island is overrun by tourists and stores selling Mexican blankets and piñatas. But back in ancient times, the only people allowed to set foot on that island were medicine men, or plant shamans. Over time, the plants came to symbolize more than fertility. They symbolized abundance of all kinds."

"But why nine?" I asked. Just to check and see if his reasons matched Exley's and Armand's. Not that I was paranoid.

"The way I think of them, and please excuse my English, I think of them as representing the nine forms of abundance: freedom, sexuality, fortune, power, magic, love, immortality, adventure, and knowledge. If you can find the plants and put them all together, then you have all of the things that human beings most deeply desire."

It was somehow comforting to know that all three men had the same story.

"People will steal from you or even kill you to get those plants."

"Yes, I heard that once before. But the man who told me that believed the nine plants were only a myth."

"The man who stole them from Armand?"

"Yes."

"Did he tell you they were *only a myth* before or after he stole them?"

"Before."

"Yet he risked his personal freedom to steal them. If he had been caught, he would have gone to prison. Believe me, a man never wants to go to prison if he can avoid it. That man believed the power of the plants was real. At least real enough to be worth risking his freedom."

"And the cycad? Which one of the desires does it stand for?"

"The cycad has accomplished what humans have not. It has been around forever. In my language, they call it the vampire plant. It is the plant of immortality, one of the deepest of the nine desires."

"Armand thinks people love death."

"I think that when people are little and they first realize they are going to die, death scares them so much that they stop thinking about it. They make up a myth. The myth of immortality. People secretly believe they're going to live forever. People are immortal right up until the minute they die. They don't have the presence of mind to love or hate death. They don't believe in death at all."

"So—I was about to kill the plant of immortality. That sounds like an oxymoron to me."

"Ah, but, you see, I came along, and so you didn't. And that's the nature of that plant. It's lucky, and it always has been."

"So I'm lucky and it's lucky."

"Yes. You didn't get shot, and it didn't get crushed."

"The gloxinia?"

"Gloxinia is the plant of love at first sight, so she's a perfect match for human beings."

"How so?"

"Humans are a very peculiar species. We don't like to work at love. We only believe love is real if it overtakes us like a sudden illness. Like the flu. When people fall in love gradually, they always question it. So the gloxinia delivers love at first sight. Just the way that people like it to be."

"How do you know what the nine plants are? I thought they were impossible to look for. That the plants have to find the person, not the other way around?"

"That's true for most people. But you and I have a big advantage. We have Armand. He is the keeper of the nine plants. He knows which ones they are."

"So the plants don't really have to find the person."

"That's right. Armand has to find the person."

"What are the other seven plants?"

"Let's dig up these two first, and start walking before night. It's not easy to walk through the jungle at night."

"I didn't realize there was any difference between night and day in here," I said, squinting into the darkness.

Diego bent down to uproot the gloxinia. Looking at him on his knees, bent over the plant, I felt an inexplicable, almost uncontrollable urge to touch him. I stood inches away from his body, watching him dig, alternately pulling and then gentling the roots out of the ground. He was intent on removing the plant and hardly noticed that I was there.

I was, in general, a very controlled person, and I wasn't sure what to do with this feeling I had for Diego. I thought of ways to entice his mind, to get his attention without actually reaching out and touching him.

"Do you like moonflowers?" I asked him. "This morning I caught sight of a vine closing at the first light."

He stopped digging.

"How far?"

"Not too far. Maybe fifteen minutes back toward the beach."

"Go get a cutting, but do it carefully. Do not cut the vine. Take a leaf cutting."

This wasn't what I had in mind at all.

"I don't want to go back there by myself. We'll be up all night walking. We'll see another vine in the morning."

"Moonflower is also one of the nine plants. She let you see her right before she closed. She waited for you, and she showed herself to you. She bared herself. She trusted you. You must go and get her. Not another moonflower, *that* moon-flower."

"Okay. Jesus. I'll get the moonflower. *That* moonflower."

"You don't understand," said Diego. "Things have gone extraordinarily well for you so far. You have two of the nine plants, and soon you will have the beautiful moonflower, the bringer of children, of procreation, and fertility, the most purely female of all the plants. You're lucky Armand sent *me* to find you. Any other man seeing what you're capable of would want to keep you here in the jungle and be with you all the time. Go get the moonflower so we can get out of here."

He looked at me with rough, soft eyes. They confused me. They were saying yes and no at the same time. I looked at him and felt so sexual I had to touch him right then and there. I couldn't stop myself. I moved toward him, but he extended his arm and put his palm up in front of my face to stop me.

"No. You found two very potent plants. The plant of love at first sight, and the female fertility vine, moonflower. The pull toward me is going to be strong, even unbearable at times. You're going to have to try and fight it by remembering that you don't know me."

"I don't want to know you. I want to touch you."

My own words seemed strange to me. I stopped talking and tried, for Diego's sake, to get a grip on myself.

He didn't make it easy.

"I know how you feel. You feel it from the crown of your head"—he placed his hand somewhere in the air over my head—"all the way down to here," he said, his hand tracing a straight line down the front of my body and ending up between my legs, not helping the situation at all.

"What you're feeling right now, it's the moonflower."

"It isn't. It's you. I feel you."

"Go back and get her or she'll never release you. You'll end up feeling this way about me for the rest of your life."

He scared me.

"Aren't you hot in that soaking-wet tee shirt?" I asked.

He laughed.

"Go. Now. Get the moonflower before I change my mind and take advantage of you."

"One touch?"

"Okay," he said. "One hug."

He felt solid. I put my nose into the hollow of his neck. It held a little pool of sweat that smelled like coconut suntan oil. I let go of him, because otherwise I'd have to make a fool of myself.

"Okay?" he said.

"Okay."

"Go."

When I returned with the fertility vine, he put the gloxinia, the cycad, and the moonflower cutting into an empty leather satchel tied to the belt loop of his jeans.

"How are you feeling about me now?"

I had to admit I felt much more in control of myself since I cut the moonflower.

"How do you know Sonali and Armand?" I asked.

"I know them the same way as you, by chance. Sonali teaches me things sometimes, like Armand teaches you."

"He doesn't teach me anything. I'm helping him get his plants back."

"I met Sonali and Armand when I was just a child, when they bought Casablanca. I lived in a straw hut, a *palapa*, with my parents, just a few hundred yards from their house. My mother still lives there today. I was young, and I was impressed with my new neighbors because they had electricity and running water, while my hut had neither. At first my parents wouldn't let me talk to them, because they were white, but when Sonali grew those giant orchids in that rocky soil behind their house, where nothing ever grew, my mother was impressed, and I was allowed to go over there whenever I wanted to."

"What did you learn from Sonali?"

"Oh, a lot of things about plants, and healing, and magic."

I looked at him sideways.

"Don't worry. Armand is your teacher, and he's much more practical than Sonali. You're literal and he's practical. It's a perfect match. I can see why he likes you. He'll teach you lots of useful things."

I could see a clearing up ahead. I felt the same joy as I had the first time I cleared the jungle, the day before.

"You don't have an affinity with the jungle, you know."

"I know."

"You only like the jungle when you're about to leave it."

"I'm like that about most things."

"You should never be alone in here again. The jungle gave you one reprieve, and you probably won't get another in this lifetime."

Scorpions

*Disgusting as it may seem, there are over two thousand species
of scorpion. Most varieties have a claw and three to four sets
of usable walking-legs. To make matter worse, the venom of
the scorpion, which appears to come from its tail,
actually comes out of its anus. Male scorpions court
females by doing a dance called the "promenade à deux."
After this dance, the male kisses the female and at the same
time injects a tiny bit of venom into her mouth, just enough
to paralyze her for a short time, so he can have sex with her.
I don't know about you, but this scenario sounds a lot like
a guy dropping a bit of Rohypnol into his date's drink
at a bar. Men are all the same. Women, on the other hand,
are not all the same, and when two scorpions are finished
mating and the venom has worn off, the male must leave
quickly or the female will set a plate and eat him for dinner.*

We stepped out into the clearing, and I stood still for a
moment looking up at the sky, the wide-open blue making me feel safe.

"This is the road to Casablanca," said Diego. "Look closely
and remember it, in case you need to find your way back at
another time. When you're alone."

We walked along the sandy road in total silence. We passed

lonely straw huts lined up on the windy beach. They were far apart, but all of them had identical rope clotheslines, with the same white sheets, blowing in the same direction, in the wind coming off the water.

Six hours by plane, two hours by boat, two days and nights on foot, and I finally arrived at Casablanca, in the middle of the night. It was black and moonlit outside the house, and the wind was howling furiously off the ocean.

From the road, Armand's house looked like another huge cement block. It was similar to the ones I'd seen at Puerto Juárez, only his was soft and rounded, with archways, and a big balcony on top. It looked solitary and lonely in the moonlight.

"This is where I head out," said Diego.

"You're not going to come in to say hello?" I asked, realizing that I was going to be alone with Armand for the first time, a man I'd met a few short weeks ago in a Laundromat.

"Don't worry, he won't hurt you. He doesn't care about you enough to expend the energy."

"Yes. That's what he tells me."

I looked toward the house across a field of patchy grass while Diego untied the satchel on his belt loop and handed it to me.

"Give the plants to Armand. They'll make him happy. He'll know his decision to bring you here was a good one."

"He didn't bring me here. He left New York without me and made me find this place all by myself. He made me travel through the jungle alone. There's a difference, you know."

I took the satchel from Diego.

"Watch out for the scorpions in the grass. They haven't had human blood since last year, when Sonali was here."

I turned around.

"Are you freakin' kidding me? Don't kid me like that. Ever."

"Human blood is a treat for them, like candy. Don't take your eyes off the ground in front of you, not for one second, and you should be okay."

Here we go again, I thought. What was it with this country? Everything in it was cawing, howling, rotting, shitting, poisonous, or deadly.

I estimated that from the shortest point between the house and myself it was still a two-hundred-yard run across the grass.

"Go," Diego whispered. "Go. Step lightly, using only your toes. Put as little of your foot down as possible. The less surface space you give the scorpions, the better."

I gripped the bag with the plants inside, took a deep breath, stood on my tiptoes like a sprinter on the blocks, then ran across the grass with my backpack banging against my spine with each foot strike.

"Go around to the front of the house," he yelled.

I looked back and saw him motioning with his arm, curving it as if he were putting his arm around the house and hugging it.

"Around to the front," he yelled again. "Go."

I tiptoed around to the front of the house, focusing my eyes on the grass, straining to see scorpions, although I had no idea what they looked like. I made it to the front, but it was hard to keep my gaze downward. The moon, which had been blocked from view by the house, was large, and so low it looked like it was sitting on the ocean, resting in a bathtub. I thought of Kody and how he wanted to see the full moon over the Yucatán and how I'd ridiculed him for that. He was right. It was something to see. His imagination was stronger than mine.

"Stand still," Armand whispered into my hair.

I screamed. I'd had no idea he was behind me. I turned

around. He was wielding a spatula in his right hand, high up over his head.

"The weapon of choice," he said, "for killing scorpions."

I looked down at the ugliest creature I had ever seen. Way worse than the mice, rats, or roaches that covered New York City. It was a large black flat circle with four pairs of legs, a separate claw, and a hard, long, prehistoric-looking tail.

"The danger is in the needles along the tail," said Armand. "They can whip that thing around and inject you with venom so poisonous you'll die on the spot."

I knew I wasn't breathing, so I made a conscious effort to do so.

"Scorpions are very slow, and that's their downfall, poor things. If you see one, all you have to do is slam it with a spatula. The whole trick is to see it before it sees you. With scorpions, it's all a game of hide-and-seek, exactly like when you were a child. You were a child once, weren't you?"

Armand bent down, scooped the scorpion onto the spatula, and flung it out onto the grass.

"Why didn't you kill it?"

"They protect my house when I'm not here. There are so many of them that an intruder is sure to get stung. Possibly even killed."

"Can a scorpion's sting really kill a man?"

"Oh sure, and a woman, too, especially if she's very young or very old. Middle-aged people like yourself have been known to die as well."

"I'm not middle-aged."

"You are to a scorpion."

"Well, *you* may not kill them, but I'm going to smash every one I come across."

Armand handed me the spatula.

"Keep it with you at all times. Everyone around here has at

least one. Some people even get theirs engraved. Oh, and never use the ones with the holes cut into the flat part. They're easier to cook with, but if you kill with one of those, scorpion blood comes up through the holes and splashes all over you. It's a nasty thing to have happen."

He opened the door to the house.

"Wait here."

I stood on the porch with the spatula high above my head, staring at the terra-cotta terrace, hunting for scorpions. My life had definitely taken a turn for the worse. My visions of sunbathing in the Gulf of Mexico and dancing on tabletops in Cancún were officially, completely gone.

"Don't waste your time looking for scorpions," Armand yelled from inside the house. "Look up!"

With no electricity to dull the light of the stars, every single constellation was clearly visible. I outlined Ursa Major and the Southern Cross with my index finger. I felt like I did when I was ten years old, strapped into a chair and staring up at the space show on the ceiling of the Hayden Planetarium.

What a strange place, I thought. If I look up, everything is so clear and beautiful, and if I look down, everything is so dangerous and ugly. I wished I could keep my head in the sky, but the scorpions brought me back to reality. Or was the sky the reality?

"Welcome to Casablanca," he said when I walked inside. He moved a candle around the dark room quickly. It was like looking at his house through a flip-book.

There were candles everywhere, and Armand walked around lighting them.

"Isn't there any electricity?"

"Sometimes, but not tonight. Someone must be watching TV out there, or listening to the radio."

"That's all it takes to kill the electricity?"

"I don't like it any more than you do. My dream was to open up a Laundromat here. But Laundromats require a lot of electricity, so I didn't get to see my dream realized. What have you lost?"

With the candles lit, I could see the terra-cotta-tiled floor and the red, turquoise, and white Mexican blankets thrown over a weathered gray rocking chair. There was a couch—a long seat, really—built right into the cement wall along the right side of the living room. There was a backyard picnic table, which I loved, and a large ceramic counter that separated the living room from the kitchen.

"Look up, look up! Must I always remind you to look up? You miss half your life always looking down."

"You've only asked me to look up twice since I've known you. Don't exaggerate."

"Okay," he said calmly. "Lila, my friend, please look up."

Huge pink-and-orange papier-mâché animals hung from the ceiling with the same kind of fishing line that was used to hang plants in the laundry. There were pigs, whales, birds, and donkeys.

"Piñatas. Made by the children in the village. Aren't they lovely?"

They were beautiful, and very expertly made.

"The children in town have a saying when they break the piñatas. They stand in a circle and yell, *Smash the piñata like there's no mañana!*"

"Are they filled with candy?"

"No."

I dropped my backpack on the floor to get a closer look at the piñatas.

"Pick that up—now! Scorpions love secret hiding places, like the inside of clothing, socks, and shoes. Bags and backpacks are an especially great find for them."

I grabbed my pack.

"You'll get the hang of it. I hope. You might even come to appreciate the scorpions. They make perfect practice prey. Later, when you get good at killing, you can conquer faster and far more dangerous creatures."

"I'm not exactly a predator. I'm from New York City."

Armand pointed his finger at a shadow on the floor. Without a moment's thought I slammed my spatula down on the dark spot as hard as I could in a tight two-fisted grip. I was actually sweating and breathing hard when I lifted the spatula off the floor.

"No," Armand said, laughing, "you're not a predator at all. Just a nice Jewish girl from Manhattan."

He showed me to my room.

"Be sure to hang all of your clothes on hangers and position them away from the back wall of the closet. Keep your shoes on top of the dresser, and check them in the morning before you put them on. In fact, the best thing to do is to wear sandals or flip-flops."

He reached for the spatula in my hand.

"Give it to me," he said, pulling on one end of it while I held tight to the other. "There's one in every room. Yours is on a nail behind the door," he said, out of breath from pulling so hard on his end.

I let go of the spatula just to see Armand fall. He didn't. Of course.

"You're getting sneakier," he said. "That's good!"

As soon as he walked out of the room, I grabbed the spatula off the nail. I took hold of a corner of the blanket on the bed and then threw the entire cover off with one fling of my arm, the spatula raised way up in the other hand. I didn't know I had that kind of strength. I checked the rest of the bed, lifting each pillow with the spatula itself and checking underneath. I knew that I would never, ever be able to use one of these things to fry an egg or flip a burger again.

———

Casablanca looked much less threatening in the morning, and in the light of the sun I noticed all of the things I had missed the night before. The bed I slept on was a double with a head-board made out of thin gnarled tree branches held together with some type of vine. Two big windows looked out across a patch of dry grass to the sea, which was the same fake turquoise color I'd seen on the boat ride over.

I sat up, sleepy. The sea was so close I felt like I could reach my hand outside the window and trail my fingers in the water. Even the grass between the house and the sea, so scary and scorpion-filled the night before, seemed like plain old grass in the morning light.

I got out of bed, still completely dressed, grabbed the satchel of plants forgotten in the scorpion turmoil, and brought it out to Armand.

He was sitting on the porch, facing the water. Even he looked less threatening in the sunlight.

"The tide is rising," he said, pointing out to the water. "If you look closely, you can see the mullet jumping out of the waves to avoid getting eaten by the bass."

"There are people out there, too."

"Lobster fishermen. At the end of the day, they'll line up on the shore and pull in their long nets filled with screaming crus-taceans. You won't be able to hear them scream, of course, but you can bet they are. When Sonali is here, the men bring us some of their catch, and in exchange she watches their chil-dren while they fish. I don't have the patience to do it without her."

I handed him the satchel with the plants inside.

I watched and waited as he opened the bag. I wanted a gasp, a compliment, a realization of my connectedness to nature. Recognition for all I had accomplished in such a short time.

"You went to the jungle and all I got were these three lousy plants? It's going to be a long trip if this is the pace you're moving at."

"I thought I did pretty well," I said. "I've never been alone in the jungle before."

"You weren't alone in the jungle, so don't be so dramatic. I sent Diego in there to keep you company. A good choice, eh?"

I looked down at myself. Was my attraction to Diego visible on the outside?

"You were always safe. Diego knows that jungle better than anyone. Better than Sonali or myself. His mother is a Huichol shaman, very respected in these parts. She was born on the rotting floor of that rain forest out there, and so was Diego. He was practically raised inside of it. You were safe even if you didn't know it."

"What good was being safe if I didn't know it?"

"It helped *me* sleep better."

I looked at him and tried hard not to get into an argument. I took a deep breath.

"What's a Huichol shaman?"

"Diego's mother is a healer, a *curandera,* and an expert in the spirit of the deer."

Armand looked me over.

"Don't go getting any feelings for Diego. You aren't ready for a man like that. Not two weeks ago, you were in love with a criminal who ruined my life's work, and now you think you're in love with the son of a shaman."

"I'm not in love with him. But if I were, wouldn't that be a good sign? A sign that I've changed and grown?"

"No, it's not a sign that you've changed and grown. It's a sign that you fall in love with anyone who crosses your path. It's a sign that you're man-hungry and desperate, too. I had to lock my bedroom door last night I was so afraid of you."

"I'm not desperate. Diego said it was the gloxinia and the

moonflower that caused me to have feelings for him. He said they exerted a strong, unbearable pull on whoever found them."

"Diego was being polite. He had work to do, and he didn't want you all over him in that jungle out there. You would have gotten both of you killed."

Armand laid the three plants on his workbench. His voice softened for the first time that morning.

"These are good specimens," he said, taking off his reading glasses, which made his eyes look much smaller and more distant and less kind. "You did good."

"Why is Diego so wrong for me?"

"That's really all you can think about, isn't it?"

"I just want to know why you think that he isn't right for me."

"Come."

We walked away from the window facing the sea and over to the one facing the mountains.

"Diego is Huichol," said Armand. "His family is descended from the great Aztec warriors, from the high mountains in Nayarit. Diego is like a hawk, or a majestic condor, floating over those mountains out there, with a wide-open twenty-foot wingspan. His great sexuality and his power come from his sense of freedom. Freedom to roam the jungle, to soar over the mountains, to heal, and to hunt. Freedom from the restrictions of ordinary day-to-day life. I'm not saying he wouldn't love you—of course he would, who wouldn't? I'm saying that, because you love restrictions, you would only hold him back."

"How can you say that? Look where I am. A woman who loves restrictions doesn't end up living with a stranger in a remote area in the Yucatán Peninsula."

"Diego is a man who is enchanted by the process of learning. He never wants to arrive at a single destination, such as a relationship. That would be like a death to him. His way of loving is not yours, and neither of you would ever be satisfied with the other."

What a load of crap, I thought.

"Unless, of course, you find the nine plants," Armand continued. "In that case, all bets are off."

"Why would that change things?"

"Because then you will have accomplished something. And you and he would be on an equal footing."

He smiled at me.

"Would you like some eggs? Or brioche with raspberry preserve?"

"I'll have eggs."

I watched Armand make boiled eggs. The kitchen was filled with sunlight, and the tiles on the countertop where he cooked were painted white with navy blue chickens and red roosters. He added a swirl of butter to each egg, which melted immediately, and a sprinkle of sea salt.

"Coffee?" he asked, pushing down on a French press.

"I'd love some."

When he finished cooking, Armand sat down at the picnic table to take another look at the plants.

"I am proud of you," he said.

"I know it's only three plants."

"There are six more to go, but I think you can do it."

"I won't stop until I have them."

"I'm counting on that."

"Why do you think I love restrictions?"

"Because you're always looking for a boyfriend or a husband to rein you in and keep you from growing and expanding."

He had a point.

"You're afraid of freedom. It's so scary that you try to find someone to put a leash on you at every turn. You're even hoping that I'll do that for you, which of course I would never do, not even if you begged me. Now, come on. Help me pot these three plants of yours."

I was trying to lift one of the big bags of sphagnum peat moss when I saw Diego walking across the grass. Thoughts of freedom and hawks and condors and Huichol shamans on my brain, I wanted to run out to meet him.

Armand looked at me.

"Don't be superficial," he said. "Don't fall in love with ideas of magic and special powers and shamans' sons. Develop power for yourself, so that it's yours. Don't fall in love with what someone else has. Do the work."

"Let me help you," Diego said when he walked through the door. He lifted the big bag of soil and brought it over to Armand.

I couldn't help noticing how strong he looked, and how tan his skin was. He looked like he'd never spent a single day in an office in Manhattan staring at a computer, swiveling around in a chair with headphones on. He looked like a different species. Like people were probably meant to look before cars and cities and endless mobile devices made us immobile, weak, brittle, and bent.

"What's up for today, Armand?" Diego asked, pouring soil from the big bags into the pots for planting. "The bass fishing looks pretty good. I heard the boats going out late last night."

"Maybe tomorrow," said Armand. "Today I'd like the two of you to do me a favor and find one of my favorite plants. *Theobroma cacao*."

He turned to Diego. "Try to find a mature plant. It should have red, orange, yellow, purple, or green pods. Make sure they're jewel-colored—that means they're ripe—and bring them to me without cracking them open. If they crack, leave them on the ground for the monkeys."

"Where do we go to find this plant?" I asked.

Armand pointed his thumb behind him toward the door. "Unfortunately, you'll have to go back into the jungle."

"Why aren't you going?"

"Because I have you to go for me."

"I'm tired. I walked at least forty miles over the last two days."

"Then you better move while you still have some energy," said Armand. "You won't be the only ones searching for cacao. It's competitive as hell out there."

Huichol Shamans

*The Huichol number about eighteen thousand, most of whom
live in Jalisco and Nayarit, rugged mountainous states in
western Central Mexico. They are descendants of the Aztecs
and part of a pre-Columbian shamanic tradition.
The Huichol say: If you have been made of corn* (eekoo)
and you eat the peyote (heekoori), *you become the
jaguar* (maye) *that hunts your deer* (maxra) *that is your
own spirit. In other words, stalk and hunt yourself
before you stalk and hunt anything else. Know yourself.*

When we left Armand's house, Diego put both of his big
hands on my skinny biceps and looked into my eyes.

"I can show you some Huichol magic if you'd like. It might
help us find *Theobroma cacao*."

He took his hands off my shoulders, turned his head toward
the jungle, and looked at me out of the corner of his eye.

"I know you want me to."

I wished Armand were here to see the majestic condor flirting with me, full wingspan.

"Come on," he said, "think of it as a shortcut. We'll have
Theobroma cacao in no time."

"Armand told me your mother was a Huichol shaman?"

"My mother *is* a Huichol shamaness," he said, "and a powerful one, too. But I'm sure it's not what you're thinking. It's not mystical and magical and full of witches and crones and spells. Huichol practices are simple and practical. All we do is listen to the song of Tamatz Kauyumari, the oldest and biggest deer. This deer gives us the power of the deer spirit and leads us to whatever we need."

"That's simple and practical?"

"Sure, why not? The deer might lead us to *Theobroma cacao*, if he likes you."

"What about you? Does he like you?"

"I grew up with him. He's like my brother, maybe even closer. Believe me, he likes me. You're the only question mark today."

I rolled my eyes. "I'm not going to have a conversation with you about whether or not the spirit of a deer likes me."

"But we're already having it."

"Why the spirit of the deer? Why not some other animal, like a giraffe, a llama, or a polar bear?"

"Do you see any polar bears around here?"

"I don't see any deer, either."

"We have to go back to your favorite place, the edge of the jungle. That's where they eat. We'll wait for them there. Depending on their mood, we could wait a few minutes, or all day, or all week."

"I thought there was just one deer we're looking for. The oldest and biggest deer."

"Tamatz Kauyumari never travels alone. He is surrounded by all of the deer who have ever loved him during his life. Deer are like that. They can't stand being alone."

We headed back toward the jungle along the same dusty, dry road that had led us to Armand's house the night before. We walked in total silence past the straw huts lined up along the beach with the clotheslines outside of them. Past the brown children and the fishermen, barely audible from a distance, holding on to long fishing nets and yelling at one another. Diego said that we shouldn't talk, that we might scare away the deer because they weren't used to the sound of my voice, which was both female and white. The silence was fine with me. I was exhausted and didn't feel like expending any excess energy on conversations about whether deer spirits liked white girls.

"The deer are not going to help us today," Diego said after we'd walked at least five miles. "We would have seen one or two grazing by now, or at least heard them rushing into the woods."

I felt sick from the intense midday heat.

"Why did it take so long for you to know that?"

"*Knowing* isn't like thinking or guessing or planning. Knowing comes over a person when it chooses to, and it didn't come over me until right now. I told you as soon as I knew."

My skin was clammy. I felt like I was going to pass out from the mix of heat and cold in my body.

"I need to sit down."

"Not here. We can't find Tamatz Kauyumari, and that means we're probably being stalked by the spirit of another animal, an enemy of Tamatz. If you sit down now, you could be killed."

"I'm not being stalked by the spirit of an enemy animal. Jesus. I'm tired. I can't walk anymore."

Diego jumped in front of me and put his hands on my shoulders for the second time that morning. The majestic condor sure was interested in touching me.

"You can't walk anymore, white girl?"

"No," I said, laughing. "I really can't."

"How are you going to get back to Casablanca?"

"I need to rest. Just for a few minutes."

"I have a better solution."

Diego picked me up in his arms. I fell asleep almost immediately with my face pressed against his soaking-wet tee shirt. The two of us, always wet from the tropical heat, were used to each other that way. His body smelled like sweat and coconuts, and I dreamt of my very first boyfriend, sitting in the lifeguard chair at the Silver Point Beach Club on Long Island. I was next to him in a bright-blue bathing suit and mirrored glasses, covered with suntan oil.

When I woke up, I felt better.

"It's okay—I can walk now."

He held me tighter against his body.

"Are you sure?" he asked, with his mouth in my hair.

"Yes. Put me down."

"But I like you here against me. I like carrying you. You're nice and light."

I liked it, too, but I wasn't going to let the freedom-loving hawk know that.

"Put me down."

He moved me from horizontal to vertical, slowly sliding my body down against his.

We walked the rest of the way back to Armand's house. I thought I walked a lot in New York, back and forth from Union Square to my job in midtown, but actually I hadn't, and my legs were stiff and sore from completely new levels of use.

We were almost back at the house when Diego stuck his arm out in front of me. He pulled me close to him, pressing my back against his chest. He gathered my hair into a ponytail and held it his hands.

"Look," he whispered into my ear, "look to the left, and don't make a sound."

I turned my head to the left. The land around Armand's house was covered with deer. Some were soft brown with white dots, some were gray and dirty, others had huge antlers. They were big and small, buck, doe, and fawn. They were everywhere. It reminded me of an outdoor music festival with people by the thousands and no visible ground anywhere.

Diego whispered in my ear excitedly.

"They came to you. They came right to where you live. Whatever happens now, understand that the deer are on your side."

"What could happen now?" I looked out at the animals through the glare of the blazing sun. "They're so gentle. I don't believe they could do me any harm."

"Don't be fooled by the soft eyes of the deer. They may not kill you with their bodies, they don't bite or have claws or venom, but if their spirit doesn't like you, you won't survive on their land. Their spirit will make sure you never find food, or shelter, or even peace of mind. Their spirit will haunt you until you are gone, either physically or mentally. Never, ever relax around deer unless you are absolutely sure you are compatible with them. Their gentleness is nothing more than a seductive shield. Behind it, they are as ferocious as a mother tiger around her cubs. You are like that, too; that's why you are compatible with the deer. Deep down inside, you understand each other."

Diego and I took baby steps toward the deer.

"Tamatz Kauyumari, the great deer spirit, is everywhere," Diego whispered. "Can you feel him?"

The only thing I felt was hot and tired and mildly pissed off that Diego thought my sweetness was just a cover.

"Kauyumari is making you feel tired so that you don't move around and scare the herd. All you need to do is sit and watch me. I'll do all the work."

That was the best sentence I'd heard all day.

"If the deer get wild and rear like horses, don't be scared. If they seem to be gathering into a stampede formation, remember, they came to where you live. You didn't have to seek them out on the edges of the jungle. They *want* to mix their spirit in with yours, so there's no reason to be afraid of them. Okay?"

I nodded. I sat down with my back against the nearest palm tree. I watched Diego. His black hair was thick and shiny as he walked into the sun toward the deer. I realized that I had no idea how old he was: he could have been twenty-seven or forty. His health hid his age. It was as noticeable as hair or eye color was on other people. His body radiated with the stuff. His white teeth, the thick muscles of his neck, his strong, tan, hairless chest, his large hands and bare feet with their clean, colorless toenails—all of it spoke of spectacular physical health. He looked like someone who would live a very long time. Or maybe someone who had already lived a long time and was still living part of a long cycle.

I tried to stop thinking of Diego's longevity as I watched him approach the herd. I felt like my life was sinking into a strange myth that wasn't my own. I tried to focus on the nine plants, the reason I'd come to Mexico in the first place, and how I would get out of here and back to my own myth, in New York City.

Diego waved his hands, signaling me to watch him. When he had my attention, he bent his arms at the elbow and pumped them up and down like a race walker, his muscles working in perfect unison, flexing and retracting with the long muscles of his back and thighs. His body seemed to move in time with the deer, and the leaves in the trees, and the rippling grass on the ground. Moving to a beat that I could feel in my body from fifty feet away. For a split second, everything around me looked like it was one thing, moving in tune to a rhythm coming up from somewhere inside of the earth.

Diego was so in tune with the animals that no matter how close he got they did not even glance in his direction. He stopped and scanned the herd, looking, I supposed, for Tamatz Kauyumari.

He lowered his body to the ground until he was crawling on all fours. He went toward a deer drinking from a watering hole, a huge reddish-brown buck streaked with gray. The deer had long, sharp antlers sticking out of him, as if someone had planted a dead tree in his head. I had no doubt that it was Tamatz Kauyumari.

Diego came to a stop and sank to his knees. I stood up quietly so I could see him over the bodies of the deer. He was kneeling in front of the old one like he was praying. I stood there, transfixed, as one by one the deer began to gather round Diego and Tamatz Kauyumari, forming a circle, until I couldn't see Diego anymore, until he was just one of the herd.

I wasn't sure what to do. Should I run over and scare the deer away? Was he in trouble? Should I toss a rock into the pack of them and make them scatter?

I was looking around for something to throw when I saw Armand standing outside his house, waving his hands at me and shaking his head no. He looked exactly like Diego did when he waved at me not to talk. Why was everyone always waving at me not to do something?

Armand was looking at me and pointing at Diego, which by this time I understood to mean: Look, you idiot girl from Manhattan, see the beautiful man surrounded by the beautiful deer.

Armand then pointed to me, and back to Diego, which I understood to mean: Go, you idiot girl from Manhattan, go to Diego and Tamatz Kauyumari.

I tried to emulate Diego's moves. I discovered that by walking with my eyes closed I could find some semblance of a rhythm. Oh, who was I kidding? I had no rhythm.

I kept walking, trying to forget about the deer, hoping that they would forget about me, too, and stay where they were. But of course they didn't. They scattered as soon as I came near, leaving me with an incredible view of Diego and Tamatz Kauyumari drinking together from the watering hole like two old friends at a bar.

Tamatz had his head bent down, his soft-looking deer mouth in the stream, and Diego was on his knees with his palms planted on the ground, his mouth in the water. Both their heads were bobbing up and down in time to that elusive rhythm of the earth.

Tamatz was the first to lift his head. Upon seeing me, he immediately turned his back and walked away.

Same to you, I thought.

Diego took his mouth out of the water and put his index finger perpendicular to his lips in the same sign for *Be quiet* that the little brown witch-boy had used, then beckoned me to follow him and the old deer. I turned to see if Armand was still there, and he was.

We followed the deer in the direction of the jungle, in total silence. Tamatz stopped to graze numerous times and to shit, twice, and finally, at the edge of the jungle, he turned and ran off into the trees.

"Right there," Diego said with excitement. "It's right over there."

"What?"

"*Theobroma cacao,* the chocolate tree, the plant of fortune, used by the great Olmec and Mayan civilizations as money and food for thousands of years."

"That deer led us right to it! How could he have known what we were looking for?" I asked.

Diego looked at me, somewhat confused.

"I told him what we were looking for. What did you think I was doing with him at the watering hole?"

"I had no idea what you were doing with him at the watering hole. How could I know that?"

"I guess you couldn't," said Diego, somewhat disappointed. "I was singing to him. I sang him a Huichol song for the spirit of the deer."

"Can I hear it again?" I asked, realizing suddenly that Diego had meant it as much for me as for Tamatz Kauyumari.

Diego sang in a high, trembly, melodic voice so unlike his deep speaking voice. The sound of it reminded me of Marco, the oboe player in Armand and Sonali's townhouse.

Spirit of the deer
Who knows the forest well
Every blade of grass
Every river swell
Let me ride with you
to find the food I seek
I won't harm your home
Or throw a stone
For you are me and I am you
I am you and you are me
Bring me to the food I seek

"My mother wrote that song for the same deer we saw today."

"Are you sure it's the same deer?"

"I told you, I've known him since I was a boy."

"It's a beautiful song," I said, realizing that Diego and I could not possibly have had more different upbringings. The closest my parents came to a spirit song was when my father sang along with the Budweiser commercials during Monday night football.

"I didn't want to tell you this before, but your spirit animal was nearby the whole day. That's why it took us so long to find the deer. Your spirit animal was chasing them away."

"What is it?"

"You really want to know?"

I pushed him on the chest with my palms. "Of course I really want to know. Who doesn't want to know what their spirit animal is?" I said, trying to relate to Diego's way of being.

He smiled.

"I know all this stuff is weird to you."

He looked into my brown eyes with his gray ones, so shocking against his black hair and tan skin. He had the kind of gray eyes that are more white than gray, as if they were lit from behind with a fluorescent bulb.

"*Panthera onca,*" he said, with a soft "c" in the *onca*. "The black panther. That's your spirit animal."

I took a deep breath, remembering the dream of the black panther I had before I left New York.

"I saw it in the jungle, twice. Once when we first met, when we found the gloxinia and the cycad and the moonflower. And then once again, today."

"How do you know it's *my* spirit animal? I read that they live in this jungle by the hundreds."

"That's true. But believe me the black panther can't be seen by a human being unless it wants to be. When it showed itself to me, I couldn't figure out why, and I was afraid that we were both going to be killed. But when it left us alone both times, I knew it must be your spirit animal. The black panther is smaller than the tiger or the lion but far more deadly. It's a stealth predator, a silent killer, quiet as the darkest, emptiest night. We are simple, easy prey, no match for *Panthera onca,* not even close, not even with a gun."

"Why didn't you tell me?"

"I didn't want it to go to your head. The black panther is such a powerful animal that panther people sometimes feel invincible when they find out. It's never good when that happens. They end up taking unnecessary risks and doing all kinds of stupid things."

"I don't think that knowing my spirit animal will make me feel invincible."

"Believe me, if you ever get the chance to see it, it will make you feel more powerful than you've ever felt. When you know, really know that you're connected to *Panthera onca*, it will change you forever."

I was intrigued. The thought of being changed forever appealed to my imagination.

"What else do you know about it?"

"See? Listen to you—you already feel special. I can hear it in your voice."

"Come on. What do you know about *Panthera onca*?"

"My mother taught me a lot about panthers, because they lived in the jungle around our home. She thought that the more I knew the safer I would be. In your world, parents worry about drug dealers in schoolyards, and crazy kids shooting up classrooms. In my world, they worry about *Panthera onca* stealing their children in the middle of the night. The end result is the same: death for children."

"What do you know?"

"I know that they have phenomenal speed, and that there's no way to outrun them in the jungle. I know they're great climbers and excellent swimmers, which is rare for cats. But it's the esoteric secrets of the panther that are the most fascinating."

"The magical parts?"

"The most incredible aspect of the black panther is its silence, which is absolute. Because of its blackness, which is a birth defect, really, and its total silence, the Huichol shamans say that the black panther knows the secret of invisibility. If it wants to kill you, it will, and that's that. You will never see it coming. And since the black panther buries its dead, no one you love will ever find you. You will disappear without a trace, and that will be the only clue that your demise came at the jaws of the panther. If you're ever fortunate enough to experience the presence of *Panthera onca* without being killed, the first thing you'll notice is its unblinking stare. It can see right through your body, and it will use its eyes to heal you on a deep, cellular level, if it wants to."

"You've got a shiny black coat and glowing eyes."

"You can joke, but you're surrounded by panthers. They're in your dreams and in the faces of your friends."

I thought about the panther commercial I'd sold to the Puma client, and the prophetic dream with Sonali's marigolds. Diego was right. I was surrounded by black panthers.

Cacao
(Theobroma cacao)

*Theobroma cacao, translated from the Greek to mean "food
of the gods," is one plant that will never let you down.
Through the good times and the bad, in times of high anxiety
and too much stress, during relationship problems when it seems
that all of the passion is gone, when there is no one around
to talk to, or when no one will listen, understand, or believe
in you, Theobroma cacao, otherwise known as chocolate,
is always there to make you feel better.*

Diego and I spent the next few hours extracting the podlike
nuts of the chocolate tree, *Theobroma cacao*. He climbed
the tree, which was about fifteen feet high and quite slender,
and shook it until the ripe nuts fell to the ground. It was one of
the strangest-looking trees I'd ever laid eyes on—tall and
skinny, with huge multicolored pods hanging down off its
main branches. It looked like a long brown stick with orange,
yellow, red, green, pink, and purple footballs glued onto it. It
was difficult for me to connect this tree and its weird pods to
Nestlé Crunch bars and double-fudge ice cream on a hot
summer day.

We collected nine cacao pods for Armand, carrying them in

nets slung over our backs. We left the cracked ones on the ground for the howler and spider monkeys, who were gracious enough to let us finish our job before screaming and fighting for the leftovers.

"The process of making chocolate from cacao seeds was first introduced by the Olmec people," said Diego. "Some scientists believe that chocolate is not even a natural plant but was genetically engineered by the Olmec themselves. They ate the chocolate, but they also used the cacao seeds as money, making *Theobroma cacao* the plant of fortune."

Diego stopped walking and took a pod out of his net.

He leaned over and banged it against a stone embedded in the jungle floor. "Never open the pod with a machete. You'll damage the seeds, and the chocolate won't taste as good. On the other hand, if you want to suck the placenta off the seeds for its sweet, lemony flavor, and you don't want to make chocolate at all, then you can open the pod any way you want to."

Diego dipped his fingers into the broken pod and offered me a handful of the white slime-covered seeds.

"No, thank you."

He took the mixture and put it in his mouth, sucking off the whitish goop and spitting out the seeds.

"It tastes good," he said, smiling, "like extra-pulpy lemonade. The pod keeps it cool, too. Are you sure you don't want to taste?"

The fact that they were cool definitely made them more appealing.

"Okay. Just a little."

Diego put the pod directly up to his mouth and poured some of the seeds inside. He came over to me and bent his head down toward mine. He put his mouth on my mouth, slightly open and soft, and let some of the seeds slide onto my tongue.

"Taste good?" he asked.

"Like extra-pulpy lemonade," I whispered.

There was something inexplicable, something a little extra, about kissing in the jungle.

"It makes you feel more alive," said Diego, reading my thoughts. "It's because every single thing around you, every-thing you're standing on, everything above you, and below you, and on the sides of you, every single thing is alive. Even the things you can't see."

He was right. Kissing in the middle of all of that life and sound and scent was not the same as kissing in a bedroom, or a bar, where nothing is alive and breathing. Kissing in the jun-gle felt completely natural and unscripted, more like eating or sleeping.

"Now you know how to quench your thirst if you're ever stuck out here without water."

"I do." And I'll never forget it, I thought.

Back at the house, Armand removed the seeds and laid them out on the table. He spun an unopened pod in his hands, and I began to feel dizzy. I looked around for Diego to see if he was feeling the same way, but he was gone.

"Don't look for Diego. He's resting now."

"I know you don't think Diego and I are a good idea, but he does like me, you know."

"Why, because he told you the story of *Panthera onca*? And maybe he kissed you out there in that sexy beast, the jungle?" Armand laughed while he continued to clean off the cacao seeds.

"He's treating you like a woman. He's flirting with you, that's all. It doesn't mean he loves you. He knows you'll pay more attention to him if he flirts with you. Me, I make you dizzy to get your attention."

"So you *do* do that on purpose!"

Armand spun the cacao pod on his fingertip like a basket-ball.

"Never mind all of that nonsense. I'm going to tell you how to make chocolate! Write this down. And, yes, you can try this at home. If you ever get back there."

How to Make Chocolate from Theobroma Cacao

Split open three or four ripened pods and scoop out the beans (seeds) and pulp.

Put the mixture into a specially prepared fermentation box, or any wooden box you can find, and cover with banana-plant leaves, or leaves from any plant in the banana family. They are easy to find, and pretty much available anywhere.

Let the mixture ferment inside the box for seven days.

Spread the mixture on slabs of wood or cement— a butcher block or a backyard picnic table will do—and let it dry in the sun. Turn the beans occasionally by raking them with your fingers or with a fork.

The fermenting pulp eventually drains away, leaving the seeds with little or no pulp residue.

Roasting

Roasting takes some trial and error, depending on how many beans you're going to roast. For a thin cookie sheet's worth, roast for sixty minutes at 250 degrees.

When you're done roasting, remove the paper-thin skin surrounding the seeds, by hand. Some people use a rolling pin to loosen the skin, but a lot of the seeds get smashed that way. Be prepared—it can take up to two hours to hull a mere nine ounces of roasted beans. What you have left after hulling is the cocoa nib, which is dark, unprocessed, unsweetened chocolate.

Next step, liquefy in a food processor. This should take about ten minutes. You might see some smoke, so check to make sure it's the cacao and not the food processor. Do this by using your nose. You'll smell either the wonderful scent of chocolate, or the not-so-wonderful scent of burnt metal or plastic.

From there, anything goes. You'll have to experiment with the amounts of milk and sugar, but here's a baseline. Add two tablespoons of melted cocoa butter, three ounces of powdered milk, five or six ounces of powdered sugar, and nuts and spices to taste. Put it back in the food processor to blend—two or three minutes, tops.

Conching

Pour your mixture into a glass and mix with an electric mixer for one or two hours. It's easy if you have a mixer that stays on all by itself without your having to sit there and babysit. If you have to babysit, you can work in shifts: on an hour, off an hour.

Pour into a foil mold, cool overnight—and not in the refrigerator—and you should come out with one highly imperfect, gritty-tasting chocolate bar. From there, all it takes is practice, practice, practice. Good luck! You'll need it.

Chicory
(Cichorium intybus)

The ancient Egyptians considered chicory a magical plant,
capable of removing all obstacles as well as opening locks, boxes,
and doors. They anointed their bodies with chicory juice from
the root of the plant in order to gain the powers of invisibility
and special favors from important people. They believed chicory
magic was much more potent if the plant was cut with
a solid-gold knife, in total silence, at midnight.
And if none of that worked, they ground and roasted
the root and blended it with their favorite coffee to taste.
A very versatile plant indeed.

"Remind me of what we have so far," Armand said.

"We have four of the nine plants: gloxinia, the plant of love at first sight; cycad, the plant of immortality; moonflower, the plant of fertility and procreation; and *Theobroma cacao*, the chocolate tree of fortune."

"Good! Now, how about if you and I go to the market and purchase plants number five and six. You've been out of the city for a while; I bet you could use a little shopping spree."

"You mean we can buy the plants? At a store?"

"The market in Xcaret sells one or two. We'll go and see if she'll sell them to us."

"Who?

"The Cashier, of course."

"Are we walking? To tell you the truth, I'm kind of tired of walking."

"Oh no. I'm not a big walker myself, and Xcaret is much too far. I've got a motorbike out back."

"You've got a motorbike out back, and I walked back and forth to the jungle about nine hundred times?"

"You would have scared the deer away. Absolutely zero chance of getting *Theobroma cacao* with a motorbike."

I followed Armand, and, sure enough, an old army-green motorcycle was leaning against the house. I'd seen it before but never thought twice about it, because it looked like a rusted old piece of junk.

"Get on," Armand said as he swung his leg over the seat. "The bike's not as old as it looks. I just made it look that way so it wouldn't get stolen. A splash of antique-green paint here and there and a steel-wool rub-down. The rust comes with the territory."

Because of his size, Armand took up most of the motorbike, leaving me with just a tiny slice of seat behind him.

"Go ahead, put your hands on my shoulders. Don't be afraid to touch me—I feel good!"

I had to put my hands on his shoulders just to stay on the bike.

"I feel pretty nice, don't I?" he asked.

"Kind of."

We bounced over the grassy patch in front of the house, no doubt crushing a few scorpions along the way.

"I was thinking this morning that it's been twenty years since Sonali and I purchased Casablanca. We bought it to be closer to our friends," he shouted over the motor.

"The plants?"

"Yep. Sonali loves it here. She would probably live here all year round if it weren't for her orchids. They love it in New York, so she doesn't get here as often as she'd like."

"How do you know they love it in New York?"

"We bring them here, they die. We keep them in New York, they grow."

"Shouldn't they grow better here? In the tropics?"

"They should, but they don't. They have an affinity for our home, and that's that. It isn't like we haven't tried, and, believe me, its no easy task bringing those plants back and forth across the border. Right off the bat, it's illegal; and on top of that, with orchid prices what they are, it's become a bit like smuggling diamonds. It's stressful for Sonali."

"Can't she find orchids here that she likes and start over?"

"Trade one orchid for another, just like that, huh?"

"Well, yeah."

"Sonali has cared for those orchids for twenty years. Some of them even longer. I'm telling you, she has a relationship with those plants that's stronger than her relationship with me."

"I doubt that."

"It's true. They give her things I can't. Great beauty, fantastic color, unusual scents, and stability, because they don't leave for Mexico with strangers. The rare ones bring her a little fame and some money. Friendships have sprung up around a shared interest in the plants. Music came into her life in the form of Marco the oboe player. Even the Laundromat was purchased with money from orchid cuttings."

Any mention of the Laundromat always made me a little tense. "I didn't know that."

"You can see how important they are to her life. And mine. Sometimes I feel as though I moved in with Sonali and her family, but it's okay, because she's never made me feel second to her plants, even though I know I am."

"What about the passion plant with no name? Did she ever look for it here in Mexico?"

"She spent many, many years searching for that plant. That was before the orchids. Before me."

"She never found it, did she?"

"She never even laid eyes on it."

Armand sounded sad.

"She lived in Mexico for a year. She worked with plant shamans, healers, hunters, and dealers. She searched. She was totally convinced that the passion plant still existed. No one could have told her otherwise."

"No one she spoke to had ever seen even one plant?"

"No. I myself visited shamans high in the mountains of Nayarit, the same mountains where Diego comes from. I asked them to call the plant. To find its name. I thought if I could find its name I could find the plant. I was wrong."

"Maybe it wasn't the right time, or the right location."

"No, it's much simpler. The plant has no name. It has only passion for life. And I knew that it would take passion to find it. Sonali had become too sad and withdrawn, so I took over for her. But my luck was not good."

Armand stopped talking, and I didn't say anything to him for a long time. It was clear that the passion plant was for him like the Laundromat was for me: a touchy subject.

"Why didn't you have children, Armand?"

"Sonali and I made the decision a long time ago to put our energy into a lot of people instead of just one or two. And the orchids, of course. And then there was the search for the passion plant with no name."

"And the people at the Laundromat?"

"Yes, and Diego, and now you."

We had almost reached Xcaret when, out of nowhere, or nowhere that I could see, three enormous black dogs ran toward us. They growled and chased the motorcycle, ripping away my melancholy mood over the passion plant and turning it into terror. I twisted my helmetless head around to look at them. They were running as fast as we were driving. They bared their teeth, which were yellow and dripping with saliva.

"Move. Faster," I yelled, grabbing Armand's shoulders and shaking them, no longer in the slightest bit hesitant to touch him.

"Don't worry," he shouted over his shoulder. "They'll all be dead soon."

Armand revved the bike, and gravel from the road tore into my hair and scratched my face.

The market was an unusual place, definitely worth the yellow-toothed devil dogs and the gravel spray.

It was made of wood—not cement, like the other buildings on the Yucatán—and it was painted sky blue. It stood alone on the side of a dusty road, nowhere near a town, and it was falling to pieces. There were large chunks of wood missing from the left side. In fact, the hole was so big that I was able to stand on the road and browse the market shelves without actually walking through the door.

"A real time-saver, eh?" Armand said, standing next to me and peering through the hole.

Inside was an old cash register on a card table, five aisles of shelving, and a few refrigerators in the back. There was nothing truly unusual in the layout of the market. It was the content of the shelves and refrigerators that was hard to believe.

For starters, the canned food was old. And I mean old, as in covered-in-several-inches-of-dust old. Armand said that the people in the village didn't eat canned food very often, because it was expensive and not as good as fresh-caught. I understood that, but, still, how hard could it be to dust off the cans every once in a while, if only for show?

I noticed the cereal right away. Yellowed cardboard boxes of Kellogg's Rice Krispies with the old red-rooster logo on the front. I'm in advertising, or at least I was, so I knew that the red rooster was a classic logo from the 1970s. That meant the cereal on the shelf was older than I was. Thirty-six years old, to be exact. I checked my pockets for cash. I was tempted to buy every single box for its resale value on the vintage section of eBay.

The refrigerated-food section was even more bizarre. Right there, between the milk bottles and the ancient cardboard tubes of Pop N' Fresh Dough, were vacuum-sealed packages of hormones. Vials of testosterone, estrogen, and proges-terone stood behind an old, faded black-and-white photo of a transvestite taped to the refrigerator door. The picture was taken in the Meatpacking district of Manhattan before Pastis, the Maritime Hotel, and the Europeans had replaced Florent and the sex trade. Items that back in the States required painful blood tests, prescriptions, and expensive insurance that no one had were practically free in this broken-down backwater market with a hole in its side.

I continued my stroll through what I now considered to be the greatest market that had ever existed anywhere, and I came across small gems at every turn.

There were boxes of Retin-A next to the Crest toothpaste. And vials of Botox—which is actually a powder, not a liquid—near the Pantene conditoner. I had no idea that people who didn't have electricity and hung cholera-warning signs in front of their houses were so concerned with wrinkles. But I was wrong. Apparently, beauty is big business, even for women who have to kill their chickens before cooking them for dinner.

The Botox was marked "$10.00" instead of the $750 that my friends back home regularly paid a dermatologist/friend/guy in the back room at Equinox gym.

I calculated that for $750 I could fly to Mexico, buy Botox, look fabulous, and have a beach vacation at the same time. What a country! What a market! I laughed out loud. I was sold. The market had revived my sense of humor. Between the deer spirits, the black panthers, and the moonflowers, I was convinced that I was losing my edge and becoming a spiritual softy. But no. Underneath the plants, the snakes, and the shamans, I was still myself. All it took was *el mercado* to bring back my city cynicism.

I looked around for Armand, but he was nowhere in sight.

"*El hombre está en el sótano,*" said the woman behind the cash register. The man is in the basement.

She was short and dark with two long jet-black braids down to her waist. Her face was very wrinkled, which was odd because her hair was thick and had no gray in it at all. She must be the Cashier, I thought.

She stared at me patiently while I looked her over. When she was satisfied that I was satisfied, she repeated, "*El hombre está en el sótano.*" She flicked her wrist at me like she was swatting a fly. I flicked mine back with equal attitude.

The flight of stairs going down to the basement was long, steep, and pitch-black. I'd had a dislike of basements since childhood, but I pushed it to the back of my mind and headed down. There were at least thirty completely vertical wooden slats that doubled as stairs. I went down backward, facing the slats like I was climbing down a ladder. The smell of plants and earth got richer with each step, and I felt like I was dropping down into the center of the earth.

"*¿La luz?*" Lights? I called out to the woman.

"*Lo siento, señorita. No hay luz. Las plantas están en el sótano. No es buena para las plantas.*" I'm sorry, miss. There are no lights. The plants are in the basement. It's not good for the plants.

Shit, I thought to myself, inching down in total darkness. What about what's good for me?

There were plenty of lights at the bottom of the stairs, but not the kind that usually light up a room. Instead, there were purple grow-lights everywhere, hovering over rectangular wooden tables jammed with plants.

The room was a long, narrow railroad-style space. It was at least five times the size of my apartment, making it somewhere around three thousand square feet. The fluorescent bulbs made the space look like one giant black-light poster from the sixties, the ones that had pictures of tigers or skulls that glowed in the dark against a purple velvet background.

As my eyes adjusted, I could see that there were thousands of plants—healthy, lush, and very green. The air was cool, sweet, and oxygenated. There were no blooms in sight, and maybe there never would be. I didn't know. I couldn't tell what types of plants I was looking at. Maybe the basement was some sort of hydroponic marijuana factory. I didn't smell any pot, but perhaps the same people selling the hormones upstairs had invented a type of weed that had no scent. A plant that could be smoked in public without detection. That would really be something, I thought. A real moneymaker. A career changer. A life changer, in fact.

"Atropa mandragora solanaceae."

I was startled to hear the faint sound of a man's voice coming from the other side of the basement.

"Armand?"

"The mandrake," said the man, whose voice was much higher than Armand's, "is the plant of magic. The great bringer of mystery."

I strained to see across the basement. I could barely make out a figure on the other side. His head was bent down over a pile of leaves, his body much too small to be Armand's. I was uncomfortable being so far down into the earth with a stranger, so I backed up toward the stairs, slowly and quietly, trying not to make a sound.

The man stood up and turned around just as I reached the steps. His skin looked grotesquely pale and sickly under the purple grow-lights.

"Hello, Lila," he said.

I froze. Something in my body felt sick. How did a man in the basement of a market in Mexico know my name? I panicked and focused hard, but I was too far away to make him out. I heard a dull thud and a click at the top of the stairs. Someone had closed the basement door and turned the lock. I knew it was the Cashier.

The man walked toward me. His blond hair shone under the lights. I sucked in a deep breath. It was David Exley.

"Do you know that the strongest mandrake plants grow beneath gallows? Or in places where a hanging death by suicide has taken place?"

I said nothing. I needed time to think.

"Severing the spinal nerves creates an erection in the hanged man. A lovely image, isn't it? When the ejaculate flows out of the dead body, it seeps into the ground, and that's where the mandrake flourishes. Plants from semen are potent hallucinogens and aphrodisiacs of extraordinary strength."

"What are you doing here?" I whispered, gripping the two wooden plant-tables on either side of me.

"King Solomon, Alexander the Great, and Joan of Arc all refused to leave their homes without having a piece of the mandrake touching some part of their body. Shakespeare wrote about it in *Romeo and Juliet*. And Homer in the *Odyssey*. Longfellow, one of my favorite poets, captured the spirit of the mandrake so beautifully when he wrote: 'Teach me where that wondrous mandrake grows / Whose magic root, torn from the earth with groans, / At midnight hour can scare the fiends away, / And make the mind prolific in its fancies.' "

I had never imagined seeing Exley again, or even if I had,

my fantasy did not include a dark basement and a quote from Longfellow.

"What are you doing here?" I asked again, trying to keep my voice as steady as the situation would allow.

"I'm telling you about the mandrake plant. She's one of the nine, you know. The plant of mystery and magic."

"But why are you here?" I asked for the third time, my brain like a car stuck in a ditch, spinning its tires, trying to get out.

Exley reached out to touch me. I backed up, away from his reach but also farther from the stairs.

"I'm here for the same reason you are, Lila. The plants."

"You have the plants already. Remember? *You stole them from the Laundromat.*"

" 'Stole' is such a harsh word. I could hardly have taken the plants if they didn't want to come with me."

"If you have the plants, why are you here? Did you follow me?"

"Are you afraid I'm going to steal the new ones you've acquired? Maybe wreck his house this time?"

"Is that what you want," I asked in a strange shouting whisper, "to hurt Armand?"

"I'm here because two of the nine plants from the Laundromat died in transit, so to speak. I'm here to replace those two plants. That's all."

"Which ones were they?"

"In the spirit of competition, you know I can't tell you that. After all, we want the same things, and the supply is so limited. But I will tell you that I don't see them in this basement."

"I don't believe you."

"It's still me, Lila, the man you met at the green market, the one who taught you about tropical plants. The man you took into your bed. The one who brushed your hair and your breasts with the soft baby-brush."

His voice sounded fake-sweet, like a man at a schoolyard

offering candy to little girls. He reached for me again, and I pushed his hand away.

"What happened in New York was not personal to you or to your friend Armand. It was about the nine plants. That's all."

"You used me to get to them. And you hurt my friend. I take that very personally. I do."

"Lila. Listen to me. When I first met you, I liked you right away. I liked you before you showed me the fire-fern cutting, before I offered you the money, and before you took me to the Laundromat. But when you told me that Armand had the plants, I had to believe that you came into my life to show me where they were. I'd spent my *entire life* looking for those plants, and there you were, with direct access to my dream. What was I supposed to do? Try for one moment to put yourself in my shoes."

"I looked for you at the green market," I said. "I looked everywhere for you, in every single stall, through the leaves of every plant. I spoke to every vendor. When I got to the Laundromat and saw what you did, it was the single most degrading experience of my life."

"Life is long," he said with a smile.

"I have to ask: why did you come home with me that night? I'd already taken you to the Laundromat. You knew how to get the plants. Why did you have to come back with me?"

"For my own pleasure. I'm a man. What can I say?"

"How about 'I'm sorry I'm a liar and a thief'?"

Exley laughed.

"I'm not sorry. I told you, it wasn't personal. It was a small thing I did in comparison with obtaining the plants. And you did enjoy our little tryst. I know you did, because I was there."

He reached out to touch my hair. I couldn't understand my own feelings. Memories of the green market, and the bird-of-paradise, and warm, earthy sex collided with the image of the broken glass window at the Laundromat. I was attracted to him and repulsed by him, at the exact same time. I wanted to run toward him and away from him, so I held the middle ground and stood still.

"I could have you arrested, you know. You just admitted to breaking into the Laundromat."

"Really? You think so? This is the wild west, baby. Try getting *la policía* in these parts to arrest me for something that took place across the border. I hope you're rich, with lots of money to bribe them."

Exley walked backward. Farther and farther down the long rows of plants, back into the farthest reaches of the basement.

"*Adiós, amiga.* It's been nice chatting with you. I'm sorry to leave so soon, but I have to get back to the business of finding plants."

I yelled Armand's name, but I was too late. Exley opened a door I hadn't seen. He seemed to pull the deadbolt right off it with his bare hands. Bright sunshine flooded the basement, and I could hear the Cashier yelling at the top of the stairs.

"*Ay, Dios mío, las plantas,*" she screamed. "*¿Quién abrió esa puerta? ¡Te mataré!*" Oh my God, the plants. Who opened the door? I will kill you.

I ran across the basement and quickly pulled the door closed. I climbed back up the slats, taking them two and three at a time. When I got back into the market, breathing hard, the Cashier was standing at the door with Armand.

"*¿Quién abrió la puerta ahí abajo?*" she demanded. Who opened the door down there?

I looked at Armand.

"Exley was in the basement."

Armand looked to his left and bit a nail.

"Did he have any plants with him?"

"I don't think so, but he was carrying a rolled-up shirt. He may have had cuttings inside."

"Did you see him take any plants?"

"No. He told me the plants he was looking for weren't down there."

I turned to the Cashier.

"Why did you close the door to the basement?"

"*¿Qué?*"

"*La puerta del sótano,*" I said. The basement door. I went over and slammed it as a demonstration. "Why?" I asked.

She seemed to understand.

"*Un accidente.*"

I didn't believe her.

"Why are they down there?" I demanded of Armand. "Why does she keep those plants in a dark basement when the sun is shining all day long?"

"They're special plants, grown to the exact specifications of particular *curanderos* and doctors in the area. They're unusually potent, and extremely dangerous in the wrong hands. They're also very valuable, both medicinally and monetarily."

"Why did she let Exley into the basement?"

Armand turned to the Cashier and translated the question.

"*Es cliente mío. Y un buen cliente, además. Lleva muchos años comprando plantas.*" He's a customer of mine. A good one, too. He has been buying plants from me for many years.

"He stole the nine plants from the laundry. He robbed Armand," I said, horrified that Exley was her customer.

"*¿Qué?*"

Armand translated for me.

"*Usted le dijo donde estaban las plantas. Usted le llevó a la lavandería,*" the Cashier shot back.

"What is she saying?" I asked Armand. "The Spanish is over my head."

"She says that you told Exley where the plants were. She says you took him to the Laundromat."

I was silent, and so was Armand.

"Is it true?" he asked.

"It was too soon after I met you," I said. "I didn't know how much the plants meant to you."

"I asked you not to tell anyone about them."

"It was a mistake."

"*¿Cómo cuando cerré la puerta del sótano?*" the Cashier said. Like when I closed the door to the basement?

I hated her.

"I still don't understand how Exley got the deadbolt off the door so quickly and easily."

"He's a man who knows about hidden doorways. He knows about openings, and about the spaces in between things. He knows how to slip in and out of these spaces. In and out of places, and situations. Knowing me as you do now, you must realize that it was no easy task robbing my Laundromat and taking the plants. He had to slide between the levels of my consciousness to do that. He had to make himself invisible to my mind. He has a great talent, the gift of invisibility, but it's one that he misuses. You have this gift, too, given to you by the black panther, but you don't know how to use it, either. You and Exley are similar in that way."

"He's missing two of the nine plants that he stole from you, but he wouldn't say which ones they were. He's here to find them."

"We'll have to be extra vigilant about the plants at Casablanca. He lived with the nine plants for a little while until the two died. He had the experience of them in completion, and he *will* want that experience again."

"How did you know the two plants died? I didn't say that."

"I felt it like a breeze. At the time, I wasn't sure what, or who, had died. In fact, for a moment I thought it was Sonali. I rolled over in bed and shook her until she was awake and very annoyed. Now I know I was right—it was the two plants."

"He said the plants wanted to be with him. He said that he couldn't have stolen them unless they wanted to go."

"Plants are immobile. That makes them very dependent creatures."

"They couldn't get away from Exley?"

"Two of them died—committed suicide, probably—so he wouldn't have all nine."

"Which two do you think died?"

"We'll find out soon enough. But right now let's get what we came here for."

Armand and I headed back down the stairs, with the Cashier behind us.

When we reached the bottom, Armand bent down and in one swift move, the kind of graceful move I could never quite get used to in someone so big, he picked something up off the basement floor. He opened his hand, and inside was a tiny lavender-colored flower with a small stem.

"Well, well, well. Look what we have here. Mr. Exley left us a present. *Cichorium intybus.* Chicory. The plant of freedom and one of the nine plants. He used it to get out of the basement, and then he left us a cutting as a courtesy. Your Mr. Exley has a good sense of humor."

"He's not *my Mr. Exley.*"

"Unimportant. This little petal tells us how he got out of here."

"He broke a deadbolt with a flower petal?"

"In a sense, yes. *Cichorium intybus* is a perennial related to the dandelion. It's cultivated in England and Ireland and from Nova Scotia to Florida and west to the plains. It is not cultivated here, in South America. He brought it with him!"

"For what?"

"For its magical properties. The plant has a long, thick taproot filled with a bitter milky-white juice. The ancient Egyptians believed that if the juice is rubbed on the body it promotes invisibility, and removal of obstacles. The Mayans called it the plant of freedom, for the same reason."

"He did not break the deadbolt with milky juice from a chicory plant. I cannot make myself believe that, even if you can."

"I'm not saying that he broke the lock with the chicory plant. I'm saying that this cutting tells us something about Exley, which may come in handy in the future."

"You're right. It tells us he's a con artist *and* a lunatic."

"Listen to me. The cutting tells us that he knows about, and, more important, that he believes in plant magic. It tells us that he's probably practiced quite a bit of it. This chicory cutting makes him a much more formidable foe than I had originally thought."

The Cashier came over, looked into Armand's hand, and slapped her forehead with her palm.

"*¡Ah chicoria! Así es cómo rompió mi cerradura.*" Ah, chicory! That's how he broke my lock.

Armand winked at me.

"Don't listen too closely to the Cashier. She's superstitious."

Mandrake
(Atropa mandragora)

If you're interested in a plant that looks like a person, has visible
sex organs, is an aphrodisiac of the first order, contains mind-
altering alkaloids such as hyoscyamine, has been known to cure
depression and insomnia, then Atropa Mandragora *is the plant*
for you. But be careful. More than one person who has pulled
this plant out of the ground has died in the process.

"Take a look at this," Armand said, bending over a large stalk.
"It's a perfect specimen of *Atropa mandragora.*"

I bent over the plant with Armand, our heads butted up
against each other, touching at the place where our open
fontanels once were.

"You want to know something funny?" his voice boomed.

"Not really," I said, backing away from him.

"They're all mandragora. Every single plant in the basement."

I'm not sure why, but that scared me out of my wits.

"What do you mean?"

"I mean that this room is a like a devotional temple, a
shrine to *Atropa mandragora.* The plant of magic."

"Why would someone do such a thing?" I turned to the
Cashier. "Why are you growing all of these mandrake plants?"

"¿Qué?"

My voice got much louder.

"I said, why are you growing all of these mandrake plants?"

"Calm down," said Armand. "She can't understand you."

"She can when she wants to."

"Some people call this plant the 'devil's candle,' because it glistens at night."

"Is she the devil?"

The Cashier looked angry.

"We grow the mandrake at night because it's safer," said Armand. "It's really for the protection of other people, who don't understand the plant and attempt to pull it out of the ground without taking the proper precautions. As soon as they do, they become ill, and sometimes they die. We grow them like this to protect outsiders from harm."

"You know a lot of things, don't you? A lot of things that you're not telling me."

"You're just figuring that out? Of course I do. And so does the Cashier. We know a few things about plants. It's nothing to be *frightened* of."

That was the first time Armand had told me not to be frightened of him, and it frightened me no end.

"Oh, come now, don't let your imagination run away with you. I'm not evil. I believe the mandragora will help you here on the Yucatán. I think it would be more than wise to befriend one or two while you're down here."

The Cashier nodded her head in agreement.

"Why does she understand your English and not mine?"

"She knows me."

I looked at the Cashier. She nodded in agreement with Armand.

"She doesn't like me," I said. "I can feel it."

"She doesn't trust you. There's a difference. She thinks you led Exley to the Laundromat because your hormones were in overdrive. She thinks you're ruled by your sexuality. In her way of thinking, this makes you a dangerous and unpredictable person."

"Do you trust me?"

"I trust you because I need to."

I looked around at the thousands of plants.

"Okay," I said, relenting. "Tell me about *Atropa mandragora*."

"The mandrake belongs to the potato family. It has large dark leaves, and white or purplish flowers that turn into yellow apple-sized berries with a lovely, fragrant scent. It's an edible plant, which is good to know if you're ever stuck in the jungle without food. While the fruit of the mandrake is attractive and good-tasting, the subterranean part of the plant is where all the action takes place. It's the part that humans have been fascinated with for ages and ages, since biblical times."

"The roots?"

"Yes, Lila, you and I are back to roots once again. Remember when we met and I asked you to try and root my fire-fern cutting?"

"How could I forget?"

"In a way, that was a test—not to see if you could grow the fern, but to see if you had an affinity with roots. Some people have an affinity with flowers, and other people with roots. If you had not been able to grow the fern, we wouldn't be standing here right now. People with an affinity for roots are drawn to the darker side of things, the underground or unseen aspects. And they are, like you, often helped and guided by the black panther, ruler of the night, the moon, and the unseen world."

Here we go again, I thought.

"I'm a root person, too, so you and I are a good match. We

understand each other. I've waited a long time for another root person to come into my life."

"You waited for me? Why?"

"I have my reasons."

I did not like that Armand had waited for me.

"We met by accident," I said.

"Some might call it that."

"If you waited for me for such a long time, then you had to make sure I stayed with you. You had to keep me close to you."

"Your paranoia is showing. All I did was entice your mind with things I thought it might enjoy. That's all. The rest was up to you."

"You have Sonali. Why do you need me?"

"Sonali is a flower person, not a root person. Her thought processes are different from yours or mine. She's generally happier and less suspicious of other people."

"But I love Sonali," I said, surprised at my passion for Armand's wife.

"Join the club. Everyone loves Sonali. That's the point. I need you because you're tougher."

Armand continued: "The mandrake has an extraordinary place in the history of plants. It's medicinal. Herbal. Magical. And folkloric. There are so many uses for this plant, I consider it the most important of the nine plants."

"You always play favorites."

"Mandrake is *medicinal* because the root contains an alkaloid that belongs to the atropine group. It's a powerful narcotic and analgesic, and, in larger doses, a superb anesthetic. It's *magical* because of the bizarre shape of the root, which looks like a human being, sometimes male, sometimes female. This root can and will exercise supernatural power over the human body and mind. It's both an aphrodisiac and a strong hallucinogen. Think about it. Those two things together can create the most mind-bending sex you're ever likely to have. And babies, too. In the book of Genesis, the barren Rachel eats the root and becomes pregnant with Joseph. The plant produces out-of-body experiences in some susceptible people, and a vastly increased sex drive in almost all men."

"Sounds good to me."

"A lot of people think so. Folks love to experiment with the mandrake. The problem is that it's poisonous in the wrong doses, and, too often to mention, people end up sick, or worse. They forget that the mandrake is in the family Solanaceae, similar to deadly nightshade."

"I don't think they forget that. I don't think they ever knew that. Nobody knows that but you, Armand."

"And now you."

"Can the root be used as a voodoo doll? Because it looks like a person?"

"Ha! Excellent question. I don't know, and I have never heard of anyone using it that way, but we must try it someday! Did you hear that?" he asked the Cashier.

The Cashier put her hand over her mouth and looked at me as if I were the devil's child.

"Let's go home now before it gets too late," I said to Armand. "I don't want to drive back in the dark."

Armand giggled. "Don't be silly—nobody's driving back in the dark. The roads are terrible. And those dogs we passed earlier—they're much hungrier and more vicious at night. We're going to stay right here. The Cashier has graciously offered us her home for the night."

I seriously thought Armand had lost his mind.

"Is she going to stay here with us?"

"Of course. It's her home. And you should thank her for inviting us."

"I don't think it's a good idea to stay with her."

"Thank her!" he shouted at me.

"*Gracias*," I said to the Cashier with an unaccustomed hatred in my voice.

"*De nada*," she said neutrally.

Sinsemilla
(Cannabis sativa)

Herb teach you to find yourself. . . . When you find
yourself, you find . . . Majesty.
ROBERT NESTA MARLEY

We left the Cashier's mandrake dungeon through the same back door that Exley had used to escape. The deadbolt was lying on the floor—split in half, like it had been struck by lightning. The Cashier looked at me like it was my fault.

"You're the one selling him plants," I said to her. "So don't look at me that way."

"She can't understand you," said Armand.

"I hate that woman."

"*¡Cómo se atreve!*" said the Cashier. How dare you!

"Oh. Now she understands?"

We headed to her house, which was across the road from the market.

"That's it right there," said Armand.

"I see sunflowers. No house, just sunflowers. What am I missing?"

"*Los girasoles mantienen el sol fuera y dejan la casa fresca.*"

"She says that the sunflowers shield the house from the sun and it stays cool."

"Yes, of course they do. But where *is* her house?"

"It's right there," Armand said, pointing at a thick, impenetrable wall of stalky yellow sunflowers with huge black velvet center pads.

I walked across the road and stuck my hand out to part the plants but Armand jumped in front of me. He spread the plants and then stood back, holding them open like a door.

"Allow me to introduce you," he said, "to the Cashier's very special garden. The garden of tortured sinsemilla."

I peered in between the sunflowers, tall as small trees.

"Don't look! Close your eyes and take a deep breath."

I inhaled.

"It's marijuana!" I said excitedly.

"It's more than marijuana. It's sinsemilla. The plant of female sexuality. The result of a special cultivation of the female *Cannabis sativa* plant."

I stepped through the sunflower stalks and into the garden. The Cashier's house was on the far side. She walked ahead of me, stroking her plants as she went, with a love and reverence she clearly did not have for the mandrakes in the basement.

"Female marijuana plants love to be petted and teased," said Armand. "They're the horniest plants on earth."

"Horny?"

"Yes, horny. You remember being horny, don't you? It's the way you get whenever you're around Diego, or Exley. Probably even me, for all I know."

"How can you tell if a *plant* is *horny*?"

"I make it horny myself, that's how I can tell."

"How exactly do you do that?"

"The same way I make a woman horny. I tease her. Unfortunately, to create sinsemilla, the teasing has to cross a line into pain. But the plant likes it that way. Female cannabis plants respond extraordinarily well to pain."

He got me with that sentence. I was definitely curious.

"To create sinsemilla, you have to treat her badly. You have to be withholding. No water. No food. No sweet talk. Nothing that feels good. And you can't feel bad about it, either; she *wants* to be hurt. When she's really dried out and about to die, deprived of everything that brings life, that's when the fun begins. That's when it's time for the torture to start. That's when it's time to take her body and bend it in half. Don't break her, but bend her to the breaking point. It's exactly like choking. It takes practice, and you might lose a few along the way. But if you do it enough times, you'll start to find that breaking point with ease."

"Why on earth would you do this?"

"To make her feel like she's going to die, without giving her the pleasure of death. To torture her."

"That's sick."

"It's beautiful. Just when she thinks she's about to die, flowers burst out of her. Big, juicy flowers just waiting to get pollinated. It's kind of a last gasp at procreation. A final attempt at passing on her genes."

Armand rolled a resin bud between his fingers and passed it to me.

"Feel how sticky it is? The flowers of the dying female get bigger and bigger, trying to attract a pollinator. They get stickier and stickier, hoping to hold on to any tiny drop of pollen that might come her way. Sound familiar?"

"No."

"She's desperate. Just like you. She'll do anything to get laid."

"I won't do anything to get laid."

"You let Exley inside of your body."

I squinted at him.

"When the flower is at its hugest and stickiest, that's when the most powerful sinsemilla is created. It's made from a female plant, reaching out to any male at all, *even as it's dying*. Sinsemilla is created from pure sexual desire. That's why it's the plant of female sexuality. Personally, I just love to watch it wait. It waits and waits for a male. It hopes and hopes. It spreads its leaves wider and wider apart, the resin bud getting bigger and riper by the day. It's quite a thing. And that's when it's ready to be smoked."

Armand spread the leaves of a plant nearby and stroked the resin bud lightly between his fingers. I sat down on a rock that looked like it had been placed there for that purpose and pressed my thighs together.

"Will you ever let her have sex?"

"Never. I will never let her have sex." Armand laughed. "Sexual satisfaction would ruin her potency."

I felt like spreading pollen on the resin buds of all of those poor plants. I would run around the garden naked and ruin the crop. I would personally satisfy each and every plant. I would make the whole damn place rock with orgasms.

"Sinsemilla means 'without seeds.' It's so potent because the plant's energy goes toward making resin, rather than babies. A seedless female is far more potent than a seeded one. Remember that next time you want to accomplish something. Do it before you have sex. Before some male comes along and shoots his seed in you, satisfying you, and making you energetically useless."

"I'm not a marijuana plant."

"Take your teachers where you can."

I could feel heat all around me in the garden. Those giant, lazy, swaying, sexed-up pot plants were completely overpowering.

"All of these poor aching females, waiting to get screwed," said Armand. "Just think of all that energy. All that unfulfilled sexual energy."

"What do they do with it?"

"They make sinsemilla! A wonderful resin that brings pleasure and creative vision to millions of people. And also reduces pain in quite a few as well. You haven't gotten laid in a while—what are you going to do with your unfulfilled sexual desire, Lila? Maybe you can create something beautiful someday. Something that will bring pleasure to many people, just like the sinsemilla plant. Maybe you'll find out that you're a tenth as talented as this horny little weed all around you."

I turned to the Cashier, in both awe and hatred of her garden.

"How do you stop the female from being pollinated?"

This time she understood my English, perfectly.

"*Matar los machos*," she said matter-of-factly. Kill the males.

"Or castrate them," said Armand. "But you have to be very careful. If you ruin a male a mile from here, a smidge of pollen could float back on a breeze and destroy the entire crop."

"How can you tell which plants are male and which are female?"

"The male plant has two balls, pardon my expression, growing on its stalk. They open up to pollinate the pistils on the female. The only way to avoid this is to cut off the balls of the male plants."

Armand began absentmindedly stroking one of the resin buds nearest to him.

"What happens if the female does produce seeds? Can she still be smoked?"

"She can, but she'll die soon after. Her life's work having been completed, genetically speaking. Unpollinated, she remains in a strong, sexual flowering state for a long, long time, capable of making much sinsemilla. In a sense, an unpollinated plant is more *female*."

"*¿Quería probar un poco?*" asked the Cashier.

"She wants to know if you would like to try some of her sinsemilla."

I was a little hesitant to have a tortured female inside of me, even if it was a plant, but too curious to refuse.

We went into the Cashier's house, which was really just a shack painted a beautiful midnight blue. On the inside, everything was bright green and woven together from plant leaves. The tabletop was thatched bamboo, and the floor and floor mats, which also doubled as beds, were all made from what looked like palm fronds sewn together with a needle and thread. There was a beautiful black Lab snoozing on a green frond mat.

"Most of her furniture is woven brand-new every day," said Armand.

I went over to pet the Lab.

"Her name is Mallorey," said the Cashier in disturbingly perfect English.

"She named her dog after Mallorey in Oliver Stone's film *Natural Born Killers*," said Armand. "It's her favorite film."

It agitated me no end that the Cashier knew the movies of Oliver Stone. I sat down and watched as she deftly plucked a resin gland from a marijuana plant and rolled it into some Mexican money.

"For good luck," said Armand. "She combines the spirit of money with the spirit of the plant to bring in a nice large cash crop."

"So she's a drug dealer?"

"She sells sinsemilla. She also owns the market, the mandrake plants, and many others, too. She deals in medicinal plants, and only with people who know how to use them."

I leaned back. The hemp mat and the wall behind me were surprisingly comfortable.

"Every inch of the Cashier's home is designed for comfort. Its walls and floors are ergonomically correct, perfectly suited for the human body. Believe me, when it's time to go you won't want to leave. No one ever does."

We smoked the Cashier's wonderful, sweet, female sinsemilla, and I fell into a dreamy, happy haze against the anatomically perfect wall.

"Get up," said Armand. "It's time to dig us up some mandrake root."

"But I feel so comfortable here," I said, not wanting to say that what I really felt was horny as hell.

"It's the longing of the sinsemilla. It's inside of you now, and we can't let it go to waste. Let's go! Now!"

The Cashier tied a rope around Mallorey's neck, and the four of us went across the street to the market and down into the basement. I was used to the steep stairs by this time, but I was not used to what I saw when we got down there. All of the mandrake plants were glowing.

"Worms," said Armand. "They rest on the leaves of the plant, and they glow at night. There's nothing magical there."

"Why is she doing that?" I asked, looking at the Cashier, who was stuffing pieces of white cloth into her ears.

"She doesn't want to hear the scream of the mandrake when we pull it out of the ground."

"But they're not in the ground, they're on the tables."

"Not the ones under the tables. They are planted directly in the ground, and they are the only ones old enough to uproot."

I looked under the tables to see hundreds more plants. It was the first time I noticed that the basement had no floor, only hard-packed dirt. The mandrake plants grew directly out of the ground, as if the market had been built right on top of them without disturbing or inconveniencing them in the least.

"Hold her for a minute," Armand, said handing me Mallorey's leash.

I bent down to look at the dog and scratch her behind her ears. She licked my face, and I put my arms around her. She seemed so human compared with Armand and the Cashier.

"Hold her tight," said Armand as he and the Cashier tied a thick rope around a mandrake plant underneath one of the wooden tables.

"Okay, give me the dog."

Armand tied the other end of the rope to Mallorey's collar.

"*Quédate atrás y cúbrete los oídos,*" the Cashier hissed at me. Stand back and cover your ears.

I looked at Armand. "Superstitious," we said at the same time.

The Cashier took a large slab of meat out of a plastic bag and held it up in front of the dog. Mallorey sniffed at it. She started to lick the raw meat, excited by the taste of blood. Just as she was about to sink her teeth into the bloody slab, the Cashier stepped back and placed the meat on the floor just out of reach. Mallorey barked and pawed at the dirt ground. Her collar, attached by a rope to the mandrake plant, strained and pulled at her neck. When she couldn't take the temptation any longer, she lunged toward the meat, growling and pulling on the rope until the mandrake looked like it was going to snap in half. In a strange game of tug-of-war, the plant seemed to pull the dog back toward it. Mallorey kept going for the meat, and finally the mandrake began to give way, sliding out of the earth like childbirth.

High from the sinsemilla, I was riveted by the sight of the plant's root coming out of the dirt. When the strange head and arms emerged from the ground, the Cashier let out a howling scream. The sound pierced through my body and made me scream at the top of my lungs at the same time.

"What the hell is she doing?" I asked, terrified by both her scream and my own.

"She believes the mandrake emits a shriek when it's pulled out of the ground that can bring death to those that hear it."

"Well, she almost brought death to me with her freakin' shriek."

"She was only trying to protect you. She was covering the plant's sound with her own. She knows these plants better than anyone, and she has seen people die, one way or another, by coming into contact with them."

I'm too high for this, I thought. I am too damn high to be in a basement in Mexico with these two witches.

"Come, and take a look at the root."

"No lo toques."

"She says not to touch it."

The mandrake root was an evil-looking thing that I had no intention of touching, ever. It was much more lifelike than I had imagined. It had two arms sticking straight up, a torso, and two legs pointing outward. There was a round, bulbous tip where the head should be, and shoots of what looked like grass on top of the head, giving it the appearance of having hair. I could see how this root had engendered so much fear and obsession. It really did look like a horrible little person, and I didn't even have to look at it sideways, squint, or use my imagination.

"Let's get out of here," I said.

"We'll let Mallorey eat first," said Armand. "After all, she did all the work."

When Armand let go of the rope, Mallorey lunged at the bloody meat and ripped it to shreds. When she finished gorging, we trudged slowly up the stairs, Armand carrying the root in the bag where the meat used to be.

"*Un momento*," said the Cashier as she took a handgun out of a wooden box near the cash register.

"What's that for?" I asked on the way out the door.

"Protection," said Armand.

The road outside of the market was covered with gray dust. It was empty and silent, with an eerie soullessness that made me think we were the only people who had ever walked on it. We walked a little way down the road, the dog in front of us, wagging her tail.

"Mallorey," the Cashier called. "Mallorey, come here."

The happy Lab jumped up in the air and turned around to look at its owner.

The Cashier unlocked the clip, aimed the gun, pulled the trigger, and shot the dog right between the eyes. Mallorey slumped to the ground with a whimper. Blood poured out of the hole in her head, turning the dusty road underneath her black and wet.

I stood there, stoned and shaking. I bent down next to the dog and held her head in my hands. I pressed my face onto her blood-soaked face and started to cry.

"Get up!" Armand yelled, grabbing my arm and physically jerking me to my feet.

"What the fuck?" I said, over and over. "What the fuck did she do?"

"It had to die," said Armand.

"Her name was Mallorey."

"Yes. And there is a new Mallorey every week. The Cashier gets the dogs from the garbage dump we passed on the way to her house. She has no ties to this dog."

"Why did that bitch kill Mallorey? I knew she was an evil bitch."

"Pull yourself together. That dog gave its life for the nine plants. The depraved, destructive parts of the mandrake spirit went into the dog when she pulled the plant out of the ground. Mallorey was great enough to sacrifice herself in order to leave us with only the good aspects of the plant. The Cashier considers the dog a savior who gave her life for the congregation of the nine plants, and you should, too. That dog did a great thing in her short life. Greater than most people will ever do."

The last I saw of the Cashier, she was marching down the road, dragging the bloodied, dead Mallorey behind her, the dog's front paws tied together with the cord that had been tied to the mandrake plant.

"She'll spend the night reciting incantations for the dead," said Armand. "And then, come dawn, she'll bury the dog. She's done it many times."

Armand held the hideous-looking root in his hands, and I walked behind him and wept for Mallorey. At the Cashier's house, I waited outside of the wall of sunflowers while Armand went inside to get our things.

"Come on, let's go home."

We got on the bike, and I did not look back at the Cashier's house.

"The closer you get to the nine plants," he said, "unfortunately, or fortunately, the more challenging things tend to become."

I was so happy to see Diego when we got back to Casablanca that I went straight over to him and put my arms around him.

"You smell like weed," he said. "Did you bring any back for me?"

"No."

"I did," said Armand, holding up a big bag of sinsemilla. "Lila was so traumatized by the Cashier, I figured it would be a good idea to have some of this stuff on hand in case we need to calm her down."

"What did the Cashier do?" asked Diego.

"The usual. She killed Mallorey after she pulled out the mandrake," said Armand.

"Mallorey *veinte*? Or Mallorey *veintidós*?"

"Mallorey *cien*."

Armand and Diego laughed. I looked at them, disgusted.

"How many Malloreys have there been?"

Diego stood behind me and put his arms around me. His soft coconut-scented hair was out of its usual ponytail. It hung free and brushed against my neck.

"It's hard to say," he said. "The Cashier has been growing those mandrake plants for years. For every plant taken out of the ground, there is a Mallorey that dies along with it."

"Why does she give them all the same name? It's creepy."

"She doesn't want to get attached to them."

"I don't think that woman could get attached to anything."

"You have three more of the nine plants," Diego whispered with his arms still around me.

"We got the mandrake and the chicory," I said, resting against him and wishing he would keep his arms like that forever.

"You got the sinsemilla, too," he said. "It's made from the female *Cannabis sativa* plant. One of the nine plants."

"Why didn't you tell me?" I asked Armand.

"I thought it would be more fun if Diego told you. Go ahead, Diego, tell her."

"Sin-se-milla," he whispered, spreading out the word, focusing on the sound of the soft "s," and pronouncing the double "l" like a "y."

Diego's body was so close to mine, it took a big effort not to turn around and kiss him like we did in the jungle.

"Armand considers the mandrake the most magical of the nine plants," he said, "but I think that honor belongs to sinsemilla. Would you like to smoke some? With me?"

Just when I was getting used to being in Diego's arms, he let go of me. I felt a cold, northerly wind blow through my body.

"Come sit," he said.

I felt as if I was being blown back and forth between two extremes—closeness and then distance—and I jumped at the chance to be close again. His caramel skin was like a kind of drug to me. I thought of Exley, with his pale skin and hair. He was no match for the deeper tones of Diego, which were a draw beyond description. Diego looked like part of the earth. As if he had grown right up out of it and was not separate from it like the rest of us.

"Come, come, sit down."

I realized I had been standing in the living room staring at him. I looked around for Armand, but he was gone.

"Armand will be back later. He doesn't smoke."

I tried to remember if he smoked at the Cashier's house, but I couldn't recall.

"Why doesn't he smoke?"

"The smoke is already inside of him. He has the spirit of the sinsemilla in his body. He doesn't need to smoke to feel it."

"You mean he's always high?"

"Whenever he wants to be. Armand is a part of everything. He feels what he wants, when he wants. Emotions go through him. Good, bad, indifferent—it's all the same to him."

Diego was sitting on the cement couch built right into the wall. He sat on top of a blue-and-white Mexican blanket with his hands over his head and his feet planted on the floor. He wore white drawstring pants, with no shoes and no shirt. I couldn't imagine being in New York City at that moment. Or anywhere else but right there, next to him.

"I see you're not afraid of the scorpions anymore," he said, looking at my bare feet. "They've let you go."

He pulled a resin bud from between the leaves of the female cannabis plant and rolled it around between his thumb and index finger.

"Smell this."

I took his hand in mine and put it up to my face.

Diego laughed.

"Not my hand, the resin bud."

I took it from him and pressed it between my fingers. It felt as sticky as warm tar. It smelled deliciously sweet and spicy, like the soil near certain plants.

"Are you going to roll it in money?"

"Only the Cashier does that, when she wants to sell the plants. Smoking that way brings her luck. Unless we smoked out of *her* money, it would make us sick."

Diego leaned down and opened a drawer built into the couch. He took out a pipe with a very long stem and a small bowl. It looked like an American Indian peace pipe.

"We'll smoke out of this."

He passed the pipe to me. It was a beautiful copper-colored wood with intricate carvings in a language I didn't recognize.

"It's Huichol. This pipe belonged to my mother's father. She passed it down to me for my birthday last year. It's a family heirloom."

"What day is your birthday?"

"My birthday is on March 17, 1979. But I was born on January 12, 1999. I was born in the winter of my twentieth year."

"What do you mean?"

"That's the year I became myself."

"Who were you before?"

"I was lots of people, but none of them were me."

"How do you know?"

"It's a feeling. Kind of like being open, but very protected and safe. Like being calm and excited at the same time. Once

I felt that way, I never wanted to go back to the way I was before; that's why I consider January 12 my new birthday. Now I stay away from anyone or anything that tries to force me back into my old ways. Believe me, when you know yourself, you never want to pretend to be anything else ever again, because it is better than anything you have ever pretended, or dreamed up or imagined, or became."

"If it's so great, why aren't people like that all the time?"

"They think they are, but the person they were born to be was covered up by years of living with parents and going to school and fitting in. Every year that passes, a person gets covered up a little bit more, like a sleeping bag slowly zipping up around a body. It's a subtle process until the day a person is totally gone. The sleeping bag is closed, and they never see the sun again."

"But they can feel it sometimes?"

"Yes. A little warmth sneaks in from time to time."

Diego dropped the resin bud into the pipe bowl and lit it. The sinsemilla sizzled. It tasted even sweeter than it had at the Cashier's.

"I hope I feel that way one day. Excited and calm."

"Oh, you will. Being around Armand will make you that way. He'll speak to all of your selves, but sometimes he'll slip in between them and speak to your real self, too."

"He's sneaky."

"Nah. He's just letting you know that you're still in there! You should probably know, if you ever unzip the sleeping bag you won't relate to very many people anymore."

"I'll have you."

"That you will."

"Is Armand real?"

"For almost forty years."

We smoked for a while in silence, and then Diego leaned back against the wall behind the couch. His legs were stretched out in front of him, his ankles crossed, and his hands were behind his head.

I felt very close to him, but I could tell from the position of his hands, wrapped as they were around the back of his head, that he was not going to touch me anytime soon. I had an incredible urge to feel his skin. The desire was so great that I actually sat on my hands to stop myself.

Diego smiled.

"Your hands are going to get numb like that. Go ahead and touch me if that's what you want."

I reached out and placed my hand over his belly button. I let it rest there for a moment, and then I stroked his stomach. He had a line of dark hair growing straight up the middle, soft as the hair of a baby. I was mesmerized by it and spent a few moments feeling its texture. I moved my hand up to his chest. The V of hair there had the same black, shiny softness. I didn't care if I ever did anything else; I already knew I would never want to take my hands off this man.

"Do you like the feel of my skin?"

I knew my answer would ruin everything, but I couldn't help myself.

"I like the feel of your skin more than anything else in the world."

Diego smiled, a lazy grin.

"What else do you like?"

"I want to put my face on your chest."

"Go ahead."

I didn't want to seem too hungry—I was afraid of scaring him with exactly how much I wanted to feel his chest with my face—so I went slowly.

"Move your face along my body if you like."

I slid my cheek across his chest. His body smelled like spice and vanilla. I could see that he liked my touch, but he kept his hands behind his head and didn't make a move.

"I like this feeling," he said. "I don't want to get rid of it too quickly."

I took my face off his chest to kiss his mouth.

"Do you want to try something new with me?" he asked before I could kiss him.

I looked up.

"Isn't this enough?"

"No. Come on, it's wonderful. I just want to try something different with you, that's all. But you'll have to take your clothes off first. I'll help you."

"Are you going to get undressed, too?"

"Not yet."

I lay down naked on the couch. It was just a thin piece of cotton lying on top of a slab of cement, but it was incredibly comfortable.

"Don't fall asleep on me, now."

I was further away from that than I would ever let him know.

Diego knelt on the floor next to me. He ran his face over my body, never once touching it, keeping his mouth just an inch above my skin. He looked at me everywhere, under my arms, behind my ears, he opened my legs and looked in between them, bringing his face so close I could feel his breath rushing in and out of me.

He came up to my face.

"Open your mouth and breathe with me," he said. And then he put his mouth over mine—again, without touching. He inhaled my breath and breathed his own back into me. We breathed together until we were perfectly in sync, our lungs and hearts and blood moving together in perfect time, like a metronome.

He placed his palm over my stomach, keeping it just above the surface. I could feel the heat coming off his hand. He was actually touching me with heat. His closeness was hard to take, his restraint unnerving. When I couldn't stand it any-more, I lifted my body and pressed it against his hand.

"It's the sinsemilla, you know, that's making you feel this way."

"It's you."

"It's the plant. All of her sexuality is inside of you. I'm just the lucky man who's here with you right now."

"Are you going to touch me?"

"Believe me, Lila, I'm touching you very deeply. Here, smoke some more of this."

I inhaled deeply from the pipe, and Diego put his hand over my mouth.

"We don't want to waste any," he said, putting his mouth over mine and inhaling the smoke from my lungs. His lips touched me for the first time that night, and something inside of me broke. I couldn't let go of his mouth. My desire for it was crazy. I refused to stop kissing him, and he pulled away somewhat violently.

"I want to show you something."

"Yes."

"I want you to breathe deeply and try to pull your breath up the center of your body. Squeeze and pull on the muscles of your inner thighs and between your legs. Then exhale deeply through your nose."

His instructions felt dumb, but I was horny, so I did what he wanted, hoping he would soon be doing what I wanted.

Diego placed his hand below my belly button. "Go deeper. Lift the energy up into your heart. That's it. Do you feel the rhythm?"

With each inhale, my body began to vibrate. The pleasure was intense, and I reached for him.

"Don't. The arousal is inside of you. It's all yours. You are so adept at pleasure, you can have sex with fire, or wind, or water. All you need to do is stand near one of those elements and inhale its energy into your body. Bring it inside of you until you feel like you do now, and then let go. You will be having sex with fire or water."

I was on an edge of a sexual arousal that I didn't find tolerable, and I knew Diego was not going to touch me. All of a sudden I knew exactly how the female cannabis plant felt as it was being turned into sinsemilla. I felt terrible for its endless arousal. I felt for the entire spread-open, tortured garden at the Cashier's house. At that moment, the creation of sinsemilla was the cruelest invention I'd ever heard of.

"You can use that energy in any way you want. Have sex, paint a painting, cook a beautiful meal. Its just energy. It's there to be used."

"I need a break from this," I said, hardly able to look at him. I was out of my mind with desire, and the thought occurred to me that Diego was mean and harmful.

I was suddenly very angry. I looked at him cross-legged on the couch, comfortable as he could be, and I knew that he had brought me to this point with no intention of releasing me. I made up my mind that even if it took all night we were going to have sex, the regular way, with him on top, pleasing me endlessly, and none of this breathing-with-my-womb crap. He owed it to me.

"I'm starving," he said. "Do you want something to eat?"

"I'll make something," I said, glad for the chance to walk away. "I wouldn't want you to get up, Your Highness," I whispered to myself.

I went into the kitchen, opened the refrigerator, and pulled out plates of leftover chicken with *mole* sauce Armand had made with the cacao beans. I slammed them down on the counter a little too hard and went back in for the bowls of yellow custard called flan. Right there behind the bowls, on the middle shelf, lay the hideous-looking mandrake root, as creepy and human-looking as when I first saw it.

It was positioned headfirst, and I pulled it out—pincerlike, with my nails—by its grassy hair. I felt the energy coursing through my body from the aborted sexual attempt with Diego. I could actually feel it vibrating out of my fingertips and into the root itself. I had a brief fear that I might animate the damn thing and bring it to life right there on the kitchen countertop.

I stared at it, remembering what Armand had told me. Remembering that it was an aphrodisiac that would produce a *vastly increased sex drive in almost all men.* I studied it for a moment and quickly made up my mind.

I took a small, sharp knife from a kitchen drawer and stabbed the root between its legs, taking a large slice of what would be its genitals if it were really human. I waited, almost expecting it to bleed.

I found a mortar and pestle hanging on a nail on the wall. I put the mandrake slice into the bowl and ground up the piece of root until it was nothing but fine brown dust. I sprinkled this into the flan, and stirred. Two could play at this game. If the mandrake root worked as Armand claimed, I would make Diego as horny as he had made me.

"The chicken is really good," Diego said. "Armand is a great cook when he wants to be."

I had to admit the chicken was superb. It was moist and tender, and it no longer bothered me that I had seen a woman in the market break its neck.

"I think Armand could have a second career if he wanted."

"I wish you could've seen his first career. The Laundromat in New York was so beautiful."

"Maybe one day," he said, smiling, "I will come to visit you and Armand and Sonali in New York."

Diego put the chicken down and dug right into the bowl of flan. Without any prompting from me, he put a big spoonful into his mouth.

I kept eating, one eye on my chicken and the other on Diego. I was enjoying myself immensely watching him eat the spiked custard.

"Do you want me to save some for you? It's really good. It's Armand's specialty."

"No, you keep eating. There's more in the fridge."

I watched Diego for signs of change, even though I had no idea how long the mandrake root would take to work. I leaned back on the couch and played Armand's words over in my mind. *This root can and will exercise supernatural power over the human body and mind. It's both an aphrodisiac and a strong hallucinogen. . . . Those two things together can create the most mind-bending sex you're ever likely to have.*

I snuggled against Diego, but when I leaned my head on his chest, his body fell over and I fell on top of him. He collapsed onto his side.

Digoxin

(sometimes referred to as digitoxin or digitalis)

*This widely used heart medication is a cardiac glycoside used
in the treatment of atrial fibrillation, atrial flutter, and
congestive heart failure. Found in the lovely purple bells
of the foxglove plant and the gorgeous, velvety black wings
of the monarch butterfly, digoxin is probably
the most beautiful medication there ever was.*

"Diego!" I yelled, shaking him.

He opened his eyes. They looked cloudy and unfocused.

"I can't breathe," he said slowly, in a low, raspy voice. "Find Armand."

Suddenly, as I sat there with my arms around Diego, the rest of Armand's sentence echoed in my head: *It's poisonous in the wrong doses. . . . They forget that the mandrake is in the family Solanaceae, similar to deadly nightshade.*

It was the second part of the teachings for the mandrake plant—the part I had chosen to ignore because of the glamour and magic of the information that came before it.

Diego's eyes were closed, and I shook him hard. "Wake up!" I screamed. "Get up!"

He didn't move. He opened his eyes, and they rolled toward the back of his head until the iris was barely visible.

I ran around the house screaming for Armand like a madwoman. I got no response. I went outside and stood on the porch. The roar of the wind off the ocean was so loud that I had to shout at the top of my lungs. I could see Armand lean over the railing of the upstairs balcony, his head surrounded by the constellation of Pisces, Diego's birth sign.

"Diego is sick," I screamed. "He won't wake up."

"What?"

"I can't get Diego to wake up," I yelled over the sound of the ocean.

"You must be very good in bed," he yelled down to me as he ran down the tiled staircase.

Armand held the lids of Diego's eyes open and peered inside. He looked all around the room, his eyes covering every detail. He searched for the cause of Diego's illness and missed it completely. I watched him assume that I knew nothing. He trusted me at all the wrong times.

I grabbed the mandrake root off the kitchen counter and held its cut-up genitals in front of Armand's face.

"You didn't."

"I ground it into his food to make him have sex with me. I must have used too much. It was too much for his system to handle."

As soon as the words were out of my mouth, I realized how obsessed I had been, mixing potions like an old crone.

Armand grabbed the mandrake root and ran toward the door.

"Are you going to take him to a hospital?"

"Sure, I'll just medevac him in. We're in the jungle, Lila. Stay with him and make sure he's breathing. If he stops, breathe into his mouth. You'll figure it out."

While Armand was gone, I watched Diego closely, never once taking my eyes off his face. I washed his body with a cool cloth when his temperature seemed to be going up. He was sweating and mumbling, but I couldn't hear a word of it. The roar of the wind from the ocean was loud, and the bugs were making terrible buzzing and raging sounds.

Armand returned with a woman I had never seen before. She looked like the Mayan woman who killed the chickens at the market. She had long black braids wound around her head like a beehive, a bright-blue dress, and flat leather sandals that crisscrossed all the way up her calves to her knees.

She was carrying some sort of a cage, like a birdcage, with a red, white, and green striped Mexican blanket thrown over it.

"Lila, this is Lourdes Pinto, Diego's mother. She is a *curandera,* a healer, as I told you before. She is here to heal her son."

I went to shake her hand but she ignored me.

"Lourdes," said Armand, "this is Lila, the woman who may have irreparably damaged your only son."

I stared at Armand in disbelief.

"I'm just getting everything out into the open, so everyone knows where they stand. It's much better for the process."

"Tell me everything that happened between you and my son, and don't leave out any details because I am his mother," Lourdes Pinto said to me. "I'll know if you do."

Telling her how much her son had turned me on was mortifying. Even worse was knowing that we had smoked the sinsemilla out of the pipe she had given him for his birthday, the pipe that once belonged to her father.

When I was done, she stood up without saying a word. She went over to Diego and laid her palms just inches over his skin, in exactly the same way he had done with me. She went over every single millimeter of his body with her palms. She was detached and emotionless.

"She doesn't seem upset," I whispered to Armand.

"Oh, she's plenty upset. But she knows that she's no use to him that way. She can't help him if she gets lost in her emotions."

Lourdes stepped away from Diego, walking backward so she could keep her eyes on him every second. She went over to the covered cage she'd brought with her and lifted the Mexican blanket. Behind the bars of the cage were hundreds of monarch butterflies.

"Close the windows and doors," she barked at me.

When I was done, she opened the cage and the monarchs flew out. They covered the room, alighting everywhere. There were so many of them, wingtip to wingtip, that the walls of Armand's living room looked like an orange-and-black mural.

Lourdes collected the butterflies that landed on Diego's body. Using her fingers like a pair of tweezers, she pinched their wings closed between her thumb and index fingers. So many monarchs landed on Diego, he looked like he was wearing a velvet suit.

When Lourdes had at least fifty butterflies, she brought them over to the kitchen and, still holding their wings together, ground up their black, inch-long bodies with the mortar and pestle I'd used on the mandrake. I cringed. The crunching of the butterflies as their bodies were crushed was nauseating. When they were thoroughly mashed, she dropped in the wings and ground them up in the exact same way.

"Is she a doctor? Diego is dying, and I don't think this is going to help him."

I was getting frantic. Diego's life was in the hands of this woman who was clearly insane, even if she was his mother. I knew that crushed butterflies were not going to save Diego. I went over to him on the couch and held his hands. Once again, just like at the Laundromat, I had done enormous damage because I liked a man too much.

Lourdes Pinto came over to her only son with the ground-up butterflies. She spooned the bloody mixture into his mouth. I gagged watching her, and covered my own mouth with a towel.

She spoke to me in a low, flat, emotionless tone.

"The monarch butterfly contains a cardioglycoside, also known as digitalis, used in your country to treat congestive heart failure, atrial fibrillation, tachycardia, bradycardia, and other conditions of the heart. I am not crazy. I am here to heal my son."

I took the towel away from my mouth.

"Diego is in heart failure?" I could barely get the words out.

"He is."

"Oh my God."

"Listen to me carefully. The monarch butterfly is a cardiotonic. It increases the tone of the heart muscle, causing more effective emptying of the chambers. The butterfly will help Diego. It will be good for him."

"Do we use monarchs, too—in the United States, I mean?" I asked desperately.

"You take digitalis from the digitoxin found in plants. Mostly foxglove. I use a digitalis-like toxin found in the monarch butterflies. Both have the same properties. The monarch lays its eggs on the milkweed plant, which also produces cardioglycosides. As the insects hatch and grow, they feed on the milkweed and ingest the heart medicine from the plant. They sequester it in their bodies, never using it and never excreting it."

"Why do they do that?"

"To keep predators away. Digitalis has a bitter taste that keeps the birds away. If you ever come across a shaman out there in that rain forest who claims to cure heart disease, he's a charlatan. He is simply using the same drug your doctors in New York are using. Digitalis. There's no magic to it at all."

"Is it working?"

"Give it some time. We'll see."

"If you don't mind my saying . . ."

"I'm sure I will, but go ahead."

"You don't seem that upset."

"I am a practical woman, and my practicality is part of my healing. Because of it, I will save my son."

I looked at Diego, who did seem to look a little bit less pale. His beautiful black hair was soaking wet and matted to his shoulders, but he appeared to be sleeping and looked more comfortable than he had in a while.

Lourdes Pinto ground up more butterflies on the kitchen countertop while I kept cool compresses on Diego's forehead. I was beginning to feel relieved when Diego's body seized.

"Lourdes!" I screamed.

Armand ran over and held him down by the shoulders. Diego was not biting his tongue, but Armand opened his mouth and held it anyway.

"The digitalis is not strong enough," said Lourdes, her voice breaking ever so slightly, which terrified me.

Armand whispered in my ear, "Get your shoes on. We're going to the Cashier's house. She never grows poisonous plants without an antidote."

"She's twenty miles away. Why doesn't anyone have a phone in this place?"

"If you're done ranting, get your shoes and let's go. Diego still has a few hours."

"A few hours? A few hours! Oh my God."

The first thing I saw when we reached the Cashier's house was a black Lab sitting in front of the thick wall of stalky sunflowers.

"Hello, Mallorey," said Armand as he got off the motorcycle.

I avoided looking at the dog at all costs. I couldn't stand knowing its fate.

"Lila, you're going to have to get a lot tougher than this. You can't let every little thing that happens rattle you to such a degree."

Every little thing? Watching a crazy woman murder an innocent dog, and another crazy woman crush butterflies to save her son? These were definitely not *little things* in my world.

Armand parted the sunflowers, and we walked through the tortured garden of sinsemilla, straight into the house, without knocking.

"No time for formalities," said Armand. "Every second counts now. Even the seconds it takes to knock on the door."

The Cashier was lying on her side on a hemp mat on the floor. She was in a perfect position for smoking opium, but she was sleeping.

"*Hola,* Armand," she said with her eyes closed, as if she could see through the lids. "*Hola,* Lila."

The Cashier rose straight up from her lying-down position, as if her body were on strings. She didn't sit up first or even bend her knees, as far as I could tell.

"See," said Armand, "did you see that? That's why we're here. That woman is capable of just about anything."

"We came here because she has the antidote," I said.

"Of course. That, too."

"*¿Qué puedo hacer por usted?*" What can I do for you? asked the Cashier.

"Diego is very ill," said Armand. "He ingested a piece of the mandrake we pulled from your basement."

"*¿Qué pasó?*" How did that happen?

"Lila fed it to him to get him to make love to her."

The Cashier looked horrified.

"Lourdes has not been able to help him."

"*¿Ella probó con las monarcas?*"

"Yes, she tried the monarch butterflies."

"*Entiendo,*" she said. I understand.

"We need the antidote," I said as calmly as possible, even though the last thing I wanted to do was to traverse those steps back down into that poison-filled dungeon of hers.

The Cashier sat back down on the hemp mat.

"What are you doing? Get up! Spring up like you did before! Make her get up," I said to Armand.

"I can't make her do anything!"

"*Siéntese, siéntese.*" Sit, sit, said the Cashier.

"I don't want to sit. We have no time. Tell her we have no time."

"If she wants you to sit, it's for a reason. She's the Cashier. She wastes nothing, especially when it comes to time."

We sat down on the hemp mats.

"*El hombre que estaba aquí, el del pelo blanco. Él llero el lirio del valle.*"

"What is she saying?"

"She says that the man who was here the other day, the man with the white hair, he took the lily of the valley."

"So what?" I yelled. "We need the antidote."

"That is the antidote," said Armand. "Lily of the valley is one of the nine plants. It's the plant of power, and the antidote to mandrake poisoning."

I stood up.

"Aren't there more?"

"*El lirio del valle es una planta común. Hay muchas, pero no aquí, en México. Ella la trajo, y la crió. Era su creación. Su bebé.*"

"What?"

"She says lily of the valley is a common plant. There are many, but they do not grow here in Mexico. She brought that one here and raised it herself. It was her creation. Her baby."

"Where are they?"

"*En los bosques secos de Inglaterra y en partes del norte de Asia.*"

They are in the dry woods of England and parts of Northern Asia.

"Ask her how many she has."

"*¿Cuántas tiene?*" asked Armand.

"*Solamente una.*"

"She had only one," he said.

I leaned back against the wall, defeated.

"Why didn't she let us know when we took the mandrake?"

"I already told you, she compresses time. Telling us about the lily of the valley back then, for no reason—she would have considered that a waste of time."

Armand stood up.

"*Muchas gracias,*" he said to the Cashier.

"*De nada.*"

"Thank her."

"*Gracias,*" I said.

"*De nada.*"

Dispassionate bitch, I thought. She probably has another one of those plants stashed somewhere in that underground dungeon of hers.

When we got back to the house, Diego looked worse.

"The antidote?" a now openly tearful Lourdes asked.

"We weren't able to procure it yet," said Armand.

Lourdes Pinto let out a sound that only a mother could make. A kind of wolflike howl. I covered my ears. I was responsible for that sound.

Diego mumbled as if he were waking up out of a long sleep, except that he never did. Even when he finally opened his eyes, he didn't seem to know who we were. He kept his hands crossed over his heart like an old woman at a funeral, except we knew that the pain in his chest was physical and not emotional. Although it could have been both.

He seemed to have gotten smaller in the hours since we

had gone to see the Cashier. It was as if his body knew that we did not have the antidote and was conserving energy by shrinking. His skin was clammy and cold, yet he was somehow hot. I went to get a cool washcloth, which turned immediately warm when I wiped his forehead. I kept on rinsing the cloth to make it cool again, and wiping Diego's head. Rinsing and wiping, rinsing and wiping, trying to wipe him back to life, back to the Diego who could communicate with the spirit of the deer, the Diego who was real, who had been born when he was almost twenty years old.

Foamy blood began to leak from the sides of his mouth. I let out a wail that was close in intensity to the one that came out of his mother. She recognized the severity of the cry and came over.

"Get away," she screamed. She threw herself over Diego, all pretense of keeping her emotions in check gone.

Armand peeled Lourdes off her son. He turned Diego on his side so that he would not choke on the foam and blood before he allowed her to go back to him. The calm movements of Armand seemed to settle her, and she got on with the business of making Diego as comfortable as possible.

"He is not stabilized," Armand said to me as soon as were out of Lourdes's earshot.

"I know," I said frantically. "I can see that."

"You are going to have to find Exley and get the lily of the valley. It isn't going to be easy. He'll covet that plant above all others, because it's exactly what he needs—life force."

"How bad is it?"

"He has deadly nightshade poisoning. First signs are nausea, dilated pupils, and tachycardia or bradycardia— heartbeats that are too fast or too slow. He'll have hallucinations, blurred vision, feelings of staggering, flying, and a sense of suffocation. His skin will turn pale, which it already has, and then he'll develop a red rash. He'll enter into a state of total confusion, his skin will completely dry out and may slough off entirely, his pulse will be rapid at first and then feeble. And then he'll die."

"How long?"

"A few minutes in some cases, to a few days at most. It depends on how much he ingested and of which type of plant in the nightshade family."

"How am I going to find Exley? He could be anywhere in Mexico."

"He's in the Yucatán, I'll tell you that. Everything he wants is here. All we have to do is pinpoint his exact location."

Datura
(*Datura inoxia*)

This one is for the men out there. Datura inoxia *is a plant*
that behaves exactly like a woman. If she lets you
spend time with her, you will begin to feel powerful.
But you will also become weak, because you will be
at her mercy. But if you treat her well, and handle her
with the utmost respect, care, and precision, she will bestow
upon you visions of a future beyond your wildest imagination.

"I've decided to bring you to the eighth plant myself," Armand informed me. "I don't like to do this, because plants will always be more powerful if you find them yourself, but right now there is no time. The plant is called *Datura inoxia*, the plant of visions, dreams, and high adventure. It's not a plant for the fainthearted."

"Will it help Diego?"

"Not directly. But if it's in the mood, it may help you to find Exley."

"Let's go. Let's get it."

We walked toward the jungle, and Armand spoke quickly, getting in as much information as he could about the plant of visions and dreams.

"*Datura inoxia* grows as a herbaceous annual or perennial.

It has trumpet-shaped flowers in shades from white to pinkish purple and, more rarely, red or yellow. The females are tall, more like short trees, and the males are spread out and bushlike. The root of the female is long, and eventually it forks. The root of the male is short, and it forks right at the base of the stem.

"*Datura inoxia* is a stronger hallucinogen then peyote, psilocybin, or LSD. It is highly toxic, and in the wrong amounts it can cause psychosis. Datura is also an extraordinarily romantic plant, exuding an unforgettably narcotic scent, at night." Armand turned to me. "Do you know why?"

"I do," I said, remembering Sonali's words from so long ago. "It's because datura gets pollinated at night, and it uses its sweet scent to attract sexual partners, or pollinators, much like human beings put on perfume to attract mates before they go out to nightclubs."

Armand smiled. "Wherever Sonali is, she's very happy right now. And, yes, *Datura inoxia* is pollinated by sphinx or hawk moths, at night."

"Am I going to smoke the plant?"

"I'm not sure yet. Datura seeds can be smoked, ground up and drunk in corn beer, made into tea, or rolled up into leaves and taken inside the body as a suppository. It is an unusual plant in that every single part of it can be used to bring about visionary states. The roots, stems, leaves, flowers, and seeds."

We walked into the rain forest, as I had done so many times with Diego.

"Take a look around and see if you can locate the plant."

"We have no time. I thought you were going to find it for me?"

"I changed my mind. I'd like you to give it one try, for Diego's sake."

We walked for more than an hour, until, as usual, my tee shirt was soaked and I was nearing exhaustion from the intense humidity and heat.

"I don't think I'm going to find the plant," I said.

"You give up too easily. We will find the plant, because we have no time and no choice, two of the greatest motivators. I'm going to show you a new way to locate the plant."

"I'm ready."

"Pick a tree that suits you. A tree that you like upon first sight. Sit down with the soles of your feet on the ground, your knees bent, shoulders relaxed, and your back against the trunk."

I saw an oak with a wide trunk that looked like it might be comfortable to lean against. When I sat down, I was surprised at how relaxed I felt. I edged my back into a hollow on the face of the trunk that seemed to be made just for my spine.

"Tree trunks have vibratory lines that go from the top branches all the way into the ground. With these lines they can *see* everything around them. You are going to close your eyes and picture these lines and then ask the tree to point you in the direction of the datura plant. When you have a feeling about the direction, get up and walk. You don't need to say anything to me. Just get up and walk."

Armand's idea sounded stupid. I was too agitated to focus on the lines of the trees.

"Don't think too much about the lines. They are not imaginary, and you cannot understand them at this point. Just picture the lines running up and down the trunk. When you have that picture in your mind, ask the tree where the datura plant is."

At first I felt nothing. But then, after maybe five minutes, I felt a pulling sensation on my left side—in my ribs, to be exact. I got up and started walking to the left of the tree. The pull was so strong I didn't even look back to see if Armand was following behind me. I just kept going. I walked and walked until I heard him yell.

"Stop!"

I looked down and saw the pink trumpet-shaped flower of *Datura inoxia* right under my foot, which was raised in mid-step. I was so shocked to see the plant that for just one moment I was free of the pain of making Diego sick.

Having found the plant, I felt imbued with a strange sort of power. Like I had done something special and magical.

"Don't let it go to your head," said Armand. "Anyone can do it. Your body is changing since you've been in Mexico, and you are much more sensitive now, that's all. It's nothing, really. If anyone deserves credit, it's the tree you were sitting against. Trees can tell us all sorts of things if we're willing to listen, and they are often very good at giving directions."

"What do we do now?'

"You walk back to that same tree and break off a short, thin branch. It is clearly a friend of datura, and it would be best for you to dig it out with the branch of a friendly tree. If you use an unfriendly branch, you can harm the datura plant, and it will not give you the visions that you need to help Diego. It may not give them to you either way, but we have to up our odds as much as we can."

I returned with the branch.

"Datura hates to be dug up with metal objects such as spades," he said. "It hides all of its power immediately in the presence of metal."

I struggled to pull the roots from the ground without success.

"Why don't you do this, for speed's sake?"

"You made Diego sick; now you have to heal him or you'll always be afraid of making people sick, or being sick yourself. You may not succeed, but you have a better chance than I do. Your guilt makes you want it more. Believe me, if I thought that I could heal him quickly, I would. That boy is like my son.

If Sonali were here, you would be dead by now. She would kill you for what you did and use your blood to heal Diego."

I let out a nervous laugh.

"You think I'm kidding. I'm not. She loves that boy more than his own mother, and you saw how protective Lourdes is."

Using the branch, I slowly dug out the datura plant. We brought it back to Casablanca, where Armand refused to let me see Diego.

"You'll be useless if you're too upset," he said. "You need all of your strength to handle *Datura inoxia*."

He ground up the seeds of the plant with a mortar and pestle until they were the consistency of heavy cream. At the same time, he boiled the root to make it soft. When the root was ready, he ground it up, too, and added it to the seed mixture until the whole concoction was a thick paste. He placed the bowl of datura goop inside a net and hung it from a rafter on the ceiling.

"To make the potion less earthbound, and more visionary," he said.

I watched the bowl rock back and forth in midair.

"How long does it have to stay there?"

"Don't worry. Soon enough, you'll be off and running. Or should I say, off and flying."

I heard Diego moaning from another room in the house, where Lourdes Pinto had moved him from the couch onto a real bed. I cringed every time he moaned.

"Shut it out of your mind," Armand said. "You're wasting energy."

The entire house smelled like vomit and illness and fever, making my guilt hard to ignore.

"The main alkaloids of datura are scopolamine, hyoscyamine, and atropine. They can produce visual journeys that will have a profound effect on your psyche for years to come, if not for the rest of your life. In other words, whether the effect of the plant is good or bad, it will definitely be long-lasting. As your friend, I feel obliged to tell you that most people do a lot of preparation before engaging with datura. They undergo extensive emotional and physical cleansing rituals. Unfortunately, you have no time for that. Your emotional and physical states are suboptimal, so you'll probably be in for a trip to hell or worse. A trip from which you may never recover."

"How am I suboptimal?"

"Your body is soft, and you don't know what you feel. You're years away from being able to handle datura correctly, but we have no choice, so we have to try."

The way he pointed out my flaws was so factual, I could hardly argue. There was no emotional content to his voice.

"Can you pull me out if it isn't going well?"

"No. I won't be able to do that. I don't mean to frighten you, but it's my job to tell you all of this. In truth, even with all the preparation in the world, your success still depends on how sincere you are in your mission. And how much datura likes you. I would say that so far she likes you very much. You had no trouble finding her, and you're still standing."

Armand took the hanging pot of datura mush off the rafter and put it on the stove. He poured two cups of green liquid over it and set it to boil.

"The green liquid is tea," he said, "for flavor."

Even with the tea, the plant was bitter and hard to swallow.

"The bad taste makes the dreams more beautiful," he said.

He led me to the couch where Diego had been. It smelled like sickness.

"Say out loud what you wish to accomplish. Say how you want datura to help you. Be as specific as possible. Do not be abstract."

"Am I abstract?"

"Focus on what you want and how you want datura to help

you, and say it out loud," he repeated in a booming voice for the benefit of someone or something I couldn't see.

"I want to help Diego Pinto. I want datura to help me help Diego."

"No! You must be much more specific! And you have to hurry. Once the plant kicks in, you won't be able to say anything out loud. You may not be able to speak at all. Hurry!"

I thought about it.

"Hurry!"

"I want to see where David Exley lives."

"Good. Keep going."

"I want to see where Exley lives so that I can get the antidote plant, the lily of the valley, and bring it back to help Diego Pinto."

"Quick. What do you want datura to show you?"

"I want datura to show me the way to Exley."

"Louder! With feeling. Let the plant hear you."

"I want datura to show me the way to Exley," I screamed.

I felt myself fade away from Armand, as if we were being separated by two lines hooked to our backs, pulling us in two different directions. I tried to reach out to him, but he was moving away from me very quickly.

"I'm here with you," I heard him yell. I knew he was yelling because of the tension around his mouth, but he sounded far away.

I saw the panther right away. A magnificent creature with shiny, silky black hair and emerald-green eyes. It was more beautiful than any living being I had ever seen. I wondered how it felt to live inside of all of that beauty, all of the time. I was mesmerized by how much it looked like Diego.

"Don't go near it," I heard Armand say from a distance. "The panther is too powerful for you. You are not ready."

We must have seen it at the same time although I don't know how. Armand hadn't drunk any of the datura tea.

I remembered Diego telling me how he had seen a black panther following me in the rain forest. I knew I was ready for the panther, even if Armand did not.

My mind tracked back to everything I knew. The amount of knowledge I had surprised me. I knew, for instance, that it killed its prey by biting through the skull to destroy the brain. I knew that it buried its dead, so that by the time the victim was uncovered the panther was far away, unable to be hunted or tracked and killed. I knew it was smart, since it ate the brains of its prey. And I also knew that it was a creature of the night. A moon-led, darkness-filled loner, trusting no one, and stealth to the core.

I followed the panther along the steaming jungle floor, imitating its movements by walking on all fours. The foliage was dense, wet, and hard to maneuver, but the massive shoulders of the animal crushed whatever was in front of it, and the padded paws flattened the ground, making a path for me to follow.

The world around the panther was silent. The hair on its body, in particular the legs, was created to absorb all sound.

Blackness and soundlessness make the panther particularly deadly. No one can see it. No one can hear it coming. Not even the most nocturnal of creatures, the night owl.

I wasn't tired crawling on my belly, because the panther was a stalker and not a runner. It prowled slowly, keeping close to its prey, which in this case was a large buck. The panther was silent and cautious. So ghostlike that the sensitive buck did not even have a chance to lift its head and sniff the air before the panther attacked. It leapt onto the buck and sank its fangs into the head, right between the antlers, crushing the skull in a single downward-thrusting bite. The panther rested for a moment on the animal's back, caught its breath, and then calmly sucked on the brains like a patron in a fine French restaurant.

When it was done eating, the ninety-five-pound cat grabbed the 250-pound buck in its teeth and dragged it up into the high branches of a nearby tree. No lie—it carried the huge buck up into the tree with its teeth.

When it came down, we didn't move for an hour. I sat and waited while the panther meticulously cleaned every inch of its body until its hair shone like the midnight sun, reflecting plants and insects in its sheen. I had never felt so much awe and respect for any living creature in my entire life.

The deeper into the jungle we went, the darker it became, and the harder it was to see well enough to keep up. I strained my eyes more and more with each step. The panther sensed my predicament, and every once in a while it turned its head toward me, and the emerald-green flashes of its fluorescent eyes lit the path in front of me.

Toward the morning, it climbed into the high branches of a tree. I tried to follow, but I could only make it onto the lowest limbs. I saw the panther's paws hanging down from above. It was sleeping. I wanted to go up and grab it and tell it that we had no time, that Diego, who had the same black hair and fluo-rescent eyes, was sick, but I didn't know how to speak to it. I looked up and stared, but I didn't say a word, because I knew it valued silence above all else, and I didn't want to lose its favor.

The sun came up, and still the panther slept in the treetop. I sat on the lowest branch, exhausted. I closed my eyes and thought about the vibratory lines in the tree. I remembered what Armand had told me, and I pictured the lines and asked the tree to show me the way to Exley. Suddenly I felt a pull on my left side. Immediately I jumped down off the branch and walked left from the tree.

There was a clearing in the jungle, and a broken-down shack made of rotting wood stood on the edge of the foliage.

I crept on my stomach. When I got close enough, I tried to look through the windows, but they were scratched, and I couldn't see anything inside. I stepped back, took cover in the jungle, and watched as the front door slowly opened. There he was. I sucked in the deep breath of the nonbeliever confronted with a truth she couldn't ignore. *Datura inoxia* had led me to the black panther, who led me to the tree, which led me directly to Exley.

I silently thanked the panther. I turned around and looked up into the tree, but it was already gone.

I woke up and sat bolt upright on the couch at Casablanca. Armand was hovering over me like a mother.

"I know where he is."

"It's too late for Diego," said Armand.

"Is he alive?"

"He is. But he'll never be the same. His fever climbed too high while you were gone."

I grabbed my backpack and some water, and headed for the door. There was no way in hell I had ruined the Laundromat, had the nine plants stolen, quit my job, come to Mexico, and taken datura, only to end up killing the one person I could love.

"Wait," said Lourdes Pinto.

I stopped impatiently at the door.

"Armand, please leave the room," she said. Then she turned to me. "Take off all of your clothes."

"No. We don't have any time left for witch-doctor games."

"Take them off now!" she screamed at me.

I hesitated, but the look in her eyes told me I wasn't going to leave the house until I did what she said. I took off my clothes as fast as I could.

"Your underclothing as well."

She wasn't satisfied until I was stripped naked.

"You must be prepared to seduce this man to get the lily of the valley."

I hadn't thought of how I was going to get the lily from Exley. I saw myself storming his cabin, grabbing the plant, and running for my life. No intrigue. No plan. Just raw speed.

"He must be narcotized," said Lourdes Pinto, "or he will kill you to keep that plant. He wants the nine plants as much as you do. Maybe more. Remember all he has done so far to get the plants that he has. He stole the lily from the Cashier, which is no simple business. For that one stupid move he will pay and pay for the rest of his life, even if he never sees her again."

"How can I get the lily from him?"

"Convince him that you still love him. That you miss him terribly. You must try to evoke a feeling within yourself. A feeling of love for him. The same feeling you had when you first met him. He has to believe in you without any suspicion. The feeling has to be real."

"Why?"

"If you love him, he will feel powerful and in control and he will desire you sexually. It is in his sexual desire that he is at his weakest. When he wants you the most, when his desire is so strong that it feels like an actual physical thing that you can touch, that's when you make your move and take the lily."

"I make myself love him. I make him feel powerful. I make him want sex. I take the plant."

"That's right."

The weirdness had already gone so far out into strangeland that I went with whatever Lourdes Pinto told me. She was Diego's mother, and I was the woman on the road to being his killer. I trusted her judgment over my own.

"Spread your arms and legs," she said. She unscrewed the lid to a jelly jar and began to massage my body with the oil inside.

"We want to make sure he goes for you. This pheromone has a subtle scent of the female sexual organs. It will drive him crazy in ways he does not understand. He will be attracted to you and need to be near you without knowing why."

She bent down on her knees and rubbed the oil into my feet and between my toes. She took her time on my calves, and moved up to my thighs, and stroked me in between my legs. She oiled my arms and back and breasts. Her hands were practiced, and I was embarrassed with pleasure, noticing that she and her son shared the same type of touch. The oil smelled floral and musky, like a flowery animal.

She kept right on stroking my body.

"It has lilac, jasmine, and musk from a rutting deer," she said.

The words for the ingredients excited me. *Lilac, jasmine, and musk,* I said to myself. *Lilac, jasmine, and musk, I must. Lilac, jasmine, and musk, I must.* They sounded like an incantation. They sounded like the sexiest words in the English language.

"Say it," she said.

I could barely breathe.

"Say what?"

"Say it," she said, moving her fingertips in circles around my nipples.

"I want to go now."

"Tell me more."

"I want to go and see Exley. I want him. I want him to touch me like you are."

"Get dressed now, and go as fast as you can."

I was almost out the door when Lourdes Pinto called me back inside.

"If you don't get the lily of the valley, don't come back to this house. Don't ever let me see your face again, or I'll kill you with my own hands."

Lily of the Valley
(Convallaria majalis)

*Lily of the valley is known to slow the disturbed action of a weak
and irritable heart, while at the same time increasing its power.
As a heart medication, it is sometimes preferable to the digitalis
made from the foxglove plant, because it is less toxic and does
not accumulate in the blood. Lily of the valley has one of the
most sexual scents of all plants and is widely used in perfume.
No wonder it causes the heart to beat stronger.*

I approached Exley's shack with extreme caution because
both Armand and Lourdes Pinto had warned me that he was
an expert in plant magic. He was not to be underestimated, not
even for one second. Lourdes and Armand said I would recognize the lily of the valley by its scent. They said it smelled like
the human female in heat, and Exley would most likely be
found sitting right near it. I wasn't sure if I'd recognize the scent
of a human female in heat, but they assured me that it was like
no other scent in the world and that I would know it instantly.

With the cabin in sight, I decided to go for a bold move. I
walked right up to the front door, but I stopped just as I was
about to knock. Although the sun was shining, the cabin gave
off a damp, yeasty, revolting odor.

The wooden door, which had once been painted a pale

blue, was chipped and appeared to be rotting, with thick, furry, black patches of mold growing everywhere. The wood looked soft, as if my knuckles would go right through to the other side if I knocked.

I walked over to a window, peeked in, and shrank away at the sight of Exley. He was sitting on an old wooden straight-backed colonial chair in a room with no lights and no sunlight. The lily of the valley was sitting on a table next to him. He seemed to be guarding the plant, as though he knew I was coming.

I took a deep breath and went back to the windowpane. Exley looked markedly different from the last time I had seen him. His hair was longer and thinner, much closer to white than the silvery blond I remembered. Had I given it that silvery sheen in my imagination? Worst of all, he was staring straight ahead at absolutely nothing, baring his teeth in a strange cross between snarling and smiling.

I leaned against the house. I could not imagine ever desiring the creature sitting in that moldy cabin.

"Lila, I'm so glad you came back to see me."

Exley's voice was a jolt. I stood up straight and tossed my hair behind my shoulders.

"I was just about to knock."

"But you're standing by the window?"

"I wasn't sure you wanted company."

"You know you're always welcome to join me, wherever I am. But, just out of curiosity, how did you know I was here?"

"A friend spotted you."

"You mean a spotted friend," he said, in reference to the panther.

"Very good," I said. "I'm here because I wasn't finished with our conversation at the market."

"The Cashier is a lovely woman, isn't she?"

"You disappeared. How did you get out of the basement?"

"Armand must have told you how I did it. I even left him a clue. It was the gentlemanly thing to do."

"The chicory plant?"

"*Cichorium intybus,* that would be the one. The plant of invisibility."

"Have you found what you came here for? Have you found the two plants that died?"

"I've been alone for a long time, Lila. I could use some company. Come in and have some tea. We can chat and catch up."

I walked to the door. I did not let Exley see me hesitate.

"I'd love some."

"I'm sorry it's not more comfortable. I haven't had time to clean the place properly," he said, holding a pot filled with water over a burner.

The cabin looked like a dump, but I pushed the thought out of my mind.

"It's fine, really," I said, looking over every inch of the room. My eyes rested on a noisy cage of rodents sitting in the corner.

"I use those to practice tracking," he said from across the cabin. "Not very pretty, I know. Not the best way to attract the ladies."

I spotted a hideous mandrake root on the dirt floor underneath the table, with the lily of the valley on top. Seeing it reminded me of Diego. The memory of him, sick and half dead, prevented me from running out the door. The lily of the valley itself was tall, robust, and obviously well cared for. I could also smell faint traces of cannabis, and I saw a purple gloxinia on a dirty windowsill. Exley was well on his way to having the nine plants.

He returned with the tea and handed me a cup. The fingernails on his left hand were long and dirty, and the ones on his right were short and clean. The rim of the cup was filthy. I put it close to my lips and faked a swallow without ingesting the tea or even touching the cup.

He sat on the straight-backed chair.

"I *am* sorry, Lila, about the Laundromat. I wanted to tell you that, but somehow it didn't come out right when I saw you at the market. I used you to get to the plants, and for that I'm sorry. Is that what you came back to hear?"

I was not prepared for him to apologize.

"Even after the nasty business with the Laundromat, I always knew you'd be back. I knew that if I waited long enough, if I just had enough patience, you would come back to me. I counted on it."

"What made you think I'd come back?"

"When it comes to the nine plants, anything goes. Any behavior used to get them is, ultimately, excusable. When I first met you, you didn't know that. But I'm sure by now you've figured it out and have forgiven me. Besides, we were good together." His long nails clicked against his teacup. "We had chemistry."

Out of the corner of my eye I saw a snake on the floor of the cabin. I lifted my feet up and tucked them underneath my legs.

"A friend?" I asked.

"Sort of. I like to think of him like your black panther friend. He's somewhat of a totem for me. He's been here since the day I got here. It's his cabin, really, not mine."

"A rattlesnake?"

"That's right. One of the most venomous snakes on earth. Don't you remember him? He was with the little-boy shaman in the jungle. The one who stole your car when you first came back to see me. When you followed me to Mexico."

I didn't follow you, I wanted to scream, but I kept my mouth shut.

"It was this snake," I said, pointing to the floor.

"It was. That's how I found you. It's how I'll always find you. Didn't you see me? I thought I showed myself to you?"

"Yes," I said, remembering the picture of Exley that came into my mind when I was with the witch boy. "I saw you."

"I saved you, you know. He could have killed you easily. The two hollow fangs in his mouth are like hypodermic needles. They release venom with pinpoint precision into the veins of his prey. When his victim is dead, he swallows it whole. It's all very neat and clean. No mess. No blood. No gore. Violence with no sign of violence. Death with no sign of death. I like that."

Exley got up and opened the cage of squealing rodents. He grabbed a large squirrel by the tail, swung it around, and tossed it to the snake. The squirrel hit the side of the cabin and fell to the floor. Quick as lightning, the snake sunk his fangs into the rodent. Inch by inch it took the thick, hairy body into its mouth, until the entire squirrel disappeared inside of the snake. I felt sweaty and sick.

"Don't look so distraught. When he's not killing, he can be very entertaining. You saw him dance for the little-boy shaman. Would you like to see it again?"

Exley got up and turned the radio on.

"I get just the one station out here. I hope you like drum music, because that's all they play, twenty-four hours a day. It drives me crazy half the time, but he likes it," he said, looking at the snake. "To tell you the truth, I keep the radio on mostly all the time. He gets testy when I turn it off. He ruins things."

"Like what?"

"The things I like most. The plants. He likes them, too, unfortunately. He likes to eat them."

"Why do you stay here with him?"

"I've moved several times," he said, staring straight out at nothing. "And everywhere I go, he's there."

"New York?"

"He's there every night, in my dreams."

"Are you afraid of him?"

"I spend my life tracking rabbit and warthogs, squirrels, rats, and other rodents, just to keep him happy. I have to kill all the time to please him. He does nothing for himself. I have to live for him, to pervert myself for him. Don't you understand? That's why I need the nine plants."

"Why?"

"To get what I want in life. To get my heart's desire, which is to be rid of the snake."

I saw my opening in his self-pity. Awful as it was, I put my dirty cup down and reached for him. I touched him. His skin felt dry and rough. I sat there holding his hand and trying to conjure up one image, any image, of the strong, rugged, silvery-blond Exley I had been attracted to so long ago, in the green market in Union Square.

"Would you like to see him dance?" he asked me again. "It's the only entertainment I can offer you. And I would truly like to offer you something besides pain."

"I would."

Exley turned the radio up until it was on full-blast. There was a lot of static, but the sound of the drums vibrated through the walls and made the shack tremble like an earthquake. I held on to the arms of my chair.

"I'll be right back," he yelled. "I need to go and adjust the antenna, get rid of some of the static."

The second he was out the door, I stood up and put my hands around the lily of the valley. As soon as I touched the plant, the rattlesnake made a horrible, explosive, hissing sound like thousands of fries dropped into boiling oil.

"Put the lily down, Lila."

I didn't move.

"I just wanted to smell it," I said, keeping my back to him.

"Well, now you have. So put it down."

I turned to face him and saw the rattlesnake blocking the

242

door. As I placed the lily back on the table, I understood that I might not be able to get out of the shack alive.

Exley adjusted the old tuner on the radio as if nothing had happened. "That oughta do it," he said. "That's much better, don't you think?"

"Much better," I said.

He held out his hand for mine.

"Come."

I took a deep breath and pictured Diego for strength. I took Exley's hand. It was the one with the long, dirty fingernails.

With the static gone, the snake moved back and forth across the dirt floor. He moved faster and faster, from one side of the cabin to the other, becoming increasingly agitated. Exley and I stood in the corner of the shack, holding hands like some strange parody of two kids at a high school dance.

"He'll go back and forth until he realizes that the cabin is too small, that there's nowhere for him to go but up," Exley whispered. "Then he'll rise until he is extended to his full height, and he'll dance for me like an Indian belly dancer. It's the only pleasure he allows me."

True to Exley's description, the rattlesnake rose up toward the ceiling of the shack. It waved its body back and forth, lifting and shaking its rattle like a tambourine, in perfect rhythm with the drums.

Exley dropped my hand. He followed the movement of the snake, undulating his body like a ribbon, making strange hissing sounds. The moldy shack shook from the drumming and dancing. Exley, with his white hair flying and his long nails in the air, was mesmerizing.

I walked toward them like a robot, staring straight out in front of me into nothing, and joined Exley and the snake in their dance.

Exley sniffed the air like a dog. He put his arms around me

and, with his face in the crook of my neck, breathed in the scent of my skin. He smelled me furiously, like an animal. The three of us danced to the sound of the drums and the rattle like that's what we were born to do.

Somewhere in my mind I remembered that the rattlesnake was a master hypnotist who struck the second its victim relaxed into the baby sounds of its rattle. The thought blew through my mind like a wind. So fast I couldn't hang on.

"Stay with me, Lila." Exley said. "Your scent is more beautiful than the lily of the valley."

I barely remembered why I wanted the lily. I had relaxed into Exley's arms, almost falling asleep on his bony shoulder, when I heard a voice. It was loud, and it seemed to come from inside my own head.

"Wake up, Lila! Wake up! Do not fall asleep!"

It was the voice of Armand. I opened my eyes as if I'd been doused by cold water. I was shocked to find myself in Exley's arms.

"Seduce him. Do it now!" Armand said.

"Don't listen to Armand," Exley said, as if he, too, could hear him. "Armand is a liar. He has the nine plants. He's always had the nine plants."

I tried to obliterate the fog that Exley had wrapped around me. He was still holding me with his face pressed to my chest, sniffing at Lourdes Pinto's perfume like a madman.

"I don't understand," I said. "What are you saying about Armand and the plants?"

"Think about it, Lila. Think of the extraordinary value of those plants. Think of their ability to bring forth everything a person could ever desire in this lifetime. If you had the nine plants in *your* Laundromat, wouldn't you take a cutting, ten cuttings, a hundred cuttings, from each plant? Wouldn't you replant them somewhere else? Somewhere secret? Just in case?"

I was stunned. Of course Armand would take cuttings from the plants. He would be stupid not to, and he was a very, very smart man. How could I have missed that?

"You have to focus on Diego," said Armand. "You have to get the lily for Diego or he will die. That's all you have to think about."

"Why am I here?" I asked Exley. "If he has the nine plants, then why am I here?"

"I don't know. But it's not for the plants."

I was confused, but I knew I couldn't think about the plants. I couldn't be sure if Armand had them or not, and I had to help Diego. If he died, I would never be able to live with myself.

"I love you," Exley murmured. "Armand never loved you like I do. He only lied to you and tricked you." Exley held me tight. "I knew you would come back to me."

"Yes, David, I'm back," I whispered into his hair. I pulled his head down and moved my scented breasts back and forth against his face. "I never really wanted to leave you."

Exley took both of my hands.

"Lie down with me."

"Do not lie down," Armand whispered in my head. "If you lie down, you will never get out of there. Ever. This is your last chance to get the lily of the valley."

Exley sat on the dirt floor on his knees, the rattlesnake sleeping and coiled up behind him. I stood next to him, and he reached for my body.

The fog around me was thick. I felt sleepy, but I fought the urge to sit down.

"I need you," he said from the floor. His hands were wrapped around my legs. He sniffed the skin on the inside of my thighs, pressing his nose into me like a dog.

I bent down and lifted his head in my hands.

"I need you, too," I said. I envisioned the best kiss I'd ever had, the one Diego had given me in the jungle when he slid the lemony-sweet cacao seeds into my mouth. And then, looking into his slit eyes, I leaned over and kissed Exley. I kissed him softly with as much passion as I could find. I did it for Diego.

I was repulsed by the texture of Exley's darting, serpent-like tongue and gray, filmy teeth. But I also knew that he loved me. Although he was corrupt and obscene and meant to follow me and keep me tied to him like a slave, he was still a person who needed me.

I remembered the words of Lourdes Pinto: *You must try to evoke a feeling within yourself. A feeling of love for him. The same feeling you had when you first met him. He has to believe in you without any suspicion. The feeling has to be real.*

I kissed Exley again and again, over and over. When I finally stopped, his eyes were closed and his mouth was wide open for more. I stood still for just one moment, to witness his passion, the most passion a man had ever felt for me in my life. And then, when I had my fill, I slid my oiled body out of his grasp. While his eyes were still closed and his mouth was still open, I grabbed the lily of the valley and ran. I left him on his knees, arms outstretched. The moldy door closed behind me, and the last thing I heard was the hiss of the rattlesnake, rising.

Tropical Air Plants
(epiphytic plants)

Air plants include orchids, bromeliads, and all staghorn ferns.
They are not planted in soil, and they do not need to be watered.
They derive nutrition from decomposing insects and leaves,
and nitrogen from lightning strikes. There's not much to
add to the story of plants that live off lightning
and death. That is drama enough for ten stories.

I ran into the rain forest as fast as I could. It was nighttime, and once inside I couldn't see an inch in front of me. I tripped over tree roots and shrubs. Leaves and branches scratched my face, and insects flew into my eyes. The pot with the lily was too heavy for me to carry, so I slammed it against a tree, shattering it into pieces. I held the plant and its dirt-packed roots against my body and continued running.

When I felt far enough from Exley, I slowed down, inching my way through the forest understory at a careful crawl. I was aware of the passage of time and the life of Diego, but I was afraid to continue running for fear of damaging or losing the lily. I had no idea which part of the plant was medicinal; I couldn't afford to have a single piece torn off and lost on the jungle floor forever.

I gave up trying to see through the blackness. I got down on my hands and knees and felt my way across the floor of the jungle as I had seen the black panther do. I had no idea which direction I was traveling in. I had no idea whether I was getting closer to Casablanca or farther away.

Exhausted, I stopped to rest against a tree. I felt a large leaf underneath my feet, which turned out to be a giant palm frond. Giant leaves were common on the jungle floor. Their size gave them enough surface space to amass the amount of sunlight required to stay alive in the extreme darkness. I lifted the frond and wrapped the lily inside of it for protection against the rain, the wind, and my own clumsiness in the dark. I kept going, stopping only once to lie on the jungle floor, which was covered in slime and rot and molting leaves, to catch my breath.

When I stood up, my hair stood on end from static electricity. This was not a good sign. It meant that a lightning storm was imminent. Armand once told me that more people are killed by lightning strikes every year than by rattlesnake bites: *You have less than three chances in one hundred of actually dying from a rattler bite. If you must ever make the choice between the reptile and the big spark, go with the snake.*

This bit of information did not bode well for me. I had just barely managed to escape the rattlesnake. What were the chances that my luck was going to hold out against the bolts of electricity?

The strike began as sheet lightning, which means it was limited to the interior of the clouds, turning them into huge oblong balls of fluorescence. They were so bright they cut right through the dense forest canopy, lighting up the treetops, creating the eerie sensation that someone had turned on an overhead light switch in the rain forest. Everything was momentarily visible, giving me a view of emerald-green vegetation and flashing points of yellow, which I knew to be animal eyes.

The sheet lightning turned out to be a momentary blessing, giving me just enough time to get some sense of where I was.

The streak lightning, which came next, was a far less enjoyable experience, with wide swaths of forking electricity cutting through the treetops and striking the ground. I knew that this type of storm was the most dangerous. It came from the negatively charged bottom of the cloud striking the positively charged ground below, and was often deadly. When people die from lightning strikes, streak lightening is almost always the cause.

I crouched on the ground, making myself as small as possible, to avoid being a target. I watched the zigzagging bolts hit small plants and shrubs on the ground, vaporizing them instantly. I looked up just in time to see the top of a tall tree burst into flames, struck by a ribbon of white light.

The fire in the high canopy lit up the jungle floor and brought me face-to-face with a plant that I had seen only in a picture. A bromeliad extinct for so long that no one bothered to look for it anymore. A plant so rare even its name was gone. It was Sonali's prize. The passion plant with no name.

There was no mistaking the mysterious bromeliad, its inward-spiraling leaves forming a small black hole in the center. A mandala, Sonali had said, created by the plant world, about the mind of human beings. I had in my sights the very plant Sonali and Armand had spent so many years searching for.

Being an air plant, it did not require any soil to live—it grew straight out of a log. It was not parasitic. It had attached itself for stability only. I waited until after the next bolt of lightning struck the ground, and then, as gently as possible, I lifted the passion plant off the log and wrapped it in the palm frond with the lily of the valley.

Armand had described it as the plant of passion because it feeds on lightning that strikes suddenly, like passion itself. He said that only another being of equal passion would ever be able to find it.

I held the two plants close to my body and kept moving. The one good thing about the storm was the loud, booming thunder. It kept the animals hidden and at bay, giving me the freedom to move without worrying about being attacked.

When the rain stopped, I could see the early morning sun coming in from the east, and I knew which way I had to go. I followed the dawn until I came to the clearing in the jungle. The road to Casablanca was just up ahead.

I had made it out of the jungle, but I had no idea if I was in time to save Diego. I was never so happy to see that gravelly dirt road as I was that morning. I ran and ran, and walked some, and ran some more. The soles of my feet bled. I had lost my shoes somewhere back in the jungle, or maybe I had left them in Exley's shack, I couldn't remember. What mattered was that I made it the seven miles back to Casablanca.

I limped through the door. Lourdes Pinto and Armand looked as though they hadn't moved an inch since I'd left. Without saying a word, I handed the palm frond with the plants inside of it to Armand. When he opened it he looked shocked to see the passion plant. He picked it up as if it were a newborn baby and held it the way he held Sonali, as if he would never let it go.

"I chose correctly," he said softly.

He held the plant in his arms while Lourdes Pinto filled a basin with warm water for my bloody feet.

Armand and Lourdes turned to the business at hand. I knew from their demeanors that I had done well. I could tell from their expressions—no crying and no tear-streaked faces—that Diego was still hanging on.

I stepped into the basin, and the water turned blood-red. I put my cheek down on the kitchen countertop, my arms extended out in front of me, like a standing-up child's pose in yoga, and watched Lourdes Pinto prepare the lily of the valley by separating the plant into root, stalk, and flower.

"Usually, the whole plant is collected when in flower and dried," said Armand, tapping his favorite anti-scorpion spatula on the countertop as he spoke, "but right now we have no time to dry it, so we'll improvise. The flower is the most active part of the plant, and its chief constituents are two glucosides. The first is convallamarin, the active ingredient. It's a white crystalline powder, readily soluble in water or alcohol, which acts upon the heart like digoxin. Next there is convallarin, which is crystalline in prisms, soluble in alcohol, slightly soluble in water, and which has a purgative action. It will force Diego to get rid of any poisons in his system by vomiting them out. Ten to thirty drops of fluid will be extracted from the plant and given to him in teaspoon doses."

When the plant had been thoroughly boiled, Lourdes Pinto poured the reduction into a tiny glass jar the size of an eye-dropper, and walked toward Diego's room. I took my bloody feet out of the basin to follow her. I was out of my mind with exhaustion, but I wanted to witness Diego's recovery with my own eyes.

"Not yet," said Armand, grabbing my arm. "We have a visitor."

"I don't hear anyone."

"Go!" he yelled at Lourdes Pinto.

She ran toward Diego's room and disappeared with the medicine in her hand just as Exley slid open the front door.

I held on to Armand's arm. I was close to fainting at the sight of Exley.

"What do you want?" I whispered.

"I want what's mine," he said in an eerie, calm voice. "I only want what's mine, Armand. I don't plan on using this if I don't have to." He held up a rusted machete. "It's not in my nature to kill."

"You followed me here?" I asked him.

"You're an amateur. You left a stinky, female trail, easy for anyone with a nose to follow."

Armand turned to me.

"Shut up," he said. "Don't say another word. Do not let him hear you speak. Do not let him inside of your mind."

Exley stared at the passion plant on the kitchen counter-top, and a look of understanding crossed his face.

"So that's what you were after. That's what you've been looking for all of this time. Tell her, Armand. Tell her the truth."

Exley turned to me.

"I was right all along. He used you, Lila. He didn't bring you here to get the nine plants. He cared for only one thing. Only one plant. The passion plant that has no name."

"Do not connect with him in any way," said Armand.

"I loved you, Lila," said Exley. "Armand never did. Not for one single moment. He only loves the passion plant. You were a pawn to him. Nothing more. He used you much worse than I did when I slept with you in New York. He almost got you killed, several times, and Diego, too. Diego is in the predica-ment he's in right now because of Armand and his desire for the passion plant, not because of you."

I looked at Armand, and he shook his head no.

"He used you to find the plant because he knows, just as I do, that it's your fate to work for a man, like a whore. But the difference between him and me is that I paid you money when you worked for me. Remember? I paid you for the fire-fern cutting. What has he given you?"

I couldn't help it. I had to think about what Exley was saying. If it was true that Armand had never needed the nine plants, if he had used me to find the passion plant, could I ever forgive him for what happened to Diego?

"Don't let him get inside of you," said Armand. "He would have lulled you to sleep in that shack and killed you, or worse."

Armand's voice sounded steady, but I could feel the muscles of his arm shaking where I was holding it. His nervousness upset and confused me.

"What is it that you want?" asked Armand.

"The lily of the valley is mine, for sure."

"Forget it. The lily has already been taken apart and boiled. It is already inside of Diego Pinto, healing him as it was meant to do."

"Then I will kill Diego to get it out of him."

"You won't touch Diego," I said, suddenly shaken out of my stupor. I racked my brains trying to remember if there was a gun or a knife or any kind of weapon at all in the house.

"What else do you want?" asked Armand, calmly, as if he knew what Exley was going to say before he said it.

"Lila is mine!" he said.

"I'm not yours!"

"Sshhh," said Armand.

"I would have had her, back at the shack, if you hadn't stepped inside of her mind."

"She's a person. She's not a puppet on a string."

"That's why I'm here," said Exley. "I'm going to slice the strings you use to keep her. The strings that bind you together." He lifted up the curved, rusted machete.

"What strings? What is he talking about?"

"You and I have lines between us, lines that connect us like the ones you saw in the tree," Armand said. And then, in one swift move, he fell to the ground, taking me down with his weight. I heard the whoosh of the knife cut through the air above us. I screamed, and Armand pushed me so hard that I slid across the Mexican tiles all the way to the other side of the room.

Armand stood up just as Exley raised the machete, but at six foot four, he was much bigger and stronger than Exley. In one of the ballerina moves that belied his size, he grabbed Exley's wrist and moved it back and forth, causing the machete to slice through the air with a whirring sound. With his bulk and strength, Armand shoved him directly underneath the pink tiger piñata that hung on the ceiling. He forced him to strike the piñata repeatedly with the machete, slashing through the layers of papier-mâché like butter. As the piñata fell apart, Armand dropped his grip on Exley's arm and dove across the room. Hundreds of scorpions poured out of the piñata and landed on top of Exley. He screamed as the prehistoric tails whipped around, injecting him with venom. In a frenzy of pain, he wielded the machete, stabbing at the scorpions that were covering his body, stabbing himself over and over with his own knife. The scorpions were in his hair and on his face, crawling down his chest and into his clothes, filling his body with poison, until he dropped to the floor. I watched him from across the room, breathing as though I had just run a marathon. I watched him until he stopped moving, until he stopped screaming, or crying, or moaning. I watched him until he was lying on the floor covered in blood and scorpions, dead.

Armand looked at me.

"Remember what the children say?" he asked.

" 'Smash the piñata like there's no mañana,' " I whispered.

"That's right," he said. "Always listen to the children. One way or another, they are always right."

My mind and body were beginning to crumble under the unrelenting pressure of the last twenty-four hours. The last thing I would remember was Armand carrying me to somewhere dark and soft. I slept for two days.

When I woke, Armand and I took a walk on the grassy hillside overlooking the ocean.

"Is it true that you were never looking for the nine plants? I have to know."

"It is. Exley was right about that. I have many, many cuttings from the nine plants."

"Why didn't you tell me what I was looking for? Why didn't you ask me to help you find the passion plant with no name?"

"Would you have given up your life in New York if I had? Would you have searched so long and so hard?"

"No."

"That's why I didn't ask."

"But you let me feel guilty about the Laundromat and the plants, for so long."

"I needed you to find the passion plant with no name. Your guilt was my only hope. It was the one thing that would get you to Mexico and keep you looking. I considered it extremely fortuitous that you were responsible for my Laundromat being robbed."

We sat in silence, watching the fishermen pull in their long nets.

"When we first met," Armand said, "you told me that you didn't like your job. You said if you could have anything you wanted in the world you would choose high adventure, love, and money. Do you remember that?"

"I do."

"Did you get all of the things you wanted?"

"I don't know."

"Did you get adventure?"

"Ten lifetimes' worth."

"Did you find love?"

I thought of Diego and myself, and Armand and Sonali.

"Yes, I found love."

"Money?"

"I'm not sure about that one."

Armand opened his leather satchel and pulled out a small cutting.

"It's from the passion plant. As far as anyone knows, except for you and me, it's extinct. There's not a single one left in the world. Take this cutting. It's valuable. It will bring you great fortune."

"Why did you want the passion plant so much?"

"I have everything I want in this world, except Sonali's happiness. The only thing that matters to her, and so to me, is the passion plant with no name. Now Sonali will have happiness. And I will have everything I want."

"I have one more question."

"Sure."

"How did you know that once I got to Mexico I would be able to find it?"

"I tested you with the fire fern. Of all the thousands of people I met going in and out of my Laundromat, of all the people I've spoken with and gotten to know, only ten people received a fire-fern cutting. Of those ten, only yours took root. That, and I liked you. Believe me, we wouldn't be here if I didn't like you. It's much too difficult to go on an adventure with someone you don't like. Especially at my age."

"How old are you?

Armand laughed. "See those hills out there?"

"What if I couldn't find the passion plant?"

"We would have stayed here until you did," he said ruthlessly. "The passion plant is the tenth plant. The beginning of a new cycle. She is part of your personal mythology. She is now *your* contribution to the legend."

"I was thinking that I might not want to go back to New York. I want to stay here with you and Diego."

"You're going back tomorrow. I've already booked your reservation."

"I'm not ready."

"You have to go back to your world and see what it looks like after all of this. That way, you can know what you really want and who you really are. You can make a choice about the direction of your life."

"Can I see Diego now?"

"He's waiting for you."

Diego was still in bed, but his cheeks were tan and healthy, and his hair, which looked like it had grown overnight, was in a long, shiny ponytail. He was as strong and handsome as ever. The antidote had worked.

I leaned over and took the rubber band out of his hair. It fell free, and I could smell its familiar coconut scent.

He lifted himself into a sitting position. I took him into my arms and held him tight.

"I'm sorry," I said, "for making you so sick."

"I know. Me, too."

"What are you sorry for?"

"For teasing you," he said. "If I had just taken advantage of you like you wanted, this wouldn't have happened." He smiled that big white-toothed smile.

"I found the antidote," I said into his hair.

"I know," he whispered. "I know what you went through."

"And I found the bromeliad with no name."

"Tell me how you found it," he whispered in my ear. "Tell me everything."

"Are you sure you want to know?"

"Yes. Tell me the story of us."

"It started when I met you in the rain forest. When I almost stepped on the cycad and the gloxinia, but you stopped me just in time."

"That's when I made you go back and get the moonflower."

"The umbilical cord, you called it."

"We walked to Casablanca through the jungle."

"And then alongside the ocean."

"I liked you already."

"I liked you, too. You introduced me to Tamatz Kauyumari. The oldest and biggest deer."

"I sang you his spirit song."

"And then he led us to *Theobroma cacao*."

"I saw *Panthera onca* following you through the jungle, twice."

"I never should have gone to the market without you, but you were sleeping."

"That's where you met the Cashier."

"And found the mandrake. And *cichorium intybus*. The plant of invisibility."

"And met Mallorey *cien*."

"Yes, Mallorey."

"And got higher than a kite in the garden of tortured sinsemilla."

"Her sinsemilla made me sexual."

"You took in all its femaleness."

"That's why I wanted to be with you so much. That's why I gave you the mandrake root."

"That, and because you love me. It made you do strange things."

"I love you."

"I know."

"I drank *Datura inoxia* and traveled with the black panther to find the antidote."

"And you saw the energy lines of the trees."

"How do you know?"

"Because I know."

"I smelled the lily of the valley, up close, but the scent of your skin is still sweeter."

"Not as sweet as yours."

"I danced with a rattlesnake."

"There are many of those in life."

"And then, under a flash of lightning, a tree caught fire and I found the bromeliad with no name."

"How strange that a tree caught fire in the rain forest. It's very wet in there."

"I found the plant of passion. The tenth plant."

"You found it with your passion. You set the tree on fire with your passion."

"I love you."

"I love you, too," he said.

"And that is the story of us."

"It is."

"It's true, then, whoever finds the nine plants really does find what they desire."

"It's true."

"Let's say them together."

We began.

"Moonflower, gloxinia, cycad, *Theobroma cacao,* mandrake, chicory, sinsemilla, *Datura inoxia,* lily of the valley, and the tenth plant. The bromeliad. The passion plant with no name."

"Would you like to see the plants?" Armand asked. "They're sunbathing on the balcony. I think they'd like to see you, too."

Diego and I walked outside and around the front of the house to the stairs leading to the balcony. It was a beautiful sunny day, and I looked out at the sea. We strolled across the rocky, grassy terrain, and I never once looked down, because I knew that the scorpions were my friends, and I trusted them now. They had killed my enemy.

We climbed the stairs to the balcony on the roof of the house, and from there we stopped to watch Diego's mother, Lourdes Pinto, standing outside of her *palapa*. She was washing clothes against the rocks in the sea, like nothing had ever happened.

"Where is Exley?" I asked Diego. "Where is his body?"

"Armand and my mother put him into the sea. She's washing their clothes right now to get the blood out."

The plants were lined up on a wooden table in exactly the same order in which we had found them. They were already potted and soaking up the sunlight, with a fine mist spraying over them from a hose on the balcony. They looked bright and happy and erect.

I walked around the wooden table to view the plants from all sides. Diego and I put our arms around each other.

"You're going back to New York, aren't you?"

"I don't want to."

"You're coming back to Mexico?"

I smiled.

"I want to."

I turned around to take a last look.

The tenth plant, the passion plant, had just begun to bloom.

❦ PART THREE ❦

NEW YORK CITY

I arrived back in the city in the middle of July, one of the hottest months of the year in New York. It was so hot that the tar on the ground near the taxi line at Kennedy airport stuck to the bottom of my sneakers. At first I thought I had stepped on gum, but it was actually melted street.

I don't want to go on about it, but the heat in New York was not the same kind of heat as in the Yucatán. I won't spout that old heat-versus-humidity argument, either. This heat was simply hotter. Period. It had no ocean breeze to cool it down, and no plants giving off cleaned-up oxygen to breathe. It was heat from motors, generators, and transformers. From plane and car engines, air-conditioning units, and exhaust pipes. A kind of heat much more oppressive than the daily heat from the sun, cooled off by late-evening ocean cross-breezes, that I had become so accustomed to. The heat in New York City tasted and smelled different, and my body rejected it like a foreign substance, resulting in coughing, sneezing, and general angst. I hated it, and I blamed myself for letting Armand talk me into coming back in the summer instead of in the fall, like I wanted to.

For fifty dollars, I took a taxi back into Manhattan. For that money, I could have lived on the Costa Maya for months.

On the plus side, I wasn't burdened by heavy luggage. I had nothing with me. Not even a backpack. I left all of my clothes in Mexico, because they were either ripped or simply worn out from so many forays into the jungle. It was great to wear out clothes instead of throwing them away because they were no longer in fashion. It was like being a kid again—the time of life when your jeans ripped, or your body grew, and you blew through your clothes like they were made of paper.

I was traveling light except for my heart, which belonged to Diego and Armand and the ten plants back at Casablanca.

I asked the taxi driver to pull over when we got to the green market at Union Square. I passed the carrot man with the dirty juicer, the half-dead rosebushes for sale, and the chocolate-chip-and-raspberry-muffin man, until I came to the spot where I had first met Exley: the plant stand where I bought the bird-of-paradise.

It was home now to another vendor, who also sold plants—muted, tiny feather plants, and withered lemon verbena. The plants looked stunted, dry, and unhappy, like zoo animals. The leaves were shriveled from lack of proper watering, and they seemed to be holding on for dear life, close to the stems, instead of spreading out toward the sun like the wings of a bird. Most of the flowers were bent toward the ground and covered with brown spots. I used to think, before Mexico, that this is what plants actually looked like.

I stood still where Exley's booth used to be, and I thought I could hear him screaming. A picture of him came into my head, covered with scorpions and dying. I wondered whether he would be in my head forever. Yes, of course he would, and he should. He gave me someone to battle and something to conquer. He made me very strong, and for that I silently thanked him.

I opened the door to my studio apartment and stood in the doorway, momentarily stunned that I lived in a space so small. Kody was sitting there on the fake Adirondack chair, in the same spot I'd last seen him. His feet were up on the glass coffee table, and he was smoking a joint.

"You look good," he said. "Not so uptight. You musta smoked a lot of weed down there in Meheeco."

"Don't say 'Meheeco.'"

"I stayed here while you were gone. The bird-of-paradise kept tipping over, so I moved in to keep it upstanding, like a good citizen."

The bird had grown huge. It was at least nine feet tall and scraping the ceiling.

"You did a good job, Kody."

"Are you staying, or are you going back to Mexico?"

"Why?"

"'Cause, you know, if you go back you're taking me with you, dude."

The bird-of-paradise didn't look like any of the plants at the green market. It clearly belonged in the Yucatán rain forest, and I decided that I would take a cutting with me if I returned. Again I thought of Exley. He had given me the bird, my very first plant, and he would never see one again. I would keep mine healthy and growing in his honor, while always remembering that he would have killed me had Armand not killed him.

Later that night, I walked east down Fourteenth Street and made a right on First Avenue, toward the Laundromat. The brand-new plate-glass window shimmered in the heat. I opened the door, and the rusty cowbell jingled. I looked around. There were plants everywhere. Sonali must have replaced them while we were in Mexico. I took off my shoes, and my feet sank into the mossy floor. For the first time since I'd arrived in New York, I felt like I was home. I took a deep breath, pulling the air up into my heart, like Diego taught me.

I searched the laundry until I spotted it. It was not in the front window, it was in the back, but there it was, a fire fern from Colombia.

I took a pair of silver nail scissors Armand had given me and snipped a cutting. I would put it in a glass of warm water in total darkness and wait. When it had long, tender white roots, I would return to Mexico.

I remembered Armand's words from so long ago, when I first took the fire-fern cutting from the palm of his hand.

Only the fern can decide whether or not it will grow roots, he said. *This week, next week, next year, maybe never. We'll see what happens.*

Acknowledgments

Many thanks to my friends and family:

Lisa Levy, Lila De La O, Phil Buehler, Marylu Lambert, Dawn Learsy, Oliver Jolliffe, Grant Collier, Geoff Council, Milton Berwin, Marianne Stewart, Anna Poehner, Claudia Berwin for being a great reader, Jenny Jackson my wonderful editor, Sam Hiyate agent extraordinaire, Al Grotell, and a special thanks to my mom, Evelyn Berwin, for her love and support the whole time.

A NOTE ABOUT THE AUTHOR

Margot Berwin earned her M.F.A. from the New School in 2005. Her stories have appeared on Nerve.com, in *New York Press,* and in the anthology *The Future of Misbehavior.* Berwin worked as an advertising copywriter and lives at New York City's Union Square.

A NOTE ON THE TYPE

The text of this book was set in Minister, a typeface designed by M. Fahrenwaldt for the German Schriftguss foundry in 1929. A modern interpretation of the classic Venetian letterforms of the fifteenth century, Minister is characterized by a calligraphic spirit, well-defined concave-shaped serifs, and broadly formed capital letters.

Designed by Maggie Hinders